Christmas Chaos
Twisted Tales of Holiday Terror

Outsider Publishing

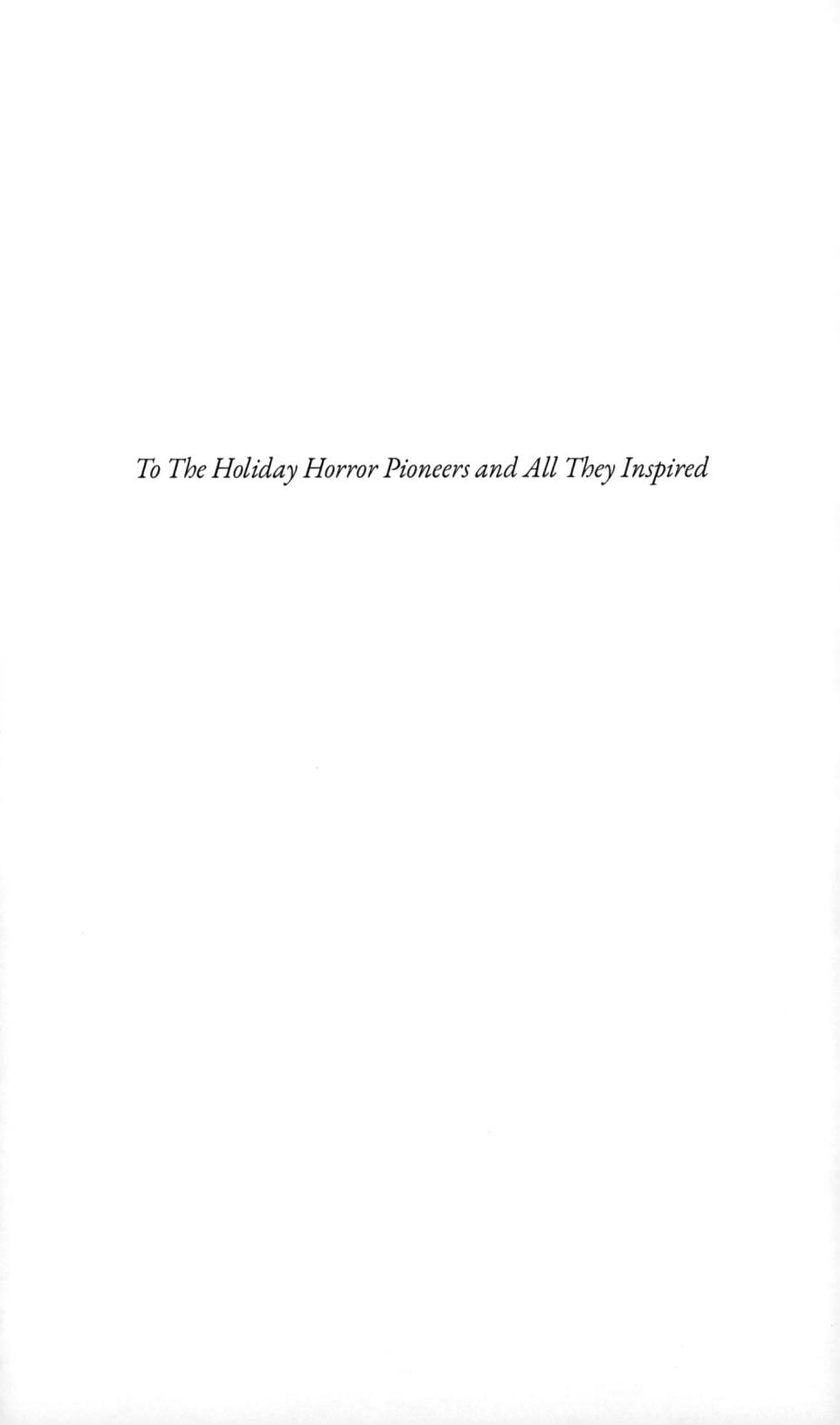

To The Holiday Horror Pioneers and All They Inspired

Contents

Foreword	vii
1. THE ORNAMENT Justin Brimhall	1
2. A KITTY FOR CHRISTMAS Max Wright	25
3. THE GREAT JHOOTHA V. Franklin	39
4. CHRISTMAS EVE Ray Prew	75
5. CHRISTMAS IN THE YEAR 2300 J. Bradford Engelsman	82
6. RETURN TO CINDER ADDRESS UNKNOWN John A. DeLaughter	99
7. THE GREED WITH IN Tiffany Vega	123
8. HOME IN A BOX Solomon Forse	132
9. HOLLY JOLLY Alexander Jose Martinez	148
10. THE ABOMINABLE FOEMAN Mark Daponte	173
11. YULETIDE BONFIRE Sam C. Tumminello JR.	190
12. GENERATION DEAD: I'M DREADING OF A NAZI CHRISTMAS SPECIAL #1 (DECEMBER 1996) Jude Deluca	210

13. BABY ITS COLD   236
    Nate Walton

14. THE CHRISTMAS WISH   252
    Mike Rusetsky

15. SACK   273
    A.J Brown

    Afterword   287
    Acknowledgments   289
    Outsider Stars   293
    About the Authors   295
    Review   303

Foreword

The holiday season often brings thoughts of warmth, laughter, and family gatherings—but what if, lurking in the glow of festive lights, something darker waits to emerge? In *Christmas Chaos*, the cheer and joy of the holidays unravel, exposing the shadows that linger just beyond the reach of the firelight.

This collection was inspired by the eerie quiet of snow-covered streets, the way silence can echo through festive halls, and how even the most joyous moments can be tinged with unease. After all, the holidays have their own kind of madness: the pressure of perfection, the tension of family, and the secrets buried under layers of tradition. Beneath the twinkling lights and merry songs, there's a chaos that thrives—and it's not always the kind that can be tidied up with a bow.

In these pages, you'll meet characters whose festive celebrations turn dark, where nightmares creep into the most unexpected places. It's a reminder that even during the most magical season, fear doesn't take a holiday.

So, as you turn the pages, brace yourself for the true spirit of the season—a little fear, a little suspense, and perhaps a deeper understanding that the holidays aren't just about joy and light. They're about facing what hides in the shadows, too.

Welcome to the chaos.

Outsider Publishing Company

The Ornament
Justin Brimhall

It had been years since Nick saw his father. He divorced his mother and remarried another woman within the following year, ten years his junior. She was closer to Nick's age. It was difficult for him to stomach. He decided he didn't want to talk to him anymore. After the first couple of years of his Father attempting to maintain their relationship, he stopped trying altogether. His Mother had a nervous breakdown, admitting herself to a mental hospital on the outskirts of town. As an only child, Nick distanced himself from the fractured family to focus on his endeavors.

Bruce, his father, reached out recently to extend an olive branch for the holidays. Every year growing up, his family would throw a large Christmas party the Saturday before Christmas, an event they all looked forward to. Nick stopped coming after the divorce, but the rest of the family and close friends continued to attend the party. He didn't understand why he wanted to go this year, but something pulled him to his father. Deep down, he still loved him but hated what he did to their family. After much deliberation, Nick decided to go to the last-minute party because he realized his anger was not stronger than his love for his father. He didn't want to miss a chance to reconcile.

    He must have driven past this small shop close to his childhood home a thousand times and never really noticed it. The lights above the dimly lit glass doors flickered while he was driving around, thinking of a gift to bring his father. The Corner Market sign burned brightly and popped off abruptly, catching his eye. Nick couldn't explain it, but it seemed like the old man behind the counter stared into his eyes, inviting him to park and enter the store. He slowed down and parked in front of the market. The old man smiled, turning away as he bent down behind the counter, his eyes twinkling with a knowing look that Nick couldn't quite decipher.

    The cold winter air chapped his skin when he climbed out of his car. He hurried carefully through the packed snow bank on the curb. His boots crackled over the salt rocks thrown over the icy sidewalk as he opened the squeaky door. The bell overhead jingled loudly upon his entrance. Faint music from an old record player filled the atmosphere. The speaker hissed and popped between the gentle saxophone tones. The air was musty. The thick dust, which seemed to have collected onto the many items littered throughout the store, forced him to cough wildly.

    "You okay, sir?" the old man asked, emerging from behind the front counter. His stringy white hair whisked as he moved.

    "I'm fine," Nick managed to answer between violent coughs.

    "You sick or just asthmatic?" he asked impatiently. The wrinkles on his face deepened with his stern expression.

    "Neither, that I know of anyway," Nick replied. He stifled his cough as his lungs adapted to the new dirty environment. He glanced around, nodding his head slightly. "I've lived around here most of my life and never noticed this place. It would be best if you had that sign outside fixed. Maybe you'll get more people in here."

"I'll consider that," he grumbled. "How can I help you?"

"I'm looking for a gift," Nick said, walking closer to him. "Something for my old man."

"Okay," he added. "What does he like?"

"I'm not sure anymore. It's been a long time since I've seen him."

"Ah, the wayward son returns," the man interjected, cackling.

"Something like that," Nick continued. "I remember him collecting old stuff, trinkets, and knickknacks, but I don't see anything like that here."

Everywhere he looked in the dimly lit store, there were various assorted items. The narrow aisles were cluttered with blankets, sheets, pillows, and soft materials. Other aisles were filled with miscellaneous items like tacks, paperclips, pens, pencils, notepads, and other junk, all covered with a prominent layer of dust. The back corner of the small area was shrouded in darkness, beyond the reach of the overhead light. In the other corner, a bright singular bulb on the opposite wall cast a faint glow on the front counter.

"I think I have something just right for you," he said. His bony fingers rested on the counter as he reached underneath. A moment later, he raised a round object hung by a thin thread or string. His thin, frail hand trembled as he held it into view. "It's Christmas. How about a new ornament to hang on the tree?"

It was unlike anything he'd ever seen. The dark green and gray appeared to clash in the middle of the sphere, creating an unsettling effect. Tiny shades of red danced, flickering throughout the forest green of the lower half of the object, giving it an eerie, almost hypnotic quality. Nick peered at the ornament as the almost swirling movement caught his eye. Initially, he thought his eyes were playing tricks, or the crafty old man was twirling them around by the string. Still, his fingers were steady, and the decoration was moving.

"Can I hold it?" Nick asked, holding his hand out.

"Of course," he replied, placing it carefully into Nick's hand.

The ornament was smooth and cold to the touch. Its surface was clear, like glass, and it had a glossy finish. Upon further inspection, the gray appeared to be clouds, and the green looked like a forest.

"It's like a snow globe," Nick remarked with a chuckle.

"Something like that," the man agreed. He snatched the sphere from Nick's hand, placing it into a small red velvet bag. "It isn't wise to stare for too long. You could get lost."

Nick snorted, squinting at the old man. "No need to try and sell me on it," he said. "I like it. How much?"

"It's Christmas. Call it a gift for a long-time neighbor," he replied, pulling the strings on the top of the bag.

"Really? I can pay you—"

"Not necessary," he interrupted. "I don't need money." Nick blinked rapidly, forcing his sarcastic remark deep into his stomach. His eyes uncontrollably glanced around at the dust-covered merchandise. "I realize that comes as a shock to you."

"I apologize; I don't mean to—" Nick was interrupted by a faint squeal followed by a feral snarl. It sounded like it came from inside the bag. The old man cocked his head to one side, peering at him in a way that dared Nick to ask where the sound came from.

A cold chill ran through his body. He stood frozen, not by fear but more from a discomfort of the unknown. This place was located in a neighborhood he knew well but never remembered seeing the market throughout his years, and the state of things around the store made him uneasy. The faint scream only added to his uncomfortable reserve, urging him to remove himself as quickly as possible.

The man reached out, pinching the bag with his index finger and thumb while his three additional bony fingers curled away from the bag. He said nothing. His icy gaze suggested he was finished with the pleasantries and no longer wished to discuss anything further. Nick obliged, taking the soft velvet bag into his hand. The ornament felt heavy in his hand. The sensation reminded him of an overfilled water balloon from playing in his backyard during the summer. He nodded and turned from the man.

"Weirdo," he scoffed, looking at the bag in his hand.

Bruce opened the front door, beaming with pride at the sight of his only son. "Nicky," he said affectionately, wrapping his thick arms around him. "So glad you came. Come in."

"Wait, how did I—"

"What's the matter, son?" Bruce interrupted. "You look like you've seen a ghost or something. Nicky? You there?" He waved his hand in front of Nick's face sarcastically.

Nick didn't know how he got there. He tried to remember what happened after the store but drew a blank. He reluctantly entered, holding the bag carefully in his hand. "Please, don't call me Nicky," he groaned.

"You never had a problem before," Bruce said.

"A lot has changed since I was nine, pop," Nick replied.

"Fair enough, Nick," he said, gripping his shoulder tightly. "I'm happy you're here. Is that for me?" He asked quickly when he noticed the bag in Nick's hand.

"Yeah—"

"Put it under the tree and head into the kitchen," he interrupted. "You're just in time for the food."

Bruce rushed down the hallway toward the kitchen. Nick

shook his head at the idea of his father full of excitement like he'd never hosted a party before. He got like that when he drank. Based on the smell of vodka on his breath, Nick guessed his father was half of a bottle in and had no plans to slow down. It was just as he remembered him.

Nick sauntered over to the tree and placed the bag down carefully on top of a tightly wrapped present closest to him. The chatter and laughter from the patrons in the kitchen made him nervous. These were people he knew, but too much time had passed. He wished it would be a smaller get-together where he could focus on only his uncomfortable exchanges with his estranged father. He took a few breaths and made his way to the kitchen.

There was a mixture of many familiar and strange faces in the crowd of people at the serving table. They stopped their conversations to look upon Nick. Most greeted him with warm smiles. "Nicky—Nick, serve yourself up," Bruce said, waving him to the table. He walked over to the assorted red and green plates, plucking a Christmas tree-themed napkin before grabbing a plastic fork. He kept his head down, serving himself with a healthy amount of everything on the table. It was all comfort food: mashed potatoes, pasta salad, green bean casserole, rolls, butter, and a tray of sliced ham. Every inch of the plate was covered with the food as he smothered it all in the thick brown gravy from the reindeer gravy boat. He made his way from the kitchen to the dining room. Nick sat at the long table closest to the end, where he guessed his father would sit. He was right. Bruce strutted over, dropping his thick frame onto the chair beside him as he grinned. Nick smirked back at him and shoveled a large helping of food into his mouth. It tasted like home, transporting him back to his childhood self, where he was overly excited about the arrival of Santa Claus and what he may bring to him. He nodded in approval as he continued scoping the delicious food into his mouth. Nick hoped it would deter people from initiating an awkward conversation with him. It worked.

As they all finished their meals, the conversations rose from the shuffling of plates and slurping cups. "Hey, Bruce," a strange man Nick never met said from the other end of the table. "Is your home fortified properly? You know, in case Krampus decides to make an appearance."

"You're funny," Bruce answered sarcastically. "I'm pretty sure only children need to concern themselves with Krampus."

"Not anymore," he said. "There have been almost two dozen disappearances since the first; many of them have been adults. There are no links or patterns. Very odd, don't you think?"

A few of the people made eerie sounds at the remark and laughed. Bruce chuckled. "People disappear all the time," he said. "It's sad and unfortunate, but it doesn't make it odd or supernatural."

"Maybe we should call those famous brothers to take the case," one of the guys in a ridiculous green Christmas sweater said. "This sounds like something they could solve."

"Get the salt," a woman added. The rest of the group burst into laughter. Nick couldn't help but join them. Bruce snickered and shoveled a couple of bites into his mouth.

The man who brought up the subject wasn't laughing. He didn't react at all. He stared at Bruce like he knew something the rest of the group didn't know. "I'm serious, man," he said after the laughter died. "It's extraordinary. Most of the time, there's something left behind, a trail to follow, or a pattern that emerges. It reminds me of before—"

"I think you watch too much true crime, Danny," Bruce interrupted. Danny leaped from his seat. The woman beside him softly pushed him from the dining room. An uncomfortable silence filled the room. "I think I put too much liquor in the egg nog this year." Everyone laughed and quickly forgot about the altercation. Bruce glanced at Nick, winking as his new wife pulled him close for a kiss.

Nick didn't understand the interaction. He tended to listen to the details of what people say. It helped him measure up any situation or individual he encountered. The fact that the man referenced a time before when his father talked about supernatural stuff and dismissed the man's words made him believe Bruce knew something or there was more to the group dynamic. He couldn't shake the old man from the strange corner market and their conversation. It couldn't be a coincidence, he thought.

The crowd dwindled as the night continued until only Bruce and Nick remained. Bruce's wife went upstairs to bed an hour before they sat by the fireplace in the living room. Nick and his father enjoyed a cigar with a glass of scotch. It was nice. Bruce didn't bring up anything from the past or attempt to apologize for his actions. Nick got to be in the moment with his estranged father without the distraction of the haunting past.

"I'm glad you came, son," Bruce said.

"Me too," he replied.

"Bianca prepared our guest room for you," Bruce said, pointing his fingers to the ceiling. "You have everything you need in there."

"I appreciate it, but that's unnecessary," he interjected. "I planned to drive back."

"Nonsense," Bruce grumbled. "Not only is it a two-hour drive, but I will not have my son drinking and driving."

"This is all I've had," he said. "I'm fine."

"I don't want to hear another word about it," Bruce said forcefully. "Just stay the night. We can have a nice morning with some breakfast, and then you can go home. Deal?" Nick knew there was no winning and nodded. "So, what did you bring me?"

They chuckled together as Nick stood up to retrieve the bag from atop the present under the tree where he left it. The sack felt heavier than he remembered from earlier. He handed it to his grinning father and sat back down. Bruce wasted no time, immediately dropping the ornament into his hand.

"It's beautiful," Bruce remarked. "Where did you get this?"

"From that old market on the main corner," Nick answered.

The blood drained from Bruce's face as he peered at him. "What market?" he questioned.

"The only one at the corner of Main," Nick said confusedly.

"There is no market at the corner of the main," Bruce said. "That whole row of buildings was abandoned after the owner vanished a little over a decade ago."

"What is with people disappearing from this place?" Nick groaned, irritated by the notion of another missing person. "It's not how I remember it."

"No, it wouldn't be," Bruce said, running his thumb along the ornament's surface. "It was far different back then. How did you find this? How much did you pay for it?"

Nick glared at his father. Bruce's eyes danced between him and the ornament. He looked upon it like it was something that drudged up a fondly faded memory. Nick noted that Bruce didn't stare at it for too long, which was what the creepy older man warned against. "Have you seen that before or something?" Nick asked.

"Something... From a long time ago," he said, placing it back into the bag. "You didn't answer my questions."

"I didn't want to come here empty-handed, so I stopped at the market when I saw the light on," Nick explained, ignoring the odd statement. "An old man that worked there showed it to me, and I thought it was neat— "

"How much did you pay?"

"Nothing."

"Nothing?"

"Yeah, nothing," Nick repeated.

Bruce's expression shifted to a hundred-yard stare like he was deep in thought. Nick snapped his fingers, and Bruce shook his head. "And he let you leave?" he asked.

"You're acting strange," Nick snapped.

His expression shifted from concerned Father to calm and indifferent. "I guess free is free," Bruce said.

"What's wrong?"

"Nothing, it's nothing," Bruce assured. "Thanks for the gift. It's a fascinating piece."

"You're not going to hang it on the tree?" Nick said sarcastically.

"Of course, duh, what am I thinking?" Bruce said, chuckling as he retrieved the ornament again. He placed it on an empty branch off the side of the tree. "There, perfect spot. Well, I'm off to bed." He doused his cigar in the crystal ashtray. "Your room is upstairs, first door on the right."

"Okay, thanks," Nick said.

"Do me a favor," Bruce said, stopping at the foot of the stairs. Nick turned around with a nod. "Try not to stare at that," he said, pointing toward the tree.

"That old man said the same thing to me," Nick grumbled. "You do know something about that. What are you not telling me?"

Bruce tapped his fingers on the fence, wrestling with himself internally. "I promise to tell you what I know and saw, which was long ago, but not tonight," he said. "I'm just really happy you're here. Goodnight." He walked up the stairs and out of view.

The whole evening, he had Nick confused. It was like a dream, bouncing around different places, getting story fragments. He couldn't make sense of any of it, especially the cryptic warning from his father. Irritated, Nick rushed to the tree where Bruce hung the ornament and stared hard at it. He snorted at the warnings and wanted to see what would happen if he stared at the ornament too long. He wondered if the boogeyman would jump from the shadows or slip into complete madness. Nick chuckled at the notion until he noticed the top of the ornament flicker. His eyes momentarily peered at the bright light before he slammed them shut as the light jumped from the object and engulfed his entire body.

A warm sensation washed over him and was followed by pure weightlessness. He felt himself sucked through some tube at an incredible speed. Once his body wiggled free from the rushing wind of the tube, he found himself in a freefall, plummeting toward the ground that tumbled through his vision. The impact was harsh and unforgiving, rendering him unconscious.

Nick opened his eyes to snow swirling above him with strong wind gusts. He turned himself over, climbing to his feet. The snow on the ground wasn't cold. It didn't appear frozen, but the winds howling overhead were as cold as a walk-in freezer at a convenience store. He scanned the area as he tried to make sense of things. Nick remembered staring at the ornament in his father's living room. Still, he doesn't remember how he arrived at this place.

A forest of Christmas trees lined the area directly in front of his position. They were fully decorated with lights of all colors, candy canes, ribbons, bows, and other festive ornaments. Each tree had a different light assortment. On some, the lights blinked or flashed, while others flickered, and very few provided a stagnant display of Christmas-themed colors. He turned around to see what was on the other side, and there was nothing but darkness. The white beneath his feet glowed from the trees and lit his path to the decorated pine tree line.

"I drank too much," he muttered, scratching his head. "This has to be a dream."

A scream cut off his thoughts from within the trees. The sound paralyzed him at first, but Nick rushed toward the illuminated path when the shouts turned to cries for help. There was a small angular opening between two smaller trees directly before him. He burst through, running toward the frantic sounds.

The lights danced around him as he ran through the narrow pathway, revealing a horror that forced him to stop dead in his tracks. The red, green, blue, and yellow lights burned brightly around him. The glow intensified with his stagnation, giving off a noticeable heat. He squinted through the radiance at two skeletons hanging from a large bushy tree like two ribbons draped purposefully across the front. They appeared to have been there a while. The bones bore ratty clothing with no semblance of rotted flesh.

Nick didn't want to approach or take a closer look. He knew what he saw and was not interested in figuring out how they got there. He closed his eyes, focusing on breathing as he tried to wake himself up from the nightmare he found himself trapped within. The branches popped and hissed around him. It was like they were being moved or chopped down based on the intense cracks that rang through his ears like thunder. He pinched his arm but only felt the pain upon his flesh. A sharp sting pulsed from his neck. He whirled around to see branches from the trees thrusting towards him as if the trees themselves attempted to stab him with their branches.

He dropped to his backside and felt his neck. His palm was soaked red with blood from the cut. The trees leaned and twisted toward his position, angling to strike him while he was helpless on the ground. Nick rolled backward. The sharp branches from the decorated trees burrowed into the ground in close pursuit. The white ground exploded from each strike, and the bones from the skeletons clinging to the branches clanked together like a morbid wind chime.

Nick clamored to his feet, darting away from the calamity, and noticed another small opening in the distance. His thighs pumped wildly as he sprinted for the perceived exit. A strong jolt from his ankle whipped him forward into the snow. Many branches engulfed him as if all of the trees in the forest fought over the right to possess him as their next decoration. The needles scraped violently at his flesh, cutting his face and ripping his clothes to pieces. One of the branches stabbed and missed under his arm. Nick pinned it under his armpit. The branch yanked him backward quickly, and another sharp branch pierced his leg just above the knee. He yelped and thrashed wildly against the thick branches as they wrapped around him. They squeezed him like a boa constrictor. Nick felt the air flee from his chest, making it impossible for him to breathe. He looked at a different tree decorated like a red and white candy cane leaning toward him. The stark white branches protruded through the eye sockets of a giant skull. It reached for him while the skull sunk back into its breast.

One of the branches fastened his hand to his thigh, and he felt the zippo in his pocket. That was his saving grace. He calmed his breathing, suppressing his panic to focus on ripping his hand free. He yanked back and thrust his arm forward into his pocket quickly. The sharp needles sliced his hand and wrist, but he managed to grip the lighter. Nick removed it from his pocket, flipping the lid and frantically striking the wheel with his thumb.

After a few clicks, the spark ignited into a flame, and Nick held it to the nearest branch. The wood caught fire instantly, spreading from limb to limb all around him. Nick fell about ten feet to the ground when the tree released its grip. He landed on his feet, but the impact jerked his knees into his chest, knocking the wind out.

A raging inferno ignited around him. The light bulbs popped, and the other decorations melted under the unforgiving heat. There was a dull hum that manifested into a wail that rivaled a train whistle. Nick covered his ears as he curled up into the fetal position. The trees were screaming from the pain of being burned alive. They whipped around, crashing into one another and tipping over. A large tree uprooted, descending upon Nick. He had no chance to escape. He scrunched his face tightly as he braced for impact. Suddenly, a pair of firm, but gentle hands grabbed his arms and pulled him out of harm's way. The falling tree missed him by inches.

Nick kept his eyes closed as his rescuer dragged him to safety. The heat faded until only the cold remained, kissing his sweaty skin. His scratches pulsed and stung from the sudden atmosphere changes. He groaned, reaching down to the puncture wound on his thigh.

"Are you alright?" a soft voice asked.

Nick struggled to open his eyes. They burned from the fire and smoke he caused, which made them water uncontrollably. "No, what the hell is going on?" he snapped, leaning upward.

"What's your name?" the woman asked as she assisted him.

"Nick," he answered and coughed. The watering in his eyes subsided enough for him to focus on her. She was covered in scratches, and her clothes were tattered. It was apparent she had been through the same thing as him but for longer.

"I'm Bernice, but everyone calls me Bernie," she said, brushing her frizzy bright red hair from her eyes.

"Thank you," he said.

"I'm the one who should be thanking you," he interjected with a snort. "Had you not come along with your quick thinking, I'd be dead."

"What is this place?" Nick asked impatiently.

She peered at him with confusion. "I was going to ask you that," she said. "You're the only person I've seen since I woke up here."

"You woke up here? How did you get here?"

"Don't know. How did you?"

"I don't know," he snapped, grimacing from the pain he felt all over his body. He shifted his weight to the injured leg, ensuring it could support him. "How long have you been here?"

"I don't know that either," she replied frustratingly. "It's not like there's a sunrise and sunset I can track."

"I don't need your sarcasm—"

"We both *don't* a lot," she interrupted and laughed. "Look, in all seriousness, I've been here a while but don't know anything exact."

"What do you know?"

"It's dark. It's cold. And there's a lot around here trying to kill us."

Her explanation was interrupted by the sweet smell of mashed potatoes and gravy that stung Nick's senses. He inhaled deeply, feeling an overwhelming sense of comfort. For a moment, he forgot where he was and the current predicament. A smile stretched across his face as he turned toward the intense aroma.

"No, it's a trick," she said, cocking her head to one side.

"What is?"

"Whatever you're smelling," she replied quickly. "It lures you in."

"What does?" he interjected, inhaling again.

"The candy land over there," she answered and pointed ahead.

"Candy? You don't smell those potatoes?"

"No, I smell peppermint and cinnamon," she snapped. "Trust me, there's nothing for you there."

In the distance, Nick saw a bright flicker of light through the darkness. He moved toward it, almost in a trance, forgetting about his injuries. His slough transformed into a brisk walk. Bernie tried to grab his arm, but he tore it from her fingers.

"I barely made it out of there—"

Dinner's ready! A voice that resembled his mother called out. "Mom?"

"That's not your mom," she said concernedly.

He ignored her and sprinted toward her voice. Bernie called out as she ran after him, pleading with him to stop and listen to her warnings. He didn't listen. Nick's feet carried him to the flickering opening that looked like a cave opening. There was no hesitation in his movements as he slid into the hole where her voice and mashed potato aroma poured from. His eyes danced around the room, scanning for the image of his mother.

It was a large room littered with candy of all kinds. There were candy canes, chocolate peppermint candies, gummies, cotton candy, chocolate-covered Santa figures, fudge, and other holiday-inspired sweets. Decorations were strung about the room and resembled Christmas in his childhood home. In the center of the room was a long table with two settings placed next to each other. Around the two plates were an assortment of table decorations, lit red and green holiday candles, a cooked turkey, and a large pan of mashed potatoes. He lunged forward, and Bernie tackled him.

"What's the matter with you?" he exclaimed.

"This is where I woke up," she growled, pushing her nose into his. "I barely made it out with my life, and if we don't leave, I fear we will die here."

"It's my mom—"

"Your mom isn't here," she snapped. "Look around. What do you notice?"

"Delicious food—"

"Where's the kitchen? Who do you think cooked it? Spoiler alert: it wasn't your mom!"

Her logic made too much sense for Nick to ignore, and somehow, it punched a hole into his mirage. He no longer smelled the intoxicating aroma of food. The smell of rot and decay replaced it. His soured expression moved Bernie to turn his face from hers forcefully. The food had transformed into maggot-filled trays, molded candy, and piles of bones around them. He jumped to his feet, frantically looking around at the horror.

"What the hell is going on? I don't understand what's happening," he groaned helplessly.

Bernie jerked him backward and pushed him down through the opening he slid into. She pulled herself through after him, tucking her feet inward as the hole slammed shut. Nick glared between her and the sealed cave of terror.

"When I awoke, there were two large openings," she explained. "The longer I lingered, the smaller the openings became until the one closed up altogether. That small opening was left when I crawled out."

"Nothing about that place made sense. The mirage...then the disgusting food—the bones," he said.

"I know," she agreed. "It was my mom's voice, too, calling me to eat. When I didn't, things began to shift quickly. Voices rang through my head, urging me to eat and become one of them. They tried to convince me to stay." She paused, staring out at the smoldering forest. "I believe that stuff was poisoned, and you would've died in there. A fate shared by the bones within. I think wherever we are, it's designed to keep us here for some reason."

"It wants us dead," Nick added.

"Yes, but I think it's more than that, and it's for a reason."

"I can't think of what that could be," he interjected. "We need to get the hell out of here. We obviously can't go back the way we came and go through the cave."

Bernie flicked her head in the direction behind him. He turned to notice tall bushes adjacent to the cave rocks with a decorative opening that revealed a dirt path. "That's the only way," she said.

"How do you know?" Nick asked.

"Look around," she suggested, spreading her arms out wide. "When I woke up and escaped the cave, I walked around this open area. There was nothing. I tried to avoid the trees like hell because I felt that was worse than the cave."

"Why didn't the trees kill you?"

She snorted proudly. "I stopped fighting them," she said. "I gave in because I didn't see a point, and their grip loosened. It still hurt, but it was manageable. I was trying to buy myself time to find a way out; you showed up."

A guttural scream interrupted their conversation. It came from the other side of the bushes. The sound reminded Nick of werewolves from movies and television. Whatever made it snarled and bellowed out another throaty growl, which made Bernie's body tense up with extreme rigidity.

"What was that?" Nick asked concernedly, inching toward the bushes.

"I don't know, and I don't want to know," Bernie replied fearfully. Nick ignored her sarcastic remark, moving toward the opening as the sounds intensified. "What are you doing?" she snapped.

"You said it yourself; there's nowhere else to go," Nick said, peering into the dark entrance.

"Whatever's in there isn't going to let us go if it finds us," she added.

"What are you waiting for!?" a beastly voice snarled from the bushes. It cackled proudly, growing closer to them. Its heavy footsteps crunched through the snow as the ground trembled beneath their feet. "I know you're there! I can smell you!"

"Whatever that is, it's guarding something," Nick remarked, turning to Bernie, who stood frozen in place. Her breath plumed as she struggled to slow down her breathing. "This has to be the way out."

"How are you so sure?" she asked as her voice quivered.

"This all feels like a video game to me," he replied. "Kind of like a maze of sorts. You're tested until you reach the main boss. That sounds like a boss to me."

"But this isn't a video game," she groaned. "We could die."

"If we stay here and do nothing, we'll die for sure," he interjected. "I don't see food anywhere, and it's getting colder. If you don't want to go, you can stay, but I'm seeing what's on the other side."

Nick rushed through the dark entrance to find another large dark green bush. Small light fixtures dimly lit the snowy path on each side. It looked familiar to him, not that he'd been there before, but it reminded him of something he saw. Bernie hurried in behind him, bumping into his back. She stumbled, and Nick caught her before she fell. The entrance they entered through closed up. The thick branches reached toward each other, entangling and intertwining like long fingers clasping together, stitching the opening closed. They were trapped inside.

"Well, you had to say maze," Bernie remarked with a chuckle.

"This way," Nick said, walking to the left.

"Welcome to my world!" the snarling beast shouted. "I cannot wait to feast upon you!"

Nick ignored the outbursts. Bernie jumped and squealed every time the beast said something. He led her through many twists and turns of the maze, locating a handful of dead ends along the way, forcing them to turn around to pursue a different route. Everything looked new and familiar at the same time. Nick wondered if the greenery had a mind of its own, shifting and changing as they moved to confuse them further on their journey.

"I see you!" the beast growled.

Nick whipped around to see a large shadow in the distance. They were at the end of a straight path. It turned the corner, stomping into view as its red eyes pierced through the shadows. The beast was giant, almost ten feet tall, and it clutched something in its hands. It growled loudly as it crouched into a running position, whatever it was planned to attack them with full force.

"Oh my god," Bernie shrieked.

"Come on," Nick said, grabbing her by the arm. They ran toward the beast. It cackled and launched toward them. Nick saw a small opening to the left, darting within, pulling Bernie with him. As they fell into the snow, the sharp edge of an axe the size of a man thrust through the bushes. It smashed into the ground, barely missing Bernie. She screamed in terror. Nick yanked her to her feet, and they darted away from the beast.

He zig-zagged through the maze, jumping through every opening he could find. He wanted to create as much distance as possible between them and the giant beast. It didn't matter. The beast's heavy hooves followed closely behind them. Bernie slipped as they turned a sharp corner, and she twisted her ankle in the snow bank. She cried out painfully, gripping her foot.

"Come on, we gotta go!" Nick shouted.

"I can't," she cried. "My ankle. I think it's broken."

Nick pulled her up carefully from the snow. "Then I'll carry you the rest of the way," he said, crouching down. He helped her onto his back and trudged on through the snow.

The silenced gripped them. Only his footsteps crunching through the snow could be heard through the calm night air. The ground didn't tremble. There were no shouts or snarls from the beast in pursuit of their position. It was strange to Nick that something so significant could vanish without a trace, mainly after it worked so hard to kill them.

"This is weird," Bernie said. "Where did he go?"

He began to answer and paused. A low hum rumbled the other side of their position. It was faint, but Nick knew it was a song. A group of people were humming a classic Christmas tune.

"Is that—"

"Yep," he interrupted, and the bushes peeled away, revealing what was at the center of the maze. They made it. Nick managed to find the center as he weaved through any turn he found to get away from the beast.

He cautiously stepped through into the open area. It was a circular space that resembled an ice skating rink. In the center was stark white ice spackled with drops of dried blood. The surrounding space had cages, like dog kennels, that wrapped around it like an auditorium. Within the cages were people, humming the song as they gripped the bars tightly. Nick and Bernie stared in horror. Their eyes were missing, exposing the dark sockets. Blood trickled from the wounds, pouring down their cheeks. The bloody tears dripped onto their knuckles, but they didn't react. They didn't seem to be in pain. They hummed with full smiles, but their teeth were rotted and chipped. Their clothes were far more tattered and torn than Bernie's, suggesting they had been there longer than her. Their hums shifted to singing the song in perfect pitch. They sang in unison, dazed like being controlled in their deep trance.

"It would be beautiful if it weren't creepy," Bernie remarked in his ear.

"I know," he replied. She squeaked suddenly and gasped. "What?" he chuckled. He felt drops of water kiss his neck. He turned to realize it wasn't water. It was blood from Bernie's mouth, dripping onto his back. The snarl of the beast returned directly behind him. He slipped, falling forward into the snow. Bernie's body remained in the air, held in place by the axe in her back. The beast struck quickly and quietly, sending Nick into a panic.

The singing ceased and was replaced by throaty howls from the decayed prisoners. It had the same sound as a recording being played backward. Noises were being made, but they sounded unnatural. The beast flung her body from his axe, standing in plain sight.

The beast was covered in dark green hair. Its red eyes sunk deep behind a protruding snout resembling a snarling jackal filled with rows of sharp teeth. He grinned with satisfaction, running his long-forked tongue over the large canines in the front. The beast had narrow, pointing ears just beneath horns curved upward from its temples. He wiggled his long-clawed fingers against the handle of his axe, the sharp nails clicking against the dense wood. Nick was frozen in fear.

"What are you?" Nick asked.

"I go by many names," he snarled. "None of that matters, boy."

"Why did you kill her?" he said, staring at Bernie's lifeless face.

"It's how I survive," he answered. "I need blood."

"Couldn't you get some from them?" he said, gesturing to the people in the cages.

"I need fresh blood," he replied. "My master supplies me with the blood I need so my power can fuel his own."

"Like some sort of a magic pet?"

"I'm through talking!" the beast snapped. "I'm starving. How about an appetizer?" He reached down, plucking Bernie's body up with one hand and placing it into his mouth. He bit down at the torso, snapping her body in half, and chewed vigorously.

"Please let me go," Nick said, frightened by the horrific sight. "I need to get back to my dad."

"You will see him again, but I'm afraid it won't be how you think," the beast grunted. He stomped his massive hooves toward Nick.

"This has to be a nightmare," he said. "I just want to wake up. Please help me wake up. I need to wake up." Nick climbed to his feet, closing his eyes to help him focus on waking himself up. The beast cackled, raising his axe high and bringing it down onto his head, severing Nick in half.

"Merry Christmas, Nicky," Bruce said, gripping his shoulder. Nick jumped and attempted to catch his breath. "Whoa, whoa, Nicky, it's alright."

"I thought I told you not to call me that," Nick groaned, scanning the living room. He patted himself and found he was wearing the same clothes, which were not ripped or torn. He didn't have any wounds from the trees. Nick found himself at the tree where he had stood the previous night before the nightmare occurred. "Did I fall asleep? Standing up?"

"Kind of," Bruce answered. "I told you not to stare at that for too long."

"Why? What's going on?"

"It doesn't matter anymore, son," he said ominously. "I'm glad to have you here...With me."

Nick squinted at him as he walked to the dining area. All the people from the previous night were there, but they weren't laughing or joking around. They stared coldly in his direction and gestured for him to approach. A small, gentle hand gripped his forearm. He turned quickly to see Bernie smiling up at him. Nick glared anxiously and shook his head in disbelief.

"I don't understand," he said. "What's happening?"

"You're one of us now," she answered.

"What?"

"Your father talked about you for years, begged you to join him here," she said. "He didn't want you to think he abandoned you."

"Here? What are you talking about?"

"The old man in the market, he's our keeper," she replied. "Our souls keep him young."

"This can't be happening," he interjected, stumbling and sitting on the couch. Bernie crouched in front of him.

"Oh, it's okay. I want to thank you," she said.

"For what?"

"I was trapped in those trees for who knows how long," she explained. "He told me if I helped you along, he would free me and allow me to join the others."

"He? The old man?"

"It doesn't matter anymore, Nick," she interrupted. "You're here now, with your dad and me. I think we can be happy here."

"Come on, son," Bruce said, holding his hand out. Nick grasped his hand and allowed his father to assist him to his feet. "It's not as bad as it seems. It's Christmas every day, forever. You always loved Christmas."

"I want to go home," Nick snapped.

"Son, you are home," he replied gently.

"Welcome to the ornament," Bernie added, kissing him on the cheek.

A Kitty for Christmas
Max Wright

Worst. *Christmas Eve. Ever.* Astrid stared out the window and picked imaginary lint from her new holiday sweater, an early gift from dad. Now, here she was, stuck with her mother's second cousin or cousin twice-removed or whatever the hell *Móðursystir* Johanna was. "You'll love her," Mom had said, when she and Jack the creepy boyfriend dropped Astrid off at the airport. "I used to visit her all the time in Iceland when I was your age."

What*ever*. Because *Móðursystir* Johanna and her little kid didn't live in Iceland, which might have been cool to visit. They lived in Iowa. In the most hick town possible, like from a goofy old black-and-white tv show. To make it worse, *Móðursystir* Johanna was one of those artsy women who wore long, swooshy skirts and lots of scarves and thought getting way from the city was cool and creative. She had a creepy, witchy woodcarvings and candles on the mantle and weird books in Icelandic and other crazy languages laying on tables and lining the bookshelves. Astrid was pretty sure that if *Móðursystir* Johanna was a kid her age, Astrid would hate her.

Why couldn't I have gone to Dad's? But Dad had decided December was the perfect time to do another rehab stint in Arizona. Leigh, her bestie since second grade, had said Astrid could spend the holidays with her, but Mom insisted the holidays "were for family." Including family you didn't even know apparently.

There was a draft through the window and Astrid shivered. She stepped back from the glass, pushed her blonde bangs back into place with a slightly sticky finger and sat on the couch. She examined her chipped nails. Nail polish was the only makeup she was allowed until she turned 13 next year. Why this, and only this, was the one and only thing Mom and Dad agreed on was extremely irritating. Leigh got to wear makeup. And tank tops.

Astrid's meditation on the injustices of the world was interrupted.

"Mom's made *piparkökur*. She says we can have some. We could have a tea party if you want." Kirsten, *Móðursystir* Johanna's daughter, stood in the doorway to the den, her impossibly blonde hair, blonder even than Astrid's, falling in untamed ringlets over her shoulders and contrasting with surprisingly hazel eyes.

"Not really." Astrid's nose wrinkled as the smell of gingerbread hit her nostrils, and she kind of regretted declining the invitation. But having a tea-party with a six-year-old would be impossibly uncool.

"Want to play something else then?" Kirsten pointed at a bookcase crammed with playthings. "I have a lot of Barbies."

"I don't play Barbies anymore.".

"If you don't like Barbie you can be Ken." Kirsten's eyes were big and earnest, like she'd just made a super generous offer.

"That's not what I meant, stu—." Astrid cut herself off. It wasn't Kirsten's fault that Astrid was here in freezing cold Iowa with people she was barely related to. "Sorry. I don't mean to be mean."

"We could go outside and make a snowman." Kirsten took a step into the den. "I'm really good at that."

"How long is your mom gone for again?" *Móðursystir* Johanna had told Astrid how long she was to watch Kirsten, but Astrid hadn't really been paying attention.

Kirsten's forehead wrinkled. "She's just going around to the neighbors. It's Christmas. We host the day after."

"Yeah, but how long will it take?" Astrid rolled her eyes, exasperated at Kirsten's inability to answer a straightforward question.

"Maybe until dinner?" Kirsten sounded uncertain.

Astrid pulled out her phone and checked the time. Still early afternoon. Plenty of time to look for stuff. She didn't really know why, but Astrid loved going through other people's things. You never knew what you might find. Like creepy Jack's collection of old porno CDs, Dad's stash of pills, Mom's sexy underwear. Astrid didn't really know if this knowledge had any application in her life or why she craved it, but it would be fun to know Auntie Johanna's secrets.

Heck, this time of year you might just find presents if nothing else. And Astrid was always curious, even about what other people were getting for Christmas. She started to come up with a story. A pretty good one, even by her standards.

"Come here, Kirsten." Kirsten walked over. Astrid leaned in close and looked the younger girl in the eye. "Since you're a *big* girl, I'm going to tell you a *big* secret."

Kirsten nodded solemnly.

"You know how Santa flies all around the world to deliver all his presents in one night?" Astrid glanced from side-to-side, pretending she was worried about being overheard.

"I asked for a Barbie Dream House." Kirsten pointed to a Barbie lying on the floor, legs splayed.

"So, think about it. There is no way he can do that. Not even if he's magical or whatever. Right?"

Kirsten's lower lip started to quiver and tears welled in her eyes. "Are you trying to say Santa's not real? Because Billy ..."

"No, no." Astrid put her hand on Kirsten's skinny shoulder. "What he does sometimes is come by early. And he puts the presents in your house. Hides them. And then he leaves your mom a note on where he's hidden them so she put them out on Christmas Eve. That way he can deliver all his presents, right?" *Where do I come up with this bullshit? Maybe Ms. Grayson is right and I have a promising career in advertising.*

"Really?" Kirsten sounded doubtful.

"Absolutely. Cross my heart and all that stuff." Astrid traced an X on her chest.

"Okaaaaaay." Kirsten's tone made it clear Astrid was going to have to spell it out.

"So that means if we look around, we'll probably find some of our presents from Santa." Astrid cocked her head and smiled her best smile, the one she practiced in the mirror to use on boys in case she met one who, unlike the guys at her school, wasn't stupid and gross.

"I kind of would like to know if I'm getting a Dream House." Kirsten started to stick her thumb in her mouth, then thought better of it and dropped her hand back to her side.

"Yeah, and you might get extra presents if you've been super good." Astrid's forced smile was hurting her face, so she dropped it.

"I don't know ..." Kirsten's voice trailed off.

Astrid stood up. "Well, *I'm* going to look."

Kirsten looked up at Astrid, and took a hesitant step forward.

"Where shall we start?" Astrid headed out of the living room. "The hall closet?" Her own mom often tried to hide things here, either up on top or buried behind a wall of coats and jackets.

"I don't know," Kirsten said. "I never looked before."

"Let's start there." Astrid opened the closet door. *How convenient.* There was a stepstool leaning against the wall. Although that made Astrid doubt she was on the right track. No grownup would be dumb enough to leave a stepstool right where they'd hidden something interesting. Still, she had to make sure. Astrid unfolded the stool, climbed up and looked on the shelf. A Dustbuster, ironically covered in grime, some floppy, vaguely witchy hats, and nothing else.

"See anything?" Kirsten asked, peering up from the foot of the stepstool.

"Nope. Let's try a different place.." Astrid climbed down and stared down the hallway, head cocked. "What about your mom's room?"

Kirsten swallowed. "I'm not supposed to go in there unless mom says it's okay. And she's not here."

"You are so du..." Astrid caught herself again. If she was mean, Kirsten would probably tattle. Or bail on the whole search, leaving Astrid to take all the blame if they got caught. Or both. "If she's not here, how can she stop us? C'mon." Astrid headed down the hall, paused outside the closed door. What if *Móðursystir* Johanna had some kind of nanny-cam or something in the room? Grownups were always spying on you, even though they told you it was rude to poke into other people's business. She took at deep breath and opened the door.

Kirsten sensed Astrid's hesitation. "Are you afraid?"

"No." *Can't turn back now.* "Let's go." Astrid fought back her nerves and stepped into the room, scanning it for anything that looked like a camera. From what she'd seen on Amazon, most nanny cams were disguised as stuffed animals or clocks. No dolls. A clock, but it was pointed away from the door, making it an unlikely location for a camera. Astrid walked up to the bed. "Let's look under here." She knelt and lifted the bed skirt.

Astrid scanned the dark space as quickly as she could. An abandoned shoe and several socks. Dust bunnies. A suitcase, which might be worth investigating, but even as she grabbed the handle and pulled it toward her, she could tell it was empty. It was locked anyway, so back under the bed it went.

"Hurry. Mom will be home soon." Kirsten sounded nervous.

"Don't be such a bay... we have plenty of time." Astrid stood and flicked the dust from the suitcase handled from her fingers. "We're just getting started." Astrid surveyed the room. A double closet. Too obvious and Astrid didn't want to waste any time in case her aunt really was on her way back. There was a weird dresser or chest of some kind, sitting opposite of the foot of the bed, with a lock that still had the key in it. Maybe *Móðursystir* Johanna had put something away and neglected to grab the key afterwards. *Best bet, for sure.*

Astrid approached the dresser. Well, it was really too short to be a dresser but too high to be an end table. Almost a kind of trunk. And the whole thing was covered in crude, creepy engravings. Creepy snakes with giant fangs. Weird slashes and other markings that kind of reminded Astrid of writing. Bearded warrior naked dudes with axes and oversized wieners and women with their boobs hanging out. That made her blush a little. Part of her wanted to look at the naked guys more and part of her was grossed out, like when she found creepy Jack's porn stash. What kind of person would keep something like this pervy their bedroom? *Never mind. I'm here on a mission.*

Astrid half-closed her eyes so the naked people weren't quite so distracting and turned the key. The lock opened with a click and Astrid tugged on the handle. *Crud. It's not opening.* Astrid fiddled with the lock for a bit. She had to open her eyes all the way. *Was that snake always swallowing that naked chick?* Astrid couldn't remember. She tried the handle again.

The chest opened, just the tiniest crack. A gust of icy wind whistled through the crack, making Astrid shudder. She stepped back, rubbing her arms to warm them up.

"Is something wrong?" Kirsten's voice was weirdly distant, like the wind was carrying her words out of the room and down the hall.

"No." *Something's weird, but I'm not going to back down in front of a baby.* "It must be rusty or jammed or something." Astrid grabbed the handle and pulled as hard as she could, planting her feet and leveraging her full body weight. Her arms strained, and she started to sweat with exertion.

The resistance gave way all at once. Astrid fell backward and landed, hard, in a sitting position. Her butt hurt, like maybe she'd sprained her tailbone or hip or something. She took a deep breath, fought back welling tears and forced herself to her feet. "See? Easy-peasy." *Were the snakes and people on the chest moving again? Or was her vision from blurry from almost crying?*

"Are you okay? I don't like this game anymore. Can we please go play Barbies? Or just eat the *piparkökur?* We don't have to have a tea party if you think that's just for kids."

Part of Astrid thought eating cookies and forgetting about the whole thing was a good idea. But part of her was even more curious now that she'd started. This dresser or trunk or whatever was a real, genuine mystery. One she was going to solve.

"C'mon, Kirsten. It's too late to stop now." Astrid walked

toward the chest. The inside was dark. She looked around the room, spotted the lamp on the end table and turned it on.

No difference. The inside of the chest was still dark.

"I want to go." Kirsten's voice was a whispery whine.

"I need you to be a big girl and help me out. Just stand guard and make sure your mom doesn't catch us. Can you do that?" Astrid said.

"I guess so." Kirsten's voice was firmer, as though knowing she didn't have to get any closer to the chest made her a bit braver.

"Good." Astrid turned her attention back to the chest. She peered into the blackness, curious but also a little afraid.

"*Meow.*"

Astrid took a step back, her hands covering her mouth as if in prayer. "Kirsten, I think we found your Christmas present."

"Prrrrrrow!" The meow was louder, more insistent. Astrid knelt and stuck her hand into the chest. *I mean, maybe Kirsten was supposed to get this gift tomorrow, but locking a kitten inside this old, creepy box? That was animal abuse.* Astrid was pretty sure you could go to jail for that.

The air inside the trunk was cold, so chilly in fact, that Astrid's fingers stiffened and she lost some of her sensation in the tips. She thought about pulling her hand out, shutting the chest and just dealing with the fallout of sneaking into *Móðursystir* Johanna's room. But what if it was so cold that the kitten died? Some Christmas that would be for Kirsten. *Look! Santa brought you a dead kitten.* Ugh.

Astrid felt around, crawling forward so that now her head and shoulders were in the chest. Her cheeks stung and her eyes watered from the freezing temperature. *This is no ordinary chest for sure.* Maybe it was even dangerous. But there was no way she was going to let that kitten die.

As Astrid crawled further into the trunk, it seemed to get

bigger. And weirder. Because her hands felt snow. Real snow. In a chest. Why would *Móðursystir* Johanna pack a kitten in a chest full of snow?

Her concern for the kitten was decreasing as fast as her worries about her own safety increased. She was about to back out of the chest and slam it closed when she felt something else.

Something small.

Something warm.

Something furry.

Astrid took hold of the twisting, struggling form and pulled it out of the chest. The kitten, panicked, sank her teeth into Astrid's thumb. "Ouch!" Astrid dropped the kitten.

"I'm getting a kitten?" Kirsten clapped her hands.

Astrid stuck her thumb in her mouth, then thought about how that looked and pulled it out again. "A kitten is way cooler than a boring toy." Astrid wasn't too upset about being bitten; the poor kitten had probably been scared half to death from being locked up and just lashed out in a panic. Her own late cat Crinkles had done that a few times. Creepy Jack said he was allergic to cats so Astrid couldn't get a new one. But she was actually kind of happy for Kirsten. Cats were cool.

"Where did it go?" Kirsten looked around the room. "Did you lose my present already?"

"It's a cat. Hiding is kind of their thing." Astrid stood and examined her wounded thumb. The bite was worse than she expected, but it wasn't like she was going to bleed to death. "Help me look for her. Him. Whichever."

Kirsten put a foot through the doorway. "Here, kitty, kitty."

"Cats don't come when you call." Astrid dropped down on all fours, careful to keep her thumb protected. Down at cat level, she started looking. Under the bed, under the nightstand, behind the door to the master bath. "Kitty, where are you?"

"I thought you said they didn't come when you call." Kirsten was closer, but still hanging back.

"Well, sometimes they do." Astrid stopped crawling around. Had the kitten gone in the bathroom? Or back into the chest? Astrid decided the bathroom was more likely. She stood and stepped in, the cold tile chilling her cotton stockinged feet. "Kitty?" Astrid remembered Crinkles liked to nap in the sink. She tippy toed toward it.

"Shit!" The bad word exploded before Astrid even had time to think about it. Something black and way too big to be a kitten shot out of the tub, ran right between her legs before she could even think to grab it.

"Ouch!" Kirsten's voice came from the bedroom. "The bad cat bit me!"

Astrid's focus shifted from the missing kitten to Kirsten. She stepped out of the bathroom and looked at the younger girl. Her eyes were watering and her lip quivered.

"Okay, where did it bite you?" Astrid asked, kneeling beside the younger girl.

"Here." Kirsten rolled down her sock. There were four little pinpricks on her ankle. There was also a little trickle of blood, but not too much.

"It doesn't look too bad." Astrid didn't know much about animal bites, but she knew you were supposed to wash them. "Let's go in the bathroom and we'll wash it."

"Do I get a princess band-aid?" Kirsten seemed to be in a lot less discomfort.

"Sure, if I can find one."

The girls went into the bathroom. Astrid found a washcloth and ran it under warm water. She put a couple drops of soap on the cloth and placed it on Kirsten's ankle. It was supposed to be antibacterial soap, and the bite wasn't that deep.

"Okay, let me see if I can find those band-aids for you." Astrid opened the cabinet and looked inside.

The growl was so loud it echoed.

That sounds like a wildcat or something.

Astrid had no idea how a wild animal got in the house, but she had to act quickly. She rushed to the bathroom door and grabbed the handle.

The impact of the wild animal hitting the door knocked her to the ground. Astrid looked up to see a black dog – no, it was a giant black cat, its eyes yellow slits against its dark fur. The cat's mouth opened, revealing fangs as long as Astrid's fingers and sharp as knives. She tried to push it away, but it was too strong. The giant feline head pushed down against Astrid's arms. She closed her eyes, waiting for the death bite to come.

Moments passed. She was still alive. Instead of killing her, the cat was sniffing up and down her, like it was fascinated by her sweater. Then, the cat sneezed.

It sneezed hard, spraying Astrid with cat snot. Then it rose, slightly, and sneezed again.

Astrid seized her opportunity. She wiggled out from under the distracted cat and dove into the bathroom, slamming the door behind her.

"Are you alright? What is that out there?" Kirsten came, wrapped her arms around Astrid's hips. "I'm scared."

"I don't know." Astrid had no idea what kind of cat looked like that. Black panthers lived in Africa or South America, she couldn't remember which, but not Iowa.

She smoothed Kirsten's hair. "Don't worry. We're safe in here. I'll call 911." She felt her hip pocket.

"Shit." Astrid could picture the phone lying on the coffee table by the couch where she'd been texting Leigh earlier that day.

"You don't have your phone?" Kirsten's voice was whiny, but Astrid couldn't really blame the kid.

"Your mom will be home soon, right? We'll be safe in here," Astrid said.

No sooner had she spoken than there was a crash against the door. Both girls screamed. Astrid looked around the room for something, anything she could use as a weapon. A toilet brush and a plunger were the only things she could see. Not much use against a mountain lion or whatever it was outside.

There was a window, but it was too high up and too small for Astrid to crawl through. She shivered.

Crash!

Kirsten started to wail. "It's the *Jólakötturinn*! It's going to get me!"

"The what?" Astrid grabbed the plunger and stepped in front of the weeping Kirsten.

"The Yule Cat. I'm allergic."

The Yule Cat. Astrid's mental gears spun, then clicked into place. Her mother used to tell her stories about a giant cat. Astrid couldn't remember all the details, but it was something about you had to get woolen clothes for Christmas and be good or the cat would eat you. But it was just a goofy story parents told to make their kids behave.

"Kirsten, it's okay. The Yule Cat isn't real."

The cat threw itself against the door again. A thin crack opened in the wood.

"Mommy said she'd protect me and that's why she sent the Yule Cat to kitty jail. And now it's here."

"Kirsten, I promise you, there's no such thing as the Yule Cat."

The door shook in it's hinges as whatever it was outside slammed into it again.

"Why did you have to open the chest? Why?"

Astrid's panicked brain began to weave unlikely connections. *Móðursystir* Johanna's strange books and witchy clothes. *Magic.* The mysterious chest. *Kitty jail.* A creature that had grown from a small kitten to a ferocious monster in a matter of minutes. *The Yule Cat.*

Astrid tried to slow her brain down, to think logically, to ignore the weird ideas in her head. *There's no way a fairy tale monster is trying to kill us.* But whether it was a bobcat or a mountain lion or Yule Cat, somebody had to get a grownup. *Now.* Astrid took a deep breath and turned to the younger girl cowering behind the toilet.

"Kirsten, you're going to have to be a big girl. Okay?" Astrid peeled off her sweater.

"How?"

"You're going out the window to get help," Astrid said.

"Why can't you go?" Kirsten started sniffling, like she was going to cry again.

"I won't fit." Astrid tugged the sweater over Kirsten's head.

"I told you I'm allergic to wool." Kirsten's voice was a full-on whine now.

"Allergic?" Astrid gave Kirsten a shake, probably harder than she should have. "You don't have time to be allergic. And you need this sweater in this cold. Even so, you'll probably free…"

Another impact against the door. A black snout worked its way through the widening crack, fangs dug into the wood and tore out a chunk.

"Hurry!" Astrid lifted Kirsten up onto the tank of the toilet, climbed to stand beside her.

Wood splintered. Astrid didn't dare look. She yanked the window open.

A guttural growl, the sound of claws on tile.

"Go!" Astrid pushed Kirsten threw the opening.

Kirsten gave a small cry as she rolled off the shrubbery below the window and into the snow.

"Run!" Astrid jumped down from the toilet, grabbed the toilet brush.

The door shattered.

Astrid jabbed at the giant cat's snout with the brush. The impact of hard bristles on soft nose slowed it.

For an instant.

Then the big cat crashed into her. She fell and hit her head on the toilet.

"But I got a sweater." The words came out in a hoarse whisper. And then she blacked out.

The Great Jhootha
V. Franklin

"Ladies and gentlemen. I must now ask, for your own safety, and for mine. Please observe absolute silence. Keep perfectly still." The Great Jhootha paused, spread his arms wide, and let the footlights augment his serious expression. "So much as a cough or the rustle of a dress." He put his arms down, cocked his head to a member of the audience, grinned. "Even so fine a dress as worn by so handsome a lady as yourself, madam." This was greeted by a chuckle from the audience, and a blush from the lady.

The magician's face became serious again. He shrugged out of the cape that hung from his shoulders and let it fall to the floor. A fellow with long, white hair materialized from Jhootha's left, snatched up the cape, and disappeared back offstage.

"Now..." The Great Jhootha wiped a drop of sweat from his forehead. "My assistant will prepare this space for the spirits... I shall produce in myself the state required to communicate with that hidden world, as taught to me by the occult masters of Ethiopia."

As the white-haired man came back onstage, Jhootha began mumbling a strange, quiet mantra. Sounds inaudible to all but those in the first dozen rows, and unintelligible to everyone.

The white-haired man placed little pots of smoking incense in a rough circle around the chanting medium. The smoke was thick and smelled bad.

Then Jhootha undressed. He pulled off his tie and unbuttoned his collar. He slipped off his jacket and then his shirt. Naked from the waist up, except for his strange, silk cap.

The crowd murmured at the spectacle. Rumors of the performance had traveled to the coast before the performer himself. But, still, here was a half-naked man, just standing there. With ladies present, no less. And, true to the stories, his body was a ruin of weird tattoos and horrible scars.

The white-haired man scurried offstage with the discarded clothing, and returned with two more clay pots and a towel. Instead of incense, one pot seemed to contain ground charcoal. The other, blood.

Jhootha put a thumb into either pot and smeared a band of color over each eye. Then he wiped his hands on the towel. "Ladies and gentlemen. My associate, Mr. Frost, will select a volunteer from the audience. I trust that one or two of you may have brought something you would like read?" There was another chuckle. Jhootha waited until the room was silent again. "I remind you. Please. Do not ask for the truth if you do not wish it. And, above all else, silence when we contact the spirits."

Jhootha turned to face upstage while the taciturn, pale man returned to the stage with some object offered up by a member of the audience. Only then would Jhootha examine the piece, never having seen its owner.

This time, it was a book. An old bible with cracked binding and frayed pages. Frost tapped Jhootha on the shoulder and the magician turned to face the audience, cradling the book. He held up the bible while Frost retreated to the edge of the stage. "Ah! Very good. Now we ask the spirits to please show themselves —" There were gasps, and a scream, from the crowd as people saw figures drifting in the smoke above Jhootha's head. Both medium and assistant threw out their hands in a frantic demand for silence. Jhootha put a finger to his lips and mouthed, "Quiet! Please!"

Then the magician sat on the floor. Absolutely still. A child's voice spoke out from the roving ghosts overhead. *This is Grandfather Isaac's book... There is writing in the margins... Grandfather Isaac told his grandchildren this was a code for sending messages past British soldiers during the war... But it was Emily... Emily practiced her letters by writing in the margin of a book.*

Jhootha slumped and held the book at arm's length. Mr Frost hurried over to take the book, then deposited it beside the footlights.

The white-haired man ventured into the audience again, returned with a tiny, metal object. Invisible, except when the light reflected just so. Jhootha held the thing to his forehead. A man's voice this time. Flinty and old. *Jonathan pricked his hand on this needle... Left on the green stuffed chair with the mending...Little Jonathan sat down and pricked his hand... Then he took fever and died.*

There was a cry from the audience. As from someone in pain. Frost and Jhootha, again, held out their hands in a demand for silence. A few people started to say "Shh!" before they seemed to recall they, too, were to remain silent.

The old man's voice spoke again. *Jonathan's appendix burst... That's why he died... His hand would have gotten better in a few days... His appendix killed him... Not the mending.* Then the needle joined the book at front of the stage.

There were other items. A telescope. A kettle. A comb. A

lady's handkerchief. He pressed each of these to his forehead in turn. A different voice came from the aether surrounding The Great Jhootha, telling the story of each object. Then the item would join a growing line under the footlights.

Jhootha dismissed the spirits, stood up and dressed, and held up the old bible. "Would the owner of this book please come on stage?" A man in his 40s climbed the steps on stage left. His suit was well made, but not gaudy. Jhootha took the man's hand and shook. "You are the owner of this book, sir?"

"Yes."

"Your name, sir?"

"Murdock. James Murdock."

"Glad to know you, Mr. Murdock." Jhootha shook his hand again. "Have we met before?"

"No."

"Very good." He turned to the audience. "Can anyone here vouch for Mr. Murdock? That you know him as an honest man?"

Scattered shouts of "Yes" came from places around the theater.

Jhootha said, "Very good" again, turned back to Murdock. "What can you tell us about this book?"

The man gave an unhappy smile. "I daresay you could tell more than I might."

Several people in the audience laughed. Jhootha said "Go ahead, Mr. Murdock."

"Well. This bible's been in our family for quite a while. Grandfather always said his father used it to sneak Yankee messages past the redcoats. It seems Grandfather was mistaken."

"Who is Emily?"

"That might be my grandfather's sister. She died when the house burned down."

"I am sorry to hear that." He handed the book to its owner. "Thank you so much, Mr. Murdock."

The Great Jhootha applauded. The audience applauded. Daniel Murdock returned to his seat. The Great Jhootha held up the needle and invited its owner onstage.

There were two. The owners of the needle were a man and a woman in their late 30s. Mr. Frost had to assist them in navigating the steps, as both had vision clouded with tears that filled their eyes and splashed down their faces.

Before Jhootha was able to ask their names, the crying man embraced him. The woman, fighting tiny sobs that fluttered in her chest, gripped the magician's hand and whispered, "Thank you."

When the embrace was over, Jhootha learned their names and verified with the audience that Oliver and Edith Blake lived in that city. Then, with several pauses to wipe his eyes, Oliver Blake told how, going on 20 years ago, their little boy sat on the chair where Edith had been mending Oliver's coat. The boy pricked his hand on a needle. Then he took fever and died.

The Great Jhootha gave a sad smile, looked into Mr. Blake's eyes, then Mrs. Blake's. "Seems to me you've been carrying something it's long past time you set it down."

More applause from the audience. Louder this time. And cheers. The magician gave back their needle and was rewarded with another embrace, another squeeze of his hand. Oliver and Edith Blake returned to their seats, heavier by the weight of one number 7 needle, lighter by the weight of years of self-recrimination.

When everyone was, again, in possession of their belongings, The Great Jhootha thanked everyone for coming. He admonished them to be wary of the spirit realm and wished them all a pleasant evening. Then the curtain fell, and the magician hurried from the stage.

***

"That was, I think, a little risky. With the needle." Mr. Frost pulled the wig from his head and became Hamelin DeClerk. He scratched where the red-brown hair on sides and back of his head grew into an ugly stubble. Probably time to shave it again.

"What are you talking about?"

"The needle. They could have gotten a different one. Then you would look at that and they would call you out for it."

"No." Jhootha, in process of turning back into James Lassiter Gordon, took a breath and ducked his head under water. He came up, snorting like a hippopotamus. "Not those two. They lost a child."

"They might have suspected."

"They got to set down their guilt for the price of a couple of twenty-five-dollar tickets. Christ, Ham. I could charge three times as much, tell them it's fake, and they'd still call it a bargain!"

"But if they suspected —"

"They thanked me. If they could still have kids, they'd probably name the next one Jhootha Frost Blake."

"But —"

"But nothing." Gordon grabbed the wood-handled brush that floated next to him and rubbed soap into the bristles. Then he set to work, scrubbing away wax scars and painted tattoos. "God's sake, Ham. I have never, in my life, been good at anything." He paused to worry at a bit of wax that clung to his chest hair. "Except now. I'm good at being Jhootha."

"I still think you should be more careful."

"Fine. Thank you for the advice."

"Then, what about that bible?"

"What about it?"

"Peter could not find anything to show it wasn't genuine."

"Yeah. Well, it's more believable when you don't just pander to whatever people want to hear... And besides, that pompous bastard needed taken down a peg."

"You are playing it to be risky."

"I'm done talking about this. Do we have anything yet for the stop in three weeks?" When Ham didn't respond, James Gordon said, "Well?"

"Our next stop, there is that rope from the hanging. There is also a teacup. Paul says the rope could be genuine. Claudia says the teacup is probably not genuine. And the owners know that."

"Hmm." Gordon splashed hot water over his now pink, smooth skin. "Not much to work with there. Maybe we can give it a good story before they got it... That's in Salem, right?"

"Pardon? Ah. Yes. We will be in Salem."

"Have to remember to make a joke about witches."

"That is a different Salem."

Porter? Didn't they find anything?"

"They did not. They can plant the crowd. But no pigeons.

"Ugh." Gordon splashed water on his face, snorted, splashed again. "What the hell am I paying them for?... It's been a while since we did the medicine bottle. We can do that one. And the potato masher... And maybe the snuff box."

"We just had the snuff box."

"Fine, then. The abacus. And those people need to get us something besides a damned teacup!"

***

Amy was lying on her side, quiet snores in perfect time with a blanket that rose and fell. Tiny form illuminated by moon and gaslight that peeked through frayed curtains.

Gordon crept to the bed, placed a gentle kiss on the child's brow. Lips still pressed to her skin, he said, "You can fool most people. But you can't fool The Great Jhootha."

"How did you know I was awake?!" The girl sat up. Mischief and indignation vying for dominance on her face.

"I'm your dad. I know you better than I know my own self." He grinned. "Also, this light is still hot." He touched the lamp beside her bed. "Your lesson book is right here." He indicated the math and grammar book beside her. "And we still haven't had a story... Did you remember to put away the lanterns tonight? And the cutouts?"

"Yep."

"Good job with those tonight. You made some people scream." The girl smiled. Gordon plunged each hand into a jacket pocket, produced a box of matches and a wrinkled book. "Now. Shove over. We've got to see whether Aladdin is ever going to escape from that cave."

Amy shoved over. "Daddy?"

"Yes, my dear?"

"Is Aladdin's turban like the hat you wear for Jhootha?"

"I don't think so. Aladdin's an Arab. And I got that hat in the Orient."

"Where you met Ham?"

"Yep."

"Where you saved his life?"

"I'm sure he would've been fine without me there."

"So... It's a Nipponese hat?"

"I don't think so, Dear. It's a one of a kind. None other like it in the whole, wide world." He grinned. "That's what makes it magic!"

"Daddy..." She tried to look serious. "Everybody knows there's not really magic."

"Well, I hope that isn't so!" He lifted the hood from the lamp, set it beside Amy's lesson book. James Lassiter Gordon struck a match, touched it to the lamp wick, replaced the hood. "Otherwise, your poor daddy would have to find new work! Now." He raised the book like it was a ticket or a letter of safe passage. "I think it's time we check up on Aladdin."

***

Tickets for the Olympia performance sold out more than a week before the show. The owners of the theater had begged The Great Jhootha for a second night, but he demurred. They offered to let him take all but $200 of the second night's take, but he told them there was a schedule to keep. They offered him all but $150, but he told them the unseen spirits might be especially riled-up after two disturbances in the same place, so close together like that, and that it would be too dangerous.

Robert Cannon, chief among those who held interest in the venue, was disappointed at the lost prospect of a second show. But he did seem to know and accept when he was beaten. And he took it in stride.

"Whiskey?" The heavyset man, not waiting for an answer, produced three glasses and a bottle from his desk. As he poured, he said, "Well, Mr... Jhootha, it is?"

"It is. And please."

"Well, I suppose I ought to have booked two shows to start with." He pushed two of the whiskeys across the desk where Mr. Frost and The Great Jhootha each took a glass and sipped. "Do you suppose that might have put the spirits in a better mood?"

The man in a strange, silk hat inclined his head. "Perhaps."

Cannon grunted, downed his whiskey, poured another. "Thought so."

Jhootha regarded this man. Here was someone not of wealthy

parentage, but neither was he born to poverty. Dressed in a suit with stitching that betrayed a wish to be seen as a man who could afford expensive suits. Hands, rough and meaty in the manner of one not a stranger to hard work in the past, but not as much as he would have others believe. A wedding band that rode his finger in the way that suggested a mistress who loved him and a wife who, maybe, did not.

Mr. Frost finished his whiskey, set his glass back on the desk. Cannon did not hurry to refill his glass. "So, tell me." The theater owner leaned back and cracked his knuckles. His chair made a similar noise. "How do you do it?"

"Do what, sir?" The Great Jhootha looked perplexed.

"All of it. The whole thing. That thing where you know all about people's things. The ghosts flying around. The voices."

"That's magic."

"Magic, huh? Great. How do you really do it?"

"Magic."

"Huh." Robert Cannon turned to Mr. Frost. "How about you?" You going to tell me it's magic too?"

Frost nodded. The Great Jhootha said, "I'm afraid Mr. Frost does not speak."

"Well, that's a terrible shame." Cannon poured more whiskey. Poured until each glass was full to the top. Then he refilled the glasses until the bottle was empty.

Frost and Jhootha left Cannon's office more than an hour and two more bottles of whiskey later. They had smoked his cigars and enjoyed his hospitality. But they hadn't given him any better explanation for the act, other than magic and disembodied spirits. Then, with breath reeking of liquor, and the floor swaying beneath them, the two performers made their way to the door and outside.

"Snow." The syllable escaped James Gordon's mouth and

remained suspended before the pair of them until the wind swept it away.

"Yea." Ham kicked a heavy clump of the wet stuff. "Going to make it hard for the pigeons to come to the show."

"They'll come. They paid too much to miss it on account of a little weather. Probably be gone by tomorrow anyway."

"I think it will not."

"Too late in the year for this. We timed it this way. It'll be gone tomorrow."

"If you say. But the weather here is not so kind."

The unfamiliar city darkened under thickening clouds and streetlights extinguished by the wind. Then the city turned white under heavy drifts of ever-thickening snow. And two drunks managed to stagger back to hotel and bed through an unanticipated winter storm.

***

"Where's my hat? Where the devil is my hat?" Gordon rifled through the contents of their small hotel room, not for the first time that afternoon. "Did one of you take it? For a joke of something?"

"I did not take it." Ham was sorting through his trunk. One item of clothing at a time, checked, restacked. No hat.

"I didn't take it." Amy called out from under the bed. "But I found four pennies!"

"Well, that's something." Gordon frowned. "What happened to my hat?"

"I think we should check outside" Ham said. "Maybe you left it in the snow last night."

"Maybe." He sighed. "Well, we can't do that now." He nodded toward the window, pattering with dots of snow and ice drumming against it. "Besides, we need to get ready for the show."

Ham donned his Mr. Frost costume. Amy checked and rechecked that her ghost-projecting lanterns were in perfect order. Then daughter and assistant painted scars and tattoos over the arms and torso of The Great Jhootha.

***

The falling curtain that evening was louder than the unenthusiastic people who comprised his meager audience. James Lassiter Gordon decided the best part of this whole mess had been the weather. At least more people stayed home, instead of coming here to watch him make an ass of himself.

Wrong. His readings were wrong. The voices were wrong. By the time the plants had come on stage, he'd lost the audience. All of it, just wrong.

No. That wasn't fair. Amy was perfect. Frost was perfect. Paul and Claudia. Jack and Clem and Porter. All perfect. Except The Great Jhootha.

Trudging through a bright white and alien world, he said as much. "That was a bad show," he said to Amy and Ham. "But that was my fault. I don't know what's the matter. But you…you two did everything just right."

Neither Amy nor Ham said anything. The trio made their way along neat, shoveled paths between the drifts. Gaslights shone off the snow, making the world a surreal daylight where fierce blizzard had ended with a failed magic show.

The noise of laughter and children drifted from a nearby alley. Gordon turned to his daughter. "Do you want to go play with the other kids?"

She gave an unconvincing smile. "No." Then, "Thank you... Maybe we should read some more of the Arabian story."

Gordon smiled back. "I think that's probably a good idea."

Ham said, "And we should get ready for the Portland show."

"Right." Gordon made a sour face. "Portland."

They returned to their hotel room and lit a fire in the stove. They lit every lamp and turned the wicks high. Gordon wished they had some whiskey, headache from last night be damned.

He stared out the window. The snow made everything almost glowing. A group of children, distorted and pale in that unwholesome light, were building a snowman.

"Hey! My hat!"

Ham said, "What are you —"

"They have my hat!" Gordon opened the window, shouted, "Hey!" Then turned to the door.

Amy said, "I'm hungry."

Gordon said, "Supper in a minute." He threw open the door and ran outside.

The street was empty. No children. No hat. No snowman. Gordon stood with numb feet and wet socks, panting. His breath made clouds in the frigid air.

He walked back to their room and closed the door and window. He took his socks off and laid them beside the stove. Then he slid his boots over his wet, unstockinged feet. "I am going to pick up some supper." He kissed Amy on the top of her little head. "What would you like?"

***

Amy lay, snuggled up on the cot by the stove. Her little chest rose and fell in beautiful, sweet quiet. Ham, asleep on Gordon's left, snored. The noise, almost a ripsaw. A particular sound

Gordon thought must be unique to a Frenchman after a meal of potatoes and cheese. Sometimes the noise would stop, and Gordon would think peace had finally come. Then Ham would smack his lips and the snoring would resume.

Gordon estimated that the snoring ended maybe ten minutes before sunlight poured around the curtains to fill their room. About twenty minutes before someone was pounding on their hotel room door.

"Dammit." He fumbled with the covers and stood, then made his way to the door. "Yes?"

He opened the door to see an unhandsome man with muddy boots and a drooping mustache. The man carried a rifle. He wore a revolver on his hip and a brass star on his lapel. Behind this man, four others stood. All similarly molded from equal parts thug and law.

The newcomer spoke. "Any of you see the bear?"

"The what?!"

"Bear."

"What bear?"

"Chinaman's boy got killed last night. On the docks. Partly eaten." The stranger pointed at the nearby river. "Couple of white kids missing too."

"I'm...We didn't see anything. We were inside all night. Except for when I went to get some supper." The man grumbled something and turned to leave. Gordon said, "Sir?"

The lawman faced him again. "Yeah?"

"A bear should be hiding in a cave right now. It's winter."

Brass star scowled. "Don't tell me my business." And stomped away.

The last of that small posse stopped to make eye contact with Gordon. Then he spat a gobbet of phlegm and tobacco juice into the snow, before catching up with his friends.

James Lassiter Gordon closed the door and sighed. He crept through the room, gathered his clothes, dressed. Careful to not wake Amy and Ham. Then he stepped out the door to a world of cold and bright.

The snow made a soft noise beneath the magician's boots as he walked. Like grinding coffee. Like a spoon taking scoops of cornmeal.

The noise of laughter, children playing, came from the adjacent street. Up early and not in school. And a bunch of little damned thieves, now that he thought about it. He would have to be sure and get his hat back from them before getting on the train.

***

Robert Cannon was not in his office. Gordon waited over two hours before the impresario materialized. Same suit as the day before, the smells of bacon and coffee joined those of cigar and whiskey.

Cannon frowned. "What're you doing here?"

Gordon said, "The show, sir. You still haven't paid us —"

"Show?!" Cannon exploded. "That wasn't a show! That was a damned embarrassment."

"I know it wasn't the best —"

"Not the best!" Cannon thrust his pudgy finger into Gordon's chest like a knife. "I got people wanting their money back. I got people going to go somewhere else next time they got a hankering to see a show. I'm not paying you to ruin me."

"But we agreed —"

"Hank!" Cannon shouted, then leaned close to Gordon until their faces were almost touching. The fat man's breath made Gordon feel nauseous, but also reminded him he still hadn't eaten breakfast. "Now you listen to me, you little bastard. The only reason you're not tarred on a rail right now is we got the law here, looking for some stupid bear. But you push me, and I'll get him to help me. Understand?"

"I'm —"

A giant of a man, presumably Hank, entered the room. Cannon said, "Hank, help The Great Jhootha, here, find the door."

***

James Lassiter Gordon made a snowball and held it to the side of his face. He prayed the bruise would be gone by their next show. The limp, courtesy of Hank shoving him down the stairs, could just be part of his wizard mystique. But who ever heard of a sorcerer with a black eye?

The noise of those children, still playing, followed him back to the hotel room. A jolt of pain shot through Gordon's knee, and he decided he could wait a little longer to retrieve the hat. He opened the door and stepped inside.

Amy and Ham were awake and dressed. The girl said, "Daddy!" and ran toward him. Then she stopped. "What happened?!"

"This?" Gordon took the lump of snow from his eye, threw it outside, closed the door. "Nothing. Just fell down and bumped myself a little bit. Slippery out there."

Ham didn't look convinced. "Did you see Monsieur Cannon?"

"I did."

"And did he pay you?"

"There was a little trouble with the bank. Because of the snow. But they're sending a telegram. Money should be waiting for us in San Francisco."

Ham looked unhappy but said nothing. Amy said, "We got sandwiches for breakfast, and we saved you one. It's roast beef."

Gordon hugged his daughter. "Thank you. I'll eat it right now. And then we better hurry up and pack. We don't want to be late for our train."

Ham said, "The train is not until late this afternoon —"

Gordon shot the man a terse look. "We don't want to be late."

Sandwiches were eaten and clothes were packed when there was another knock at the door. Gordon stood, hobbled to the door, and opened it. Robert Cannon was there. His little dewlap quivered in the late winter cold. Beside him were the frowning lawman Gordon had seen earlier, and Hank.

There was an awkward silence until Cannon snatched Gordon's hand and swung it up and down like a pump handle. "Mr. Jhootha! Oh, Mr. Jhootha! How I have misjudged you! That is just amazing! Simply amazing! I would ask how you do it, but a magician never reveals his secrets, isn't that right?"

Gordon said, "That's...that's right."

"Oh! And here's your assistant, the versatile Mr. Frost. It is Mr. Frost, isn't it? Hello, Mr. Frost. And this lovely, young lady. Is that your daughter? What a charming girl."

They stared at each other, the uncomfortable quiet louder than the distant, yet growing noise of cheers. Children.

Cannon said, "Hank has something to say to you." He slapped the giant on the arm. "Go ahead."

The big man frowned, wrinkled his thick forehead. "I apologize for what happened. There was a misunderstanding, and I did wrong, and I hope you accept my apology."

After a beat Cannon said, "Fine. Now get out of here, you big lummox." Hank scurried away. Cannon smiled and said, "Now, Mr. Jhootha. I believe I owe you something." He produced a stack of green paper from inside his jacket and thrust it at James Gordon.

"What —"

"Why, it's yours. All of it. And a little something extra for your troubles."

"Um. Thank you."

"Thank you, Mr. Jhootha. What you did. It's just...Well, it's magic."

"I'm... Right."

"But please. Please promise that, whenever you are in the area, you will play my theater. Just my theater. Whatever you want. We'll pay it."

"Another thing." Bronze Star spoke up this time. "Could you please try to keep it out of the main thoroughfares when people are trying to move? Just that things are bad enough right now, with the snow. Then a parade like that can really block up traffic."

Gordon said, "Traffic?"

"Not that there's any problem," Cannon put in. "Is there, Sheffield?"

Bronze Star frowned. "No. There isn't any problem. Just worried about the bear attacks, I suppose."

Gordon wasn't sure how. But by the time the two had left, they had extracted a promise from him. When in Olympia, The Great Jhootha would only ever play Robert Cannon's theater.

He closed the door and turned to the others. "Well. We got paid."

Ham looked as if he didn't know whether to be happy or angry. "So, we see."

Amy said, "Is there a parade?"

"No, dearest. I don't think that man knows what he's talking about."

Amy said, "What's that noise?"

Ham peered out the window. He wiped the glass, stared some more, then said, "It is a parade."

Amy and Gordon rushed to the window. The three pressed their faces against the glass.

Impossible.

A riot of children marched up the street. They laughed. They sang. At the head of this column, staff in his hand like a drum major, keeping perfect step, a snowman.

Gordon said, "Is that a snowman?"

Ham said, "That is a snow man."

The golem of ice marched past, a bit of cloth almost discernible inside. And maybe a shirt button. Maybe a pipe. Maybe a row of very small teeth.

Gordon said, "Is that a broom?"

Ham said, "I think that is an oar."

The snowman hurried on its way. *Catch me if you can.*

A little girl, her father, his assistant. All three stood at the window and stared down the lane where crowd and snowman had disappeared.

"Wait! My hat!" Gordon tore himself from the window and rushed to the door.

Ham said, "What —their goddamn snowman!" Gordon ran outside and down the road, after the parade.

He knew it was too late. But he ran and he shouted. He searched. He paced the streets of Olympia, hunting a snowman in a stolen cap. A cap that was the rightful property of The Great Jhootha.

***

"It has been three days." Ham pleaded with his employer, his friend. "We had to cancel the Portland show, and will have to cancel the Salem show if this keeps going."

"Goddammit, Ham. I can't go on without the hat."

"Yes. You can."

"No, I can't. Have you seen me get anything right, anything, since I lost the hat?"

"You are just having a bad confidence. That is all."

"It's not confidence. Don't you see? I only started getting it right after I had the hat. And now that it's gone, nothing."

"You are saying it was a real magic?"

"You want to tell me how a snowman started moving around?"

"Maybe it was a man in a costume."

"Do you believe that?! You saw that thing!"

"...Yes. I did... So, what do you do now?"

"Just...just keep looking."

"But the snow is all melted now. There is no snow man."

"Then we look for the hat somewhere in a puddle or something."

Another day combing the city. Then Amy told them about the bear attacks. "A cleaning girl got killed," she told them. "In Tacoma. They said it was a bear. And then two kids got lost in the snow. Because nobody could find them."

Ham and Gordon looked at each other, then back at the girl. "Where did you hear this?"

"I was playing dolls with Karen Vernon. Her daddy works at the telegraph office. And then two people got killed by a bear last night in Seattle."

Gordon cursed. "Ham, we need tickets. Something fast. To somewhere north of Seattle."

Hamelin DeClerk frowned. "But we will be out of monies. "

"We're not going to have any money ever again if we don't get my hat back. And guns. We're probably going to need a couple of guns. And maybe a couple of dogs."

"But the money is low."

"Just get it." James Lassiter Gordon turned to his daughter. "Now, let's go and get you some candy."

***

The SS Durante stank of coal smoke and unwashed men. Engine huffing like an angry bull, she labored against the waves, butting into every breaker, also like an angry bull.

"Can't you go any faster?" Gordon demanded of the captain.

"I'm beatin' her up as it is." Captain Frees squinted at the clouds up ahead.

"But I paid you extra to go fast."

"This is fast."

"But the snow's still ahead of us."

"I'm not in charge of the weather." Captain Frees glared at Gordon. "But I am in charge of this ship. This is fast enough."

Gordon nodded and left the bridge. Hands against the walls, he struggled down the staircase that was almost a ladder. The Durante bucked and rocked, trying to throw her demanding passenger down the remainder of those steps.

Amy and Ham were crouched in a portion of hold that had been left empty to serve as the trio's cabin. The shifting floor had canceled their checkers game when the pieces kept sliding from the board. Instead, the two placed a ball in the center of their makeshift quarters, then shouted and giggled to one another as they argued where the ball would roll next.

Gordon sat and watched the two, his tired form leaning against the bulkhead. Just beyond that thin barrier of tarred planks, the sea threatened to crash in like a mad beast and snatch away everything Gordon had. Everything he had left.

The ball wobbled, seeming uncertain which direction to follow on the shifting deck. Then it tumbled over to stop in the lap of a man who, again, would be The Great Jhootha.

Amy and Ham cheered. The Durante shifted and creaked, promising in a language none understood that she would keep them safe in her grandmother's womb of cargo and beams and creosote.

Ham said, "What did he say?"

Gordon answered "You were right. He said this is as fast as we can go in the storm." As if to emphasize that point, the Durante struck a large wave. She pitched forward and shuddered. Cargo strained against its ties like a pack of dogs, eager for the hunt.

The ball fell out of Gordon's lap and bounced toward the bow. Not moving his lips, Gordon made the ball talk. *Here I go! Faster than the rest of you! Catch me if you can!* Then the Durante reared back, and the ball rolled toward the stern. *I can't tell where I'm going because I don't have any eyes! Whee!* Amy laughed. Ham grinned. The ball changed direction and rolled toward the front of the ship with Amy in pursuit.

Ham said, "Is that the ball talking, or you?"

Gordon scowled. "Not this again."

Ham said, "You are making the ball talk without the hat."

"That's different and you know it is?"

"Is it? How old is the captain?"

"Shy of fifty."

"Is he married?"

"Widowed."

"Children?"

"Two living. One dead."

"Drinks?"

"Never on ship. Gets whiskey drunk on shore."

"Ahh." Ham smiled, tented his fingers. "And he told you all this when?"

"He...he didn't."

"He didn't what? I am sorry. My English is not so good sometimes."

Gordon scowled. "He didn't tell me any of that."

Ham clapped his hands to his face, formed his mouth into a letter O. "Alors! How did you know?"

Amy returned with the errant ball, placed it on the deck between the two men, then ran after the toy as it rolled away again.

Gordon said, "I am done talking about this. We need to get the hat back. Those kids stole it. That thing has it. It's mine and I need it back."

"And your plan?"

"Silver's supposed to kill magic things in the stories. That's why we got cap and ball guns. I had that jeweler cast slugs out of silver —"

"That is not what I —"

"We track it down with dogs, kill it, and get my hat back."

The Durante leaned starboard, and Amy ran past, still not in custody of her wayward ball. Ham said, "I mean what of the plan for where we make shows until there is enough money? You buy a farm and maybe find a mother for Amy? I buy a farm and get a wife? Do you remember that plan, James?"

Beyond a stack of crates, Amy shouted in triumph, then shrieked when she set the ball down and it rolled away again. Gordon said, "Look. The plan is the same. We just...I need the hat."

"I will buy you a new hat."

"I need that hat. Just...without it there's no more shows, no money, no farms, no wife for you…nothing to leave for Amy after I'm gone."

Two men sat in the dark and greasy cargo hold of the SS Durante. The gap in their conversation was filled by the creaking of timbers, a chugging steam engine, and a little girl shouting, "Come back here!"

James Lassiter Gordon wiped his eyes and said, "Goddamn little bastards stole my hat."

Ham said, "Then a bear ate them during the winter and snow."

The Durante shuddered against the waves. Amy yelled something unintelligible at her ball. Gordon said, "It's not supposed to be real, you. Magic, I mean. It's not supposed to be real."

Ham's mouth curled into what might have been a smile, if the rest of his face had shifted with it. "No. It is not."

***

The only dogs for sale were a sad pair of mongrels. Better suited to napping beside a stove than tracking a golem of snow. Any use these two might have had was long spent years before. Amy called them Toka and Mootoo. When asked why, she said, "Because that's their names."

The old trapper who offered the dogs for sale, argued with Ham for what seemed like hours. The backwoodsman, unimpressed with Ham's Continental-French, conversed in his own, New-World dialect of that same tongue. While Amy patted the dogs, Gordon watched a debate in a language he didn't understand. Mountain Man, there, was missing a couple of fingers on his right hand. Most likely a trap went off when he was setting it. At least two wives, maybe three. One dead in childbirth, and one left him. He'd been a brute to them both, all, whatever.

Ham wore a sour look as he pushed the dogs' lead ropes into Gordon's hand. "We are paying too much. But there are not any other dogs. Everyone is gone to look for gold, and they buy all the dogs."

Gordon looked down at the mangy pair. Mootoo was having her ears scratched by Amy, while Toka seemed to feel it was her turn, and Mootoo should get out of the way. "Then I guess we're stuck. Pay him."

"We do not have to keep doing this."

"Yes, we do. Pay him."

"He says we are stupid for chasing a bear in the winter. He says the bears will not be out in the winter."

"Well, he's right about that."

"He also says there are some children who were missing."

"Where?!"

"He just came from there. The whites are blaming the Indians. And the Indians are blaming the whites. He just wanted to go away from there." Ham sighed, looked resigned. "He also said he can make a map for us."

"Get the map!" James Lassiter Gordon tugged the dogs' lead with one hand, grabbed his daughter's arm with the other. "Come on, Amy! We've got to get supplies! Quick!"

Cold weather clothing, food, tent, and matches. Sled and show-shoes. Compass, ax, and bedrolls. All of it priced for sale to desperate men on a northward dash for gold.

**

"It should be here. Somewhere." Ham pointed at the valley before them, and then stared back at the map. "It should be here. We should see the smoke."

Gordon stood beside his friend, gazed at the valley of drifts and snow-blanketed trees. "Maybe they moved?"

"Winter would be a bad time for them to move."

"I suppose." Gordon turned to his daughter. "You okay up there?"

"Okay, Daddy." Amy had insisted on riding the old gelding they bought to pull the sled. "Star keeps me warm. Don't you, boy?" She patted the ancient creature's neck.

If there had been a better horse in town for sale, Gordon couldn't have bought it. Purchase of this swaybacked nag, suitable only for the knackers; and then storage of The Great Jhootha's equipment, had eaten the last of the savings. Gordon wasn't sure how they would buy passage back on the show circuit, once they had the hat back.

They were lucky. The weather had been clear. And the snow was just deep enough for the sled, but shallow enough to allow easy passage of horse, dog, and man.

It has also been quiet. No sign of people since they started along the trail. No animals either, save the trio of ravens that sometimes flew near to croak at them before flying away again.

Gordon raised a hand to shield his eyes, more from cold than sun, and said, "I think your trapper friend gave us some bad directions."

"I think he did not." Ham pointed. "Look there."

A series of black shapes and outlines set against the dark of forest ground, covered in snow. Invisible until pointed out by the erstwhile Mr. Frost.

"Is that it?"

"I think it is." Ham frowned. "But there is not smoke. No sounds. Something is wrong."

"Your gun handy?"

"It is right here."

"How do we do this?"

"I will go down. You wait with Amy." The Frenchman waved at the dogs. "Chiens! Allons-y!"

Mootoo whined and didn't move. Toka sniffed at a bush, apparently deaf. Ham made a rude gesture at the dogs, cursed, and stomped down the trail.

They hadn't been eager to set out on this trip. Two tired, old hounds, straining to return to the comfort and safety of town. Then, as they neared their destination, Toka and Mootoo seemed ever less willing to follow the humans to this place.

Toka joined Mootoo in whining. Gordon told them to hush. Amy had some jerky, a biscuit, some water. Then she braided Star's mane. When that was finished, she combed the braids loose, then braided it again.

Gordon blew on his hands and stomped his feet. Just off the horizon, three black specks, ravens, against a grey sky. Aside from man and daughter, horse and dog and raven, all was still. Frozen.

He saw the smoke, a thin finger of grey on grey, at the same time he saw Ham. The man waved his arms, pointed north, then started toward them.

When he reached them, the Frenchman said "Most of the buildings burned. And all of the people are gone."

Amy said, "I'm cold."

Ham smiled. "Well. It is a good thing I made a fire." He slapped Gordon's shoulder, pointed north again. "Look there."

Gordon squinted. "What?"

"There is rain and a warm spot there."

"So?"

"If your snow man is here, he is trapped."

"Are you sure?"

Ham grinned. "If I can take a ship from Calais to Nippon, I think I know what a rain looks like."

Gordon nodded. "Right. Why don't we go see to that fire of yours?"

***

They had to drag the animals to the valley. Gordon pulled Star's halter rope while the horse balked and shook his head. Ham towed the dogs to their new quarters, cursing at them in three languages.

The former occupants, while maybe not in a panic, had left in a hurry. Valuables and food were gone. As were blankets and clothes. But there was ample firewood. And decent stoves in the houses that hadn't turned to ash.

Most of the homes on the village perimeter had burned. Whether that was deliberate or accident, neither Ham nor Gordon could say. Although, they both guessed it was intentional. A ring of cinders, several homes deep. Surrounding an unblemished big-house.

Not one of those massive, long-houses of bygone days, the big-house was still impressive. A great hall of planks and logs. A place for the village to meet and be together. A place for the chief to administer justice. A place for the community to shelter while, outside, their houses burned.

Rows of benches and chairs. A good stove at either end of the place. Plenty of lamps and tins of kerosene. A few books. A piano.

Ham pointed to the books and told Amy, "You are behind on your lessons. You should do some work now." Then he said to Gordon, "Outside with me."

Back in the ankle-deep snow, Gordon said, "What is it?"

Ham pointed at the sky. "It is warmer and raining north. Your snow man is trapped here. But we will have more cold and snow."

"How long?"

"Soon."

"We're stuck here."

"I think. Yes."

"What do we do?"

"All the wood we can. Bring it inside. Stack it against the walls. Like under shirt. And all the kerosene we can find. For the lamps. And food. We need more food."

"How long are we here for?"

"I do not know."

Toka and Mootoo were only too happy to curl up by the stove with Amy. Star had been less keen on being in the big-house, until he seemed to realize it would be dry and warm in there. An impromptu corner stall was made with a pair of tables, and the gelding settled right in.

Gordon felt claustrophobic, with tins of kerosene and piled logs on every side. But he deferred to Ham's instinct for weather. The Frenchman had been a decent sailor, not some infantry deserter and variety show charlatan.

The snow was tentative at first. Tiny, invisible pinpricks against the background. Then it came in earnest. Great, heavy clusters of snowflakes that tumbled to earth and whispered *Shh!*

***

Amy laughed until she hiccupped. "Do it again, Daddy!"

"Me?!" James Lassiter Gordon tried to look confused. "I'm not doing anything!"

"Do it again!"

Without moving his lips, Gordon made Toka say *The best part of a ham is the part with fat on it!*

No, it isn't! Mootoo said. *The best part of a ham is the rind! The fat is the best!*

That's not even a ham! The fat is what goes on bacon!
No, it isn't!
Yes, it is!

Amy screamed with laughter. Still not moving his lips, Gordon made Star say *Oh, stop it, you two. Somebody get me a sugarlump!*

Ham made his way to the piano while Amy tried to catch her breath. Gordon said, "That's enough you three!"

Then he made Toka say *Fat!*
Mootoo said *That's bacon!*
Fine then! Bacon!
Rind!
Fat!
Somebody get me a sugarlump!

Ham started playing the piano and singing. "Oh! Some like the fat part! And some like the rind! You can call it bacon, and that will still taste fine! There is some who want a sugar lump —"

The song came to a rude ending when both dogs sprang to their feet and began a frenzy of barking. Snarling and baying, they faced the wall, ready to attack any intruder who might appear in that spot.

Star pinned his ears back and stomped his foot. The horse snorted and turned in his poor stall before he seemed to decide he might best express displeasure by kicking the stack of logs behind him. Amy had stopped laughing. Her little, round face, still flushed, wore an expression of incomprehension and fear. Gordon and Ham looked at each other, then at Amy. Gordon said,

"What's—" And then they heard it.

A low throbbing, more a vibration through the ground than any real noise. *Tum. Tum. Tum. Tum. Tum. Tum. Tum.* Gordon might have sworn it sounded like a giant's heartbeat, save that it was in perfect rhythm to the song they had just been singing. *Some like the fatty bit. Some like the rind.*

***

"What is it?" Gordon whispered to keep from waking the little girl asleep on his lap.

"How do I know that?" Ham whispered back.

"What do you reckon it is?"

"It is a snow man."

"How?"

The Frenchman shrugged. "Magic?"

"Is there any such thing?"

"I think maybe there is."

They sat, wordless and pensive. Fire hummed in the stove, accompanied by the snoring of dogs and girl. Outside, wind cried and falling snow told it to *Hush*.

Gordon said, "Why did it take those kids?"

Ham shrugged again. "It must have something in mind?"

"Something in mind?" He made a sour face. "You think it thinks now? It's a...a pile of snow does not think."

"It thought to move north because spring time will be coming."

"That's...quit talking crazy."

Ham smirked. It was not a happy expression. "We are in a snow storm in Canada, because you are chasing the people-killing snow man that stole your magic hat. It is a time for crazy talking, I think."

"Goddammit." Gordon started to move, then stopped when he remembered the sleeping Amy on his lap. He inclined his head to the stove. "Put some more wood on there, will you?" Ham fed the stove while James Lassiter Gordon sat and tried to puzzle his way around why chase after a magic hat.

**

He woke. Senses coming to confused, gradual focus like a rusty stereoscope. The dogs were baying at the far end of the big-house, hackles raised and teeth bared. Rickety old bitches, finding courage inherent to any creature that finds itself threatened and no place to flee. Star reared and snorted. Hooves lashing against tables and firewood. Ham was shouting curses in French. Pistol in his right hand, he pushed Amy behind himself with the left.

Gordon struggled from his bedroll and tottered to his feet. "What's happening?!" Then he felt the cold. Every breath heavy in his lungs and throat. His face aching. Everything so cold.

Ham yelled, "The stove is gone out! I think it dropped snow in the —"

The building shook. Floorboards shifted under Gordon's feet and he stumbled. Like being on-board the Durante again. But with screaming. Ham cursed again and stepped away from where they were clustered by the cooling stove. He unscrewed lids from the kerosene tins and threw them across the room.

Gordon called out over the racket, "What the hell are you doing?!" Then the building shook again and the front wall tore away in a din of creaks and splintering.

The blizzard rushed inside like a musket volley. Slivers of ice stung his exposed face and hands. Frigid wind struck him in the chest like a club. Gordon flailed with his left arm, searching for Amy.

The creature, thing, Gordon wasn't sure what to call it in those brief seconds, stepped into the big house. Into the dome of light cast by glass lamps. It wasn't really a snowman. Not anymore. It had been made of snow, once. And that was still the primary ingredient to this figure of winter and suffering. But there was more.

The snow had gone to ice. Hard, transparent ice that showed what was inside. And inside were bits of children. Pieces of hair and skin. Strings of sinew and splinters of bone. Tiny fingers and toes and immature little organs. Little eyes that stared, blind, through their frozen sepulcher. Teeth.

Most of the new body, for this thing that wouldn't have to fear the melt, would be the teeth and gums and jawbones of children. Gordon saw those grisly mouths of babes, behind the glint of lamp on ice, when the thing stepped into view. Hundreds of little teeth, set into little gums and little, purloined jawbones. Little mouths, forever in a noiseless, screaming rictus. A snow full of mouth.

The dogs broke their invisible slips when that winter giant opened the house. They rushed at it, grey jaws snapping and yellowed fangs ready to shred the monster.

It reached out with a claw formed of ice and the irredeemable loss of grieving families. It swatted both dogs away with a single, wet, red *pop!* that rose above the noise of storm and Amy's screaming. For less than a second, the snow flurry turned into rose petals. Soft, red droplets that shot away from the point of impact like rays of a now-forgotten sun.

What was left of Mootoo struck a wall of the house, leaving a dark stain and shattered planks. Toka sailed through the opening left by her killer, disappearing into the howling, shifting starscape of winter night.

The creature advanced. Too tall for the roof of the big-house, it tore away the cover of that building as it waded into the great hall. Star, bucking and snorting, pushed against the wrecked side of his stall and fled into the swirling night. The monster didn't seem to notice.

Gordon and Ham fired their weapons Gordon wasn't sure who started shooting, they just emptied their pistols into the thing. Twelve silver balls. Deadly charms for a lady's bracelet spat from the blued muzzles of the men's guns. Gordon saw the bullets hit the creature. Points of hard contact rippled. A pond sprinkled with gravel.

The snowman convulsed and fell to what would be its knees. There was a noise like a death rattle and the monster lurched to the side.

"Is it..." Amy asked, no longer screaming as she peered from behind her father.

"I don't know." Gordon wished he had another cylinder for his gun, a long stick, something. "Ham?"

And then it laughed. The goddamn thing made of snow and parts of stolen children laughed. It moved back to a kneeling position. One of its claws came down on top of Ham and the Frenchman disappeared in a red mess and brief cry.

Amy screamed again. James Lassiter Gordon screamed. This snowman-thing, still laughing, pushed itself to a standing position. Ham, Hamelin DeClerk, was dead. And this thing was laughing.

The monster's head broke the ceiling into kindling as it took a step toward them. Still laughing, it tapped Gordon back and snatched up Amy in its claw. *Happy Birthday. Happy Birthday to me!* It lifted Amy to its huge, snowman mouth and bit.

There was no spray of gore. Just a little squirt of blood. A little splash like the juice that Amy would get on her face when she ate a ripe peach. Peaches had been her favorite.

Gordon screamed again. But louder this time. No names or

words. Just the sound of grief. He threw his gun at the thing. He threw silverware. He threw a lamp. He missed.

The lamp shattered against a wall and tumbled to the stack of logs below. The wick seemed to drift like a confused firefly. Then it settled on the wreckage of log and lamp before realizing it still had a part in all of this.

The flame that spread from wick to kerosene-soaked wood moved like murmurs through a crowd on one of The Great Jhootha's best nights. It moved like a wounded French sailor fleeing Nipponese soldiers. It moved like the fluff that a breeze carries, after a little girl blows on a summer dandelion.

The fire took and roared. But the din of conflagration and winter storm were lost under the howling of that thing. The snowman turned to flee. But there wasn't any direction not blocked by flame.

Gordon smelled his clothes and hair burning. Felt his skin cook and blister. Mirroring the creature, he crawled across the fast warping floor in a search of someplace he might shelter from the cyclone of heat and light that turned around him.

***

He guessed it must be about eight o'clock. Maybe seven. Faint sunlight from the west colored the world in varied shades of blue and grey. A painting given movement.

They were gone. All of them. So was the big-house. Reduced to a patch of black ruin on black ground. Clouds of ash blew away like swarms of hungry mosquitoes. The only mosquitoes anybody would see this time of year.

Gordon staggered to the place where all things had given over to the fire. Amy. Ham. The creature. Even bones and teeth and pieces of iron had been lost in that little spot of Hell, summoned to take back one of its own.

Except the hat. The hat perched atop a pile of smoking ash. Unburned. Not crushed. Not even smudged.

He found the blade of a shovel in one of the smaller houses. The handle was burned. But the blade would still work. Hands alternately frozen and burned in places, James Lassiter Gordon dug a hole.

The hat spoke to him while he dug. *Be The Great Jhootha.*

"Shut up."

You're The Great Jhootha.

"Shut up."

You need a hat, so you won't freeze.

"I said shut up."

He wasn't sure the hole was deep enough; wasn't sure it could be deep enough. But Gordon knew he couldn't last much longer. And he needed time, energy to back-fill the hole. He nudged the hat with his shovel blade, not wanting to touch it. The hat told him *You'll be sorry.*

"I'm sorry now." He piled dirt and stone over that strange, silk hat of indeterminate make. Then he rolled onto his back, too exhausted for anything else.

He wondered if it would be the cold or the burns to claim him. Maybe wolves. He tried to fall asleep, wishing he could unhear the last thing he heard from that small hole in the ground. *I'll be back again someday.*

The End.

Christmas Eve
Ray Prew

I stood by the bay window, watching the storm drop a foot of snow on the city. The carving knife in my hand had stopped dripping blood. Over in the corner, the elderly couple made a final death rattle and expired. How cute, I thought to myself; they both died at the same time.

I had no use for their money or presents, so I left them where they were. The pain the old couple went through, and their deaths were entertaining enough.

All the people in my life were mean to me. Guys wouldn't shake my hand, and girls laughed at date requests. I learned to be my friend. After a few years, I knew I could talk things over with myself in two voices. The other voice is very mean but has very good ideas. It was his idea to kill the elderly couple. I looked the room over carefully before I left to ensure I left no trace of my identity.

This makes the fifth killing this year. It's a good thing he only wants to do this once a year. It's the one night of the year I can walk down the street dressed like Santa, and no one looks twice.

Last year, he had me kill 12 people; the year before that, it was 10. The papers call me the Christmas Eve slayer.

I exited the apartment building and began walking toward the lights of a busy intersection. I looked at the next name on my list. It was all the way across town. Maybe if I found someone closer, that would be just as good. As long as it's someone innocent, the other voice shouldn't mind.

I crossed past an alley and saw a homeless man rummaging through a garbage can, looking for something edible. He would certainly be innocent, but he had nothing to lose. The voice only wanted us to kill people with nice things and happy lives.

I still remember my worst Christmas ever. My father bought board games, which required finding someone to play with. No one played with me, so the games were an insult. The voice told me that the more these people enjoyed their Christmas, the more they deserved to die.

As I walked to the bus stop, I passed a house with pretty Christmas lights. Through the front window, I saw a family exchanging presents. A young father and lovely mother, a young son of about five years, and a little girl of about seven; a playpen held a small baby. They looked so loving and happy, and it made me want to puke. I found my next victims, and the voice would be very happy with these...

I snuck around to the back of the house. I used my burglar tools to open the lock and quietly slip inside. They were all laughing so hard and having such a good time that they never heard me enter the house. I took out my hatchet and braced myself for what was to come.

With a hearty "ho ho ho," I burst into the room and buried my hatchet in Dad's head. As he lay there twitching in an expanding pool of blood, I picked up the fireplace poker and wrapped it across Mom's head as hard as I could. She hit the floor, twitching like her husband. I took the hatchet from Dad's head and chopped off Mom's head with it. I tossed the gory severed head into the playpen with the baby. The little guy shrieked and jumped at the sight of his mommy's head in his playpen with him. I wished the children a merry Christmas and reminded them they had to be asleep on Christmas Eve or else I wouldn't bring them any presents. Well, the kids wouldn't be so happy now with their mom and dad gone, so no point in killing them. I had to be consistent and stick with my business if I ever wanted to be a legacy like John Wayne Gacy. My motto was very simple and in keeping with a theme: Only. Kill. Happy. People. As the kids wailed, "Mommy, Daddy," I left.

As I resumed my stroll down the sidewalk, I thought to myself that it was fun. I was certain the other voice would be proud of me. We often discussed that as a grand finale, I should kill myself, but I objected to that as I had more presents for people.

I remember a Christmas party for a company I worked for years ago. I asked a pretty co-worker to be my date. She smiled condescendingly and explained she wasn't going to the party but wished me a good time. She showed up at the party with a date and laughed at my dismayed expression. She declined to dance with me but danced with five other guys, some of whom she clearly met for the first time that night. I considered looking her up and giving her a present.

Christmas was such a hard time. I have no family and no friends, just my other voice for the company. The voice wants me to kill other nights of the year, but I only agreed to Christmas Eve, and I only agreed to kill people with nice lives.

I decided to call it an early night. To hell with the voice if it doesn't like it. I wanted to go home and change my blood-spattered clothes. I'm cold and hungry; I want something to eat. I entered my one-room apartment. It always smelled damp and musty. The fridge was empty, and the voice didn't remind me to buy more food.

My family has all passed, and friends always deserted me. Mine was a sad and dismal life, but the killings perk me up a little. I sat on my roach-infested chair, wondering if next Christmas would be as sad as this and as sad as all the others have been.

Perhaps the voice was right; maybe it was my time to die. But how do I go about doing it? I've tried before with no success. The voice tells me to do it but not *how* to do it.

I could try to cut my wrists, but that takes too long, and I am a slow bleeder. I could stick my head in the oven, but that wouldn't work. I cook with electricity instead of gas. I wondered if it would hurt much to take a bath with the toaster. I decided to try an overdose of pills. I knew a drug dealer two blocks away; he would have what I needed.

I changed from my Santa suit into my ordinary clothes. He had no idea that I was the Christmas Eve slayer. I needed it to stay that way. As I walked down the sidewalk to the dealer's house, I heard the wailing sirens. Apparently, they found the mom and dad. It seemed like everybody was having a busy Christmas Eve.

God, I want my death so fucking badly. I'm tired of the voice and the horrors it made me do. I remember Christmas Eve two years ago, that poor family. It was right about the time the voice went from making suggestions to giving instructions. It told me to kill that farmer and his family, Friday the thirteenth style. We compromised and settled for a quick hack job rather than one at a time, which would have been very time-consuming. Unlike Jason or Mike Myers, I was not indestructible; I'd rather take my victims by surprise.

I reached my friend's house and he lets me inside. I showed him my money and asked for all the sleeping pills and painkillers he had. He brought out his supply and started to fill a baggy. He wasn't even aware I had moved when I brought the edge of my blade across his throat. I pulled his head back and sliced his throat all in one move.

As he lay there bleeding out, I put my money back in my pocket and took his money as well. I took all of his pills and all the weed I could find. All this was done without the sound of an argument or a struggle. It would be days before anyone even looked for him. He fit the criteria for a present. He had a happy life and nice things. In this case, however, it was a public service. The guy was a discredited doctor that sold phony drugs to blind people. Even I don't like him, and I'm a serial killer!

I walked back to my home. I had all the things I needed to kill myself. One final conversation with my other voice and I was on my way to the spirit world. As I continued on my way, I passed a darkened alley where I saw some punk had a lady up against the wall. He was pulling off her clothes with one hand and brandishing a knife with the other. The lady saw me and called for help. Oh well, what the hell? What's one more thing, I thought?

I walked into the alley, shaking my head at the clumsiness of this amateur. He lashed out at me with his knife. The punk picked himself up slowly. I took out his eyes with my left hand. I gave him a full minute to realize he was blind. With my right, I cut his throat.

The lady shrieked and fell to the ground at the sight of my actions. I wished her a very merry Christmas. Wait...was he happy in his attempt at killing her, or did I just violate my one sacred rule? This was the last year, I thought to myself as I left the ally. Once I got home, I would take my pills and be gone. I wondered what Charles Dickens would say about my night tonight.

Most of the evening, I remembered the ghosts of my past Christmas,' and I saw the underbelly of Christmas and the happiness I could never have. This was the spirit of my Christmas present. Now, I sought to end my life to determine my Christmas future.

I returned to my bleak little shithole of a home. I put down the pizza and bottle of vodka I picked up on the way home. I might as well have a decent last meal. I looked around as I thought how it was going to suck to die alone.

I downed the first handful of pills, took a big swig of vodka, and began munching on my pizza. I think those were sleeping pills; the next would be painkillers. The pizza tasted good; it would help to absorb the drugs so I wouldn't puke them back up. The vodka was a top-shelf brand that went down smoothly. I downed a handful of painkillers and washed them down with another drink. I started on my second slice of pizza. I wondered if it was legal to die without a suicide note. I could have admitted that I was the Christmas Eve slayer, but that would have taken all the fun out.

I started to feel the effects of the pills. I downed a handful of each and ate my third slice of pizza. The bottle was half empty now, depending on how you look at it. My father and his Goddamn board games, that bitch from the old job, the girl who refused a dance, they have all ruined my life My other voice hated them, too. It's one of the few things we agreed on. How many pills has it been now? Probably about thirty or so...

I tried to turn on my radio to listen to some goodbye music, but the batteries were dead. Dead like I'll be soon. The voice didn't remind me to buy more. Not even music for company. Even the voice won't come back now. I felt so miserable, and the end couldn't come soon enough.

I poured the last of the pill bags into my mouth and ate another slice. My head was light, I was sleepy, and the room was growing dark. I downed the last of the vodka. I could see trails swirling before me. I could see the faces of all the people I had killed. They were still laughing at me, at my weakness in taking my own life. People have always laughed at me like this right up to the end.

I'm lying on the floor now, and my limbs are too heavy to move, and it's hard to breathe. This is it, I'm...

The End

Christmas In The Year 2300

J. Bradford Engelsman

"What's wrong, baby? You seem nervous." Nasha asked her fiancé, Zell. They were both fairly uncomfortable, having spent the previous hour in a two-seater transport pod; decked out in their finest evening attire. Zell's discomfort was more profound, however.

"Nothing—it's just, this is my first Christ's Mass celebration, and I know how seriously your family takes everything. I'm worried I'll mess something up. I want to respect their traditions."

"You're respecting *my* traditions by learning about them ahead of time and talking to an old pro like me." Nasha leaned over and kissed Zell on his cheek. "Besides, you can't mess up because nobody expects you to do anything. Everyone knows you were raised as a Scientist. Be polite and follow my lead at the Mass tomorrow; tonight's just a party. You'll do great."

Just follow Nasha's lead, thought Zell, running through his list of dos and don'ts: *It's rude to walk away from a conversation, don't take communion tomorrow, and it's bad luck to accept a present tonight.*

Ultra-Modern Christians have always been secretive about their rituals and celebrations, especially on their two most holy days, Christ's Mass and Resurrection Day, which commemorate the birth and execution of their foremost saint and prophet, Jesus the Nazarene Christ. People celebrated bastardized versions of these holidays worldwide in the Ancient Days, but their popularity declined during The Hopelessness. The story goes that the founder of UMC had been given a vision by their Triune God and hacked his way through the ruins of the old server farms and data mines to find the true meaning of the Holy Days. Non-believers are only permitted at these festivities when they have bound themselves to a UMC family through marriage.

After a long pause, Zell sighed contentedly and once again looked to his fiancée for reassurance, "They're not going to think I'm an idiot?"

"Not an idiot, just ignorant." Nasha teased. Zell groaned.

#

Zell had already met Nasha's immediate family, but this was the first time he'd spend a major holiday with everyone together in the ancestral manse. For people whose religion was called Ultra-Modern, UMCs had a tradition of leaning into distinctly old-fashioned styles. The main home and its outbuildings were all spheroid domes made of paneled wood or something that looked like it. Nothing like the stately A-frames you see today.

"Sometimes I forget you're rich," Zell gawped as the pod took them over a stone wall, the first security measure, rendered superfluous by their flying transport.

"We're not rich," Nasha replied, using that specific tone rich people use when they resent that there are still more affluent people.

"What did your grandmother invent?"

"My great-grandmother, but she didn't invent anything. She was on the team that created the fungus which helps photosynthetic plants absorb and process carbon dioxide into oxygen at an advanced rate, which helped to restore the ozone layer." Since entering college, this sentence has become a repeating mantra of her life.

"You're not rich; your grandma just invented supertrees."

"She just patented the technology. Anyone else on the team could have done the same; she thought of it first." Another often-repeated refrain, this one with an air of defensiveness. The pod landed on the snowy ground, and Zell stepped out with a soft crunch.

"How do you have snow if it's not freezing?" he asked.

Nasha shrugged, "I don't know, Christ's Mass magic? It's just a thing they do every year for the holiday spirit."

"Whoa, whoa, whoa. Who or what is the Holiday Spirit? Is that like the Holy Ghost? Why does it need snow?"

Nasha rolled her eyes. "It's not a real spirit, doofus. It means ambiance, getting in the mood."

"Hmph. I didn't expect this much trudging through the snow."

"We usually have a carriage, but I wanted you to get the full effect. The approach is part of the experience. Shhh, listen, you can almost hear it." Nasha stopped and held out her hand for Zell to do the same. In the still silence, he could hear old-timey music from the decorated dome and see strange, flickering light coming through the windows.

"Is that a fire? Like, actual fire in there?"

"Yeah, we have special places made of stone to have a fire inside."

"Indoor fire spaces in a wooden home?" he asked incredulously. *Rich weirdos,* he thought to himself. As if on cue, a wooden carriage drawn by half-sized creatures who had no business on this latitude or longitude, an elephant, wildebeest, and rhinoceros came jingling by, with a family of four all dressed in seafoam green formalwear and a driver wearing a great cloak.

"Friends of yours?" asked Zell, nudging Nasha.

"That would be Uncle Zeb, Aunt Bertie, and their two kids. I'm sure you'll meet them inside."

"And the couriers? More of your grandma's inventions?" To Zell's surprise, Nasha took this question entirely at face value.

"No... Someone in Zimbabwe, I think, invented them like fifty years ago. We've had them for as long as I can remember. Be careful, though; they're smaller but not properly domesticated. The drivers are the only people who are allowed to handle them."

"Noted. Stay away from the livestock."

Nasha stopped and squeezed Zell's hand. "I'm serious," she said. "They can fuck people up. Promise me you won't go near them by yourself."

"I promise," he responded. "I don't plan on taking any chances this weekend." He hugged her tight and kissed her. "Unto the breach?"

As they approached the main door to the massive house, it was immediately opened by someone wearing an old-fashioned black suit. Zell put his hands together and gave a formal head bow. "Good evening, thank you for inviting me–" Nasha grabbed his elbow and dragged him inside to a discreet corner. "Whoa, hey, that seems rude. Who was that?"

"Nobody, that was staff. I'm sorry; I should have told you. Staff all wear black, they call it a tuxedo. There are so many of us, that's how you can tell who isn't family and you won't end up asking an uncle to get you a nog."

After Nasha finished her explanation, the server spoke:

"Drones will have your luggage in your room within the hour. " Nasha simply nodded in response.

"Don't talk to them any more than you need to. It's not like you'll ever see any of them again." Zell looked confused. "They're all temps; they'll return to the agency after the party. Tomorrow morning, a new batch will show up with breakfast."

"So, just ignore them?"

"Unless you need something. That's their job."

"Right, got it." He thought briefly, "That's why you told me to wear the plum suit."

"That, and you look good in the plum suit."

"And it's my most expensive suit."

After his initial faux pas, Zell felt so self-conscious that he expected the massive room to fall silent as he entered. Luckily, it was already so noisy and crowded with people donning old-fashioned three-piece suits and dresses in every color of the rainbow that they slipped in inconspicuously.

"Oof, this is a lot of people."

"It's okay; you already know all the important ones. The rest are just aunts, uncles, cousins, and niblings. Hopefully, you'll have plenty of time to meet them all in the future."

"Hopefully? What does that mean?" Zell was getting the distinct impression he was being teased.

"Nothing, it's fine. Go mingle. This isn't a test." Despite her reassurances, this very much felt like a test.

#

The main party area, referred to as a ballroom for some esoteric reason, took up half of the dome's first floor. Zell learned this from Uncle Einar, a man with a prodigious mustache and an emerald green suit. Despite not knowing exactly whose uncle he was or how he was related to Nasha, Zell assumed it didn't matter much. He would likely forget it soon, anyway. He was pleased to have someone to talk to, and Einar seemed equally happy to have an audience.

"Of course, the room isn't always so grand; you can see how the retractable walls go across there and there. Ordinarily, this would be the drawing room, parlor, and library." Of these words, Zell could only identify 'library.' "Another quarter of this floor is the kitchens and lodging for the regular servants. Of course, they're all home for the holiday now. Have to make do with temps."

Zell nodded along.

"Yes, Nasha told me about the temps."

"Yes, of course! You're Little Nashi's man, aren't you? Her room will be on the third floor, I gather." *Her room? Does that mean we'll be separated?* thought Zell, *she didn't warn me about that.* "I hope you don't think me rude, but you seem somewhat out of sorts. I heard this is your first celebration of Christ's Mass; how are you faring?"

"Oh, um, pretty well," Zell replied, equally relieved that someone cared how he was feeling but distressed that now he had to talk about his feelings. "Holidays are a strange experience for me; we didn't have any growing up."

"None at all? I thought your people had a few, Hubbard's birthday, and the like."

"No, that's Xenun Scientism; it shares the name but is quite different from being an Athein Scientist. We don't have any prophets, gods, or holidays in general."

"Nothing to celebrate?" Uncle Einar said with a touch of curiosity and pity.

"Well, we have New Year's and... birthdays." Zell knew how UMCs felt about 'self-celebration', and bringing it up on the birthday of their Lord seemed especially daring. Still, he didn't want Uncle Einar to think he was ashamed of his faith.

The older gentleman simply replied, "Yes, well..." as he caught the attention of someone across the room and escaped. As Zell watched Einar leave, he saw him greet a man in a red suit, who offered him a small box of something. *I wonder what that's about,* he thought to himself, *party game?*

Before Zell could muse too profoundly, however, Einer was swiftly replaced by a man of around thirty, not too much older than Zell, wearing a canary yellow ensemble with matching rose boutonniere.

"You're Nasha's boyfriend, right? I heard you telling Einar you're an Athein. I've gotta ask you, man, do you think we should be trying to bring dead people back to life?"

"What?" This was a far cry from the architectural conversation he was having moments ago. Still, the urge to be polite won out, and he shifted gears as best as possible. "Oh, well, I mean, it hardly seems fair to bring fully dead people back to life if only because they can't consent."

"Fully dead?! Ha. There are no degrees of death, my friend. People either are or they aren't." This seemed like an intense conversation to initiate before even introducing oneself. Zell wondered how many nogs the man had had.

"That's true to a certain extent, but one could argue that if somebody is in a position where the doctor could bring them back, maybe they weren't dead at all. Just nearly dead. It's not like anyone is trying to bring back week-old corpses."

"Jesus did."

"What?"

"Lazarus had been dead four days when Jesus brought him back. John 11:17. I bet he could have done it at a week."

"Well, yes, but I mean no one these days." Zell realized he

might inadvertently start an argument if he didn't watch his words. It's not a good start to your first Christ's Mass.

"They better not be. The prophets warned us about that: Shelley, Romero, and Kirkman each warned us of the dangers of reanimation." Zell nodded along; he was familiar with the prophets; their stories were well known even to those who didn't take them as divinely inspired. The man in yellow continued, "The only time in recorded history where reanimation did not end is when Jesus brought back Lazarus and later self-reanimated. And one day, he'll bring all believers back from the dead."

"Yes, but that's a whole different holiday!" Zell said jovially, trying to lighten the mood. "I hear the children are doing a play in a little while. What's the word? Nativity?"

The man nodded gravely. "Then you'll learn what this is all about," he said as he stalked towards the punch bowl.

#

After what felt like two failed conversations, Zell elected to fetch himself another eggnog, the thick, sweet, alcoholic beverage that had a way of growing on you. He sequestered himself in a corner, hoping his betrothed would rescue him. Despite its luxury, he was beginning to appreciate that he would only have to attend this party once a year. Like most people who did not grow up with servants, the practice made him intensely uncomfortable. *Am I going to marry into a family where we have people we just ignore? Did I just think the words "have people"? Am I being infected already? It's only been a few hours!* He looked around, trying to keep a pleasant look on his face but not so inviting that someone might talk to him. Everyone looked friendly enough, and it was charming how they all wore different colors. *There's Red Suit again. What is he giving everybody? Whatever it is, Nasha will tell me if it's essential to the festivities. Oh, speaking of...* Nasha approached in her lilac dress.

"Hey sweetie, making friends?"

"Yes, so far, I've offended Uncle Einar and some fellow in yellow."

"Theodore, he's a cousin. And a turd. Used to try to get me to play with the tigers when we were little."

"Tigers? Since when are there tigers?"

"Since forever." Zell noticed a subtle slur in Nasha's voice, "I'll show you tomorrow. Don't try to play with them." She punctuated each word emphatically. "They-will-eat-you. And you're all mine." She growled and gave him a nip on the neck.

"Maybe I'm falling behind." Zell was not much of a drinker to begin with and was pacing himself this evening.

"Eggnog for Zell," said Nasha as she sauntered away.

"Oh, I guess I'll wait here then." He replied to no one.

#

"Hi! Zell, right? You're Nasha's new fella?" The man in red finally made his appearance.

"Well, we've been engaged for most of a year, but yes."

"I'm Jack, one of Einar's. Soon to be Cousin Jack, I guess. Anyway, I just wanted to give you a little welcome-to-the-family present."

Zell hesitated, "Isn't there something about not accepting presents during Christ's Mass that it's bad luck?"

"Hey, you've been doing your homework! Yeah, but that's just for kids. Since this is the first time we've got a chance to meet, I figured, what the heck?"

"I told Nasha I wouldn't do anything without her say-so. Where did she go?"

"She's caught up talking to my sister about wedding planning. It's fine." He set the box in Zells's hand. "Just don't open it until you get to your bedroom." He added with a wink.

"Well, thank you very much." Zell said, somewhat confused as he pocketed the small box, "I was starting to worry that no one in your family liked me much."

"What? No, they're just a bit old-fashioned."

"It's surprising how much I hear about the Ultra-Modern being old-fashioned."

"Think of it as a modern reclamation and reinterpretation of old ways."

"Reinterpretation?"

"Maybe we just have hindsight, but it's amazing what the ancients missed even though it was right there."

"What do you mean?"

"Like how they would *celebrate* tempting children with sweets and presents and, Oh! The pageant's about to start! Better find Nasha."

The crowd moved towards one end of the ballroom, where a platform was set up and a curtain strung through as a makeshift backstage area. Some guests brought chairs for the older people, who had already been standing for hours. Zell quickly found Nasha, who Cousin Jack had already seen. She turned and hugged her cousin as he approached. "How did it go?" she whispered in his ear.

"You'll see," he replied coyly. She gave him a playful bat on the arm and stood beside Zell.

The room darkened, and a small boy came onto the stage wearing what looked like a well-worn costume of black pants, an orange coat, and a green hat. He was holding a blue blanket.

"Oh, they've got little Gemma playing Linus this year," cooed someone behind the trio.

"I never got to be Linus," Nasha muttered.

The crowd fell silent, and a small voice came from little Gemma: "Lights, please." The crowd applauded as a drone with a single spotlight shone on the child as she began her monologue, "And there were in the same country shepherds abiding in the field, keeping watch over their flock by night. And, lo, the angel of the Lord came upon them, and the glory of the Lord shone round about them, and they were sore afraid. And the angel said unto them, 'Fear not! For, behold, I bring you tidings of great joy, which shall be to all people. For unto you is born this day in the city of David a Savior, which is Christ the Lord. And this shall be a sign unto you: Ye shall find the babe wrapped in swaddling clothes, lying in a manger.' And suddenly there was with the angel a multitude of the heavenly host praising God and saying, 'Glory to God in the highest, and on earth peace, goodwill toward men." Many of the adults in the crowd, having heard it countless times, murmured along with the child. Several of them were probably the child onstage in years past.

There was a second applause, and a new voice from off stage began to speak while children acted out various scenes:

"The great reanimator, who would save us from death, was born on this day in the town of Bethlehem. He was born of a woman who had never known a man, which in those days was a miracle." The light expanded, illuminating two children wearing simple robes. One held a shepherd's crook, while the other placed a baby doll gingerly in some sort of old-fashioned bed.

"What on Earth is a manger?" muttered Zell under his breath.

"He spread the good word, performed miracles, and gathered disciples," the voice continued, "He reanimated Lazarus and later himself after being betrayed by one of the Holy Dozen." A child wearing a fake beard marched to the stage, waving his arms elaborately. Zell was relieved when the rest of the audience started chuckling, as he was beginning to fear he wouldn't be able to contain his laughter.

Eventually, the child approached a body lying on the stage, and with great fanfare, the child shouted, "Lazarus, come forth!" Yet another applause erupted from the audience as Lazarus got up, and the two walked off stage together.

"He ascended into heaven and sent inspiration to the prophets telling why we must never attempt to reanimate without Him. He alone holds that power." At this point, two children dressed in old-fashioned clothing meant to evoke *Night of the Living Dead* (the prophet Romero's first offering) appeared on stage. Another, made up like a zombie, shambled on the stage to menace them as they ran away.

"We love Him as He loves us, and we trust Him as He trusts us. But Lo! An imposter comes to tempt us from His ways! The devil, Santa, tries to lure us with gifts, just as he tempted Christ in the desert. He tempted Christ three times, and three times was rebuffed."

"Ho ho ho," a child shouted as he hopped onto the stage wearing the most elaborate outfit yet: a red suit with horns, a floppy pointed hat with a pompom, some sort of trident Zell did not recognize, and a large sack slung over his back. As the child walked across the stage, he approached the Christ figure, who sat serenely meditating under a tree. The devil elaborately pantomimed, tempting Christ with his sack of gifts, which were consistently refused.

"With his magic sleigh and reined deer, the devil flies the entire world to tempt us each and every one. But does he succeed?"

"No!" shouts the crowd, startling Zell. The devil figure pranced off the stage into the crowd and attempted to persuade the adults to accept gifts from the bag he had slung over his shoulder. The adults all chastised him with mock enthusiasm.

"Has the devil in red tempted anyone here?" The crowd quieted down, and everyone began to look around. *The devil in red?* Thought Zell as he recalled Jack distributing small boxes to everyone. All eyes shift towards Jack, in his red suit, and Zell, standing next to him. "Has no one been plied by trinkets this night?" All eyes were now firmly on Zell.

"Well," he stammered, his voice surprisingly loud, as he realised a boom mic drone was hovering above him. He suddenly had the feeling of being on trial. "He said it was a welcome-to-the-family gift. I didn't realise it was part of the game."

"Were you not warned about the prince of lies?" The voice addressed him directly.

"I *was* told not to accept any gifts tonight, that it's bad luck or something," Zell admitted, chuckling nervously.

"Is it mere bad luck to trade your soul for a bauble?"

"No!" The crowd responded in unison. Nasha looked at Zell and smiled sympathetically.

"I told you," She mouthed.

"But other people-" Zell cut himself off, realizing he had not seen anyone accept the gift from Jack. "Yes, well, I apologize. But this does seem like a planned bit of hazing for the new guy." The crowd shifted as an older man stepped onto the stage, undoubtedly the pater familia Zell had not yet met.

The voice echoed through the room, but Zell could now see from whom it came: "What was *planned*, young Zell, was for you to marry our Nasha and join us in our Holy Days. Hopefully, you would have eventually found the grace of God and joined us in faith."

"What—what do you mean 'was'? I'm still going to marry Nasha." Zell's voice cracked a little. "Right?" He saw his fiancée's eyes getting misty. "You won't break off our engagement because of one little mix-up. Right?" He looked at Nasha with pleading, confused eyes. He didn't notice the crowd splitting until the unmistakable sound of a giant, animatronic suit shaped like a demon made its presence unavoidable. Its horns, hooves, tail, and a strangely long tongue hanging out of its mouth unmistakably marked it as a malevolent entity. An ominous empty sack completed the effect. "What is that?" asked Zell as it approached him.

The man on stage continued his speech from moments ago as though the conversation interlude never took place. "Behold, the Lord has sent Krampus to punish those who place themselves on the naughty list, defiled by the devil Santa!"

The crowd tightened, forming a circle around Zell and whoever, if anyone, was in the Krampus suit. Zell frantically looked around, only to discover that the temporary workers had left for the evening, leaving only the family. Krampus approached Zell and attempted to trap him by casting the bag over his head. Despite its menace, however, the machine lacked dexterity and fumbled with haphazard movements. The crowd cheered with each repeated attempt and when it seemed that Zell might pose an actual challenge to the creature, two men whom he hadn't yet had the pleasure of meeting grabbed Zell by the arms. The child dressed as a zombie wrapped himself around Zell's legs, hobbling him. Only now, as he noticed the other children making their way to the circle and moving between the adults' legs, did Zell feel a genuine sense of danger. He saw the devil, Linus, one of the zombie victims, and others who had already doffed their robes.

"Naughty list! Naughty list! Naughty list!" The children and some adults started chanting, keeping the rhythm by stomping on the floor and using their props from the play.

Unsure if this is all an elaborate scheme he is playing a part in or if the danger is in fact genuine, Zell frantically made eye contact with Nasha one last time.

"What's happening?"

"I'm sorry," she replied, "I really did like you." With her use of the past tense, he finally realized the gravity of his situation and redoubled his efforts to break free. As he did, his body hurled forward, and the sack covered his head and shoulders, clamped around his ribs. As he tipped over, he felt the child loosen his legs, and his shoulder struck the hard floor. *Oomph!* He looked towards his feet just as the opening of the bag was drawn shut and blows from half a dozen sticks battered down all over his body as the children gleefully continued their chant.

"Naughty list! Naughty list!" Still on the floor, he realized his best bet would be to focus on escaping his scratchy cocoon, ripping and clawing as best as he could. He attempted once to bite through but received several immediate blows to the face, one resulting in a sharp *crack!* as it hit his nose, quickly dissuading this strategy.

"Ha!" someone shouted, "they always try that. It just gives the little ones a target." A few seconds later, the voice continued, "Isn't it about bedtime?" *Yes!* Thought Zell, *bedtime for the children; they've had their fun.*

"Come on now, give the kids their chance; who knows when we'll get another one?" a gruff, jovial voice replied. "We gave you longer than that when you were Linus." *Is that Uncle Einar, that prat?*

Zell was unsure if he had passed out, but the next voice he heard was unfamiliar: "Alright, settle down, you lot, off to bed. We'll tell you all about it in the morning." *Tell them about what?* Thought Zell wearily as he began to whimper. There was one final blow as a child began to pout and sniffle.

"Oh, somebody's overtired. Come on, I'll tuck you in. We'll all go to Mass in the morning. Won't that be lovely? Yes. Shhhhh, shhhhhh." Zell heard the soothing words of a doting parent recede across the room.

There was a brief reprieve as Zell's bag was hoisted into the air, no doubt by the Krampus creature. "Come on now; even if he is dead, we've got to do this properly." *Thunk, thunk, thunk,* the thumps of Zell colliding with the creature's back were gentle by comparison to what he had just endured. He realized that he was upside-down now, unable to speak with the pressure of his entire body on his head and neck. He was unsure he'd be able to form a coherent sentence anyway.

Suddenly, Zell felt a breeze as the front door opened, and he was carried outside. *That's nice,* he thought and made a contented cooing noise.

"Oh! He is still alive," exclaimed a voice as sweet as sugar plums.

Zell heard the crunch of the snow turn to slush under the feet of the assembled crowd. When the thumping had stopped, several hands grabbed the bag and untied the opening where Zell's feet were. They then dumped him over a fence into a muddy pit.

"Oh no!" Someone shouted, "Zell's gotten into the carriage animals!" *What,* thought Zell, *no I*–but he heard the plodding and snuffling as the elephant, wildebeest, and rhinoceros approached him.

"Nasha, didn't you warn him they were dangerous? The authorities always ask if they were warned about the animals," Zell heard another voice shout as he realized he could no longer stand of his own accord and began attempting to drag his body up and over the fence. *Always ask?*

"I did," Nasha wept. "I made him promise not to go near them."

"They'll still make us build a taller fence again and put up some tacky sign, no doubt," some unseen figure lamented. The wildebeest lunged forward, slamming into Zell with a cracking sound that shot through the crowd. Its two horns punctured Zell on either side as bits of his spinal column became dislodged.

"No, you mustn't try to save him," shouted Uncle Einar to no one. "You'll only get yourself killed." The rhinoceros jammed its horn through Zell's legs, shattering the tibia and fibula on one side and going through his knee on the other. He wailed and thrashed as his hands could no longer hold his weight, and he fell to the ground on his back. The collected crowd held its breath, and Zell could see the elephant's trunk swaying as it approached him. It trumpeted majestically as it stood back on its hind legs, and its front feet came crashing down, one squarely on Zell's chest, shattering his ribcage and several organs.

"They never listen, do they?" Zell saw Jack say to Nasha as life ebbed from his body, "It's a simple rule."

Return to Cinder
Address Unknown
John A. DeLaughter

The thud on the roof was a time-honored sound to the Old Man's reindeer familiars.

For centuries, beginning in the ancient city of Patara through the present, they became associated with Nicholas the Wonderworker, Nicolas the Gift-Giver, or Nicolas the Calmer of Seas. The Old Man acquired many names across the ages and among the many cultures he visited. He was even rumored to have cast a demon, one of Beelzebub's main underlings, from a tree destined to become a chief graven image in the hidden courts of Constantinople, where Eastern Emperors worshipped in secret the Gods of Power, those who once emboldened Alexander the Great to achieve his great exploits.

The rulers of the great Byzantine Empire wore polished piety in public. At the same time, in private, they kept company with dark denizens who dwelled in inconceivable, unlighted halls beyond the known spheres.

The demon agreed to leave the magnificent tree under Nicholas's mightiest exorcisms. Instead of casting the infernal princeling into the lake of fire, where it would be tormented eternally, the Wonderworker permitted It to roam the corridors of the earth freely again. In return, the nameless One granted Nicholas a vision that was the path that led to endless life on this earth rather than in the next. The pious but naïve Nicholas never realized that he endangered his immortal soul by making such a pact with the demon. He sealed his fate to walk the earth alone, banished to the Northern Climes among the races forgotten by time until the sun darkened.

The Old Man had only one vague promise that gave him a ray of hope and prompted his continuing mission on the earth. A being of light wrote in Nicholas's journal over his shoulder not long after he established a cottage in the far north; this one thought that the only chance for his repentance while walking the earthly, eternal purgatory was to spread joy and cheer once a year, at the time of the winter solstice and the yuletide, to the children of the world through the giving of gifts.

Around that penitent act, the Old Man accumulated magic from the forgotten peoples of the North. His reindeer familiars, his sleigh that floated like a feather in the air, an army of bored dwarves and elves, and a magical, four-dimensional toy sack, small on the outside and voluminous on the inside, a gift from a lost Time Traveler: all were gathered to him. The dwarves mined raw materials from the virgin North. At the same time, the elves turned those materials into fabulous toys for children and adults who saw life through the eyes of a child. Both tribes also made a myriad of enchanted conveniences that made his solitary life bearable.

But fear for his eternal soul wasn't the Old Man's only motivation. A spirit of empathy, a psychic gift that allowed him to read the negative and positive emotions of others across vast distances and among many people, guided him. It took him a mortal's lifetime to learn how to manage the dizzying effects of such a paranormal attribute, to distinguish the line between his own troubling emotions and bothersome moods and those of many others across the globe. The psychic language of the souls of millions was as clear to him as the writing in his many journals despite the myriad conflicting and confusing tribal tongues they spoke. That most were naughty and some were nice made his gift-giving endeavors simpler, though he often gave things to raise the spirits of those who dwelt in dim shrouds of personal darkness.

The Old Man had learned many sorcerer tricks to enter a home. Among the few times he allowed a mortal to see him, his most famous device was to descend a cold chimney. Of course, over the centuries, having food as his only therapy and claustrophobia as one of his weaknesses, the Old Man's girth prevented him from going down a chimney in his "plump as a bowl of pudding" body. So, a fire mage, a rarity in the Northern Climes, taught the Old Man how to transform himself, for short intervals, from a human being into a single element, like a variation of fire. The mage also taught the Old Man how to use psychokinesis to manipulate inanimate objects—such as causing a Xmas tree to break dance—to distract parents or children who caught him in the act.

He even learned the martial art psychic-judo to protect himself from a nervous robber should he happen on a burglary-in-progress.

After much trial and error, the Old Man found a way to transmute himself into a sentient ash, which could float down the chimney and then reform into his Ho-Ho old self below. Next, he could open a door or window to get his bag of goodies for the good children of the household.

#

Tonight, something different happened. The Old Man had done the same routine untold times. He checked the chimney, found it cool, and transformed his person into his ash pseudo-self. He simultaneously cut himself on the jagged metal edge of an old chimney pot. A bit of his blood fell down the chimney as he, the sentient Ash, floated down the flue.

Some coals in the home's hearth were still aglow as the Old Man's immortal blood struck a redwood ember. When he came to himself, shocked at the heat, he stamped his boots on the hearthstones and swatted out the small flames that clung to his red suit.

Breathing a sigh of relief, the Old Man, spooked about the chimney's red-hot coals, opened the house's back door and began distributing the presents, a practice he timed down to a millisecond.

He shut the backdoor quickly as he left the house, leaped into the sleigh, and sped off to another home. The reindeer familiars flew near the speed of light, bringing time to a standstill around the Old Man's sleigh and allowing him to work a lifetime of effort into a single night.

Unbeknownst to the Old Man, something dark occurred as his immortal blood spilled when he became sentient ash.

That casual act transmuted the essence and being of a single burning redwood ember, turning it into something alive unto itself, awake with its thoughts and aware of the wider world, as it was endued with a tiny dose of the Old Man's paranormal abilities and a bit of his psychokinetic powers.

#

The Peoria County sheriff deputies sifted through the living room of the burnt-out home, searching for clues among the charred remnants of Xmas presents intended for children. They examined the suspected arson, with the fire beginning as a ring of destruction around the home's chimney and hearth.

A short video taken by exterior cameras outside the house baffled the deputies. A human-like form appeared, all ablaze, floating to the ground as a feather might.

Immediately, the fiery ghost went to the front door and walked straight through it as if the metal door didn't exist. The camera soon stopped working as a fist of fire poured forth from the doorway, engulfing the front porch in a fiery holocaust. It also recorded piercing screams in the background before it suddenly went dead.

The deputies might have passed the video off as a Halloween hoax if it had not been for what they found. The front door still stood in its charred frame, and its face bore the scorched outline of the flaming thing that walked through it in the video. Above the metal door, burned in rough letters into the brick, was the nonsensical phrase, "Return to Cinder, Address Unknown!" So, the perpetrators didn't even know their Rock and Roll song titles? Pieces of the door were removed for analysis by the Sheriff's crime lab for a more thorough explanation of the apparent phenomenon. The deputies on-site were ordered to keep silent about what they found.

No one in the family that occupied the house escaped alive.

#

A year passed uneventfully in Peoria. The case grew cold as the evidence proved a forensic dead-end. Also, there were no witnesses to the crime other than the odd video and the cryptic message that spoofed one of the King of Rock and Roll's songs.

Sam Burston made a living anyway he could. His main gig, working counters at a major gas station chain in Peoria, paid for his rent, food, and an occasional bender with his on-again, off-again girl pal, Amy. Around the holidays, at least the Xmas season, Sam hated Halloween because he feared skulls; he liked to pick up extra money by playing Santa at the local food court near a line of outlet stores. Not many children came to sit on Santa's lap, but many thought he was the real deal. He let his already gray hair and habitual beard grow to believable "Jolly Old Elf" lengths.

Like one little girl, Emily, who tugged his beard, said, "It's just like in the story!"

Sam sat on a bench in the food court employee's locker room, his cabinet with a simple "Santa" written on plain paper, scotch-taped to its lockable door.

They don't even know my name, he thought as he took a slug from a whiskey flask to keep up his holiday spirits.

Sam smelt something burning nearby and turned to see what caused it.

He fell back against the locker and took another shot of his whiskey before dropping the flask.

A flaming pillar stood behind him, somehow reflecting in its face, a fun-house reflection of good 'ole Saint Nick.

Sam swatted the air as he tried to avoid hearing the voice of God inside his head.

"Thief, murderer, desecrator! Are you Old Man Nicholas?" the voice asked.

"Me, who?" a puzzled Sam replied as he stepped back from the hovering inferno.

"Die, pillager of the elders and the ages," the voice resounded as the flames roared.

A dozen burning skulls flew from the flaring pillar, gathering around the screaming Santa like a swarm of red-hot raptors.

The fiery flock descended on him, their eyes aflame with

vengeance, devouring Santa Sam as his shrieking died out and his flaming bones slid to the concrete floor.

The extended finger of a blazing hand wrote like a welding torch across the face of the dead man's locker, "Return to Cinder, Address Unknown."

Hideous laughter filled the backroom as the flaming thing formed wings like a resurrecting phoenix, then sped away, burning an outline through a skyline window pane.

#

Chuck Atkins's wife always volunteered for him to play Santa at the hospital's holiday party. She often obligated him like that. While Chuck was good-natured and took such things in stride, there were instances where her bossy nature graded on his sensibilities. He seldom felt appreciated by her for anything he did. But his costumed presence brought joy to the hospital employees' kids and children in the hospital wards.

So, Chuck put up with her indifference as he saw the joy in the children's eyes.

He practiced his, "Ho, Ho, Ho," outside the house in the shed out back because his son was still young enough to believe in good old St. Nick. He didn't want to burst Leonard's bubbly belief.

Chuck kept his Santa costume in the shed because it helped him get into the season's spirit. His "Ho, Ho, Ho" was the one thing kids remembered about his characterization of the old gent beyond the outlandish outfit.

It was two weeks out from the holiday, and since his wife and Leonard were off to her sister's house, he decided to take the opportunity to practice.

He felt like preparing inside the house that night since it got cold in the shed, despite his furry suit. After all, it was a costume, not a full-weather outfit meant to be worn at the North Pole.

The one thing Chuck did not like, a concession to the Mrs. and his son, was a holiday tree in the house. When he was young, such a tree caught fire and burned down his family's home. That incident was the first in a series of calamities that caused him to grow up fast, leaving behind, too soon, the fantasies of childhood.

Chuck found some festive holiday music on one of the many stations that carried such nostalgic hits. He liked the older versions of songs sung by crooners of long ago, from Bing Crosby to Nate King Cole and Frank Sinatra.

He caught Dean Martin on the dial, flirting with Marilyn Maxwell in the crooner rendition of "Baby, It's Cold Outside..."

He had just donned his suit when behind him, he heard the crackling sound of burning wood and smelt smoke.

Since he'd never lit a fire in the hearth, Chuck bolted to the kitchen counter, grabbed a fire extinguisher, and then turned to investigate the source of the smoky fumes.

A pillar of flame appeared in the fireplace, then arose like an avatar of flickering flames, with the hearth's painted bricks framing its multi-colored fires.

Puzzled by what he saw, Chuck pulled the safety pin on the fire extinguisher, pointed it at the fiery pillar, and pressed its plunger.

Nothing happened, as the fire extinguisher had sat on the kitchen counter for over a decade, years beyond its expiration date.

Chuck felt his skin crawl like a swarm of army ants pouring over him from a broken overhead pipe in an abandoned building. He dropped the extinguisher and swatted at the unseen insects.

"Argggg..."

He heard a voice inside his head that sounded like an angry God.

"Murderer! Killer of the Elders, are you Old Man Nicholas?" it boomed.

Chuck's hands went to his ears, trying to shut out the thunderous words. He backed into the Xmas tree as the flaming pillar followed his movements like a mirror image.

He screamed as he felt himself lifted and thrown back against the holiday tree. Its thickest branches coiled around his legs, arms, and neck like a hungry boa constrictor.

"No bother, you shall die according to your worst fears!"

Babbling incoherently, the last thing Chuck saw in his mind's eye was a vast forest of massive tree stumps atop rolling desolate hills that faded into a dark horizon.

The Xmas tree burst into flames, as the shrieking man caught fire and tried to escape, but could not due to the tree's seizure of his thrashing limbs.

The flaming thing exited the home, burning its way through the front door. Then, hovering over the driveway, it wrote with a fiery finger into the concrete:

"Return to Cinder, Address Unknown."

#

Jamel Hernandez stamped his booted feet and pulled his dime store Santa costume tight around his person. It was early evening, and he was cold. The temperatures in Illinois during December were brutal.

No one had stopped to look at his wares for an hour.

His cheap Sterno stove gave off some heat. But not nearly enough to warm his person. It barely kept his cup of instant coffee warm. Street lights overhead gave off enough light that he didn't need to supply his own.

He often thought, "What the hell am I doing selling yard elves and garden gnomes from the back of my car in the dead of winter?"

Jamel, down deep, knew why.

His strict mother, Rosalina, God rest her soul, ingrained in his person through her constant paddle to his butt the idea of earning an honest living. So, during the Winter, when his lawn care business was slow, he made an honest living as best as possible.

He wasn't sleeping in his car poor. But he lived out of a storage locker, where he kept his lawn care equipment.

The only thing left to him by his father, Jorge, was a stainless-steel neck chain and a medallion containing a radiating sun disk crossed with a fiery snake. Jamel's readings symbolized the Aztec Sun God, Huitzilopochtli, who wielded Xiuhcoatl, the fire serpent, as a weapon. The pendant had been fashioned in a shiny but cheap metal. Otherwise, he would have hocked it at a Pawn shop.

Jamel was thinking about calling it a day when he felt intense heat behind him and saw a sudden flash of light.

Turning, he saw a pillar of fire.

He fell backward against his car, knocking the Sterno stove into the snow.

Jamel heard a voice like thunder shout at him, "Desecrator! Killer of the Elder Woods! Are you Old Man Nicholas?"

"Who, me, Santa Claus? Where the hell are you?" Jamel said, thinking it was a prank.

"Liar! You will die for your insolence!" the fiery thing roared as Jamel's Santa costume burst into flames.

Screaming in agony, he dove into a snowbank, trying to doze the fire.

The blazing thing followed him, toying with its prey.

Through the fiery melee, reflecting the streetlights, the burning thing saw Jamel's pendant through his charred Santa suit.

"What's this? You wear a symbol honoring the Great Old One, Cthugha, the most ancient burning One who sired us all?"

Clouds of steam arose as the flaming thing descended on the howling man.

"You will forever bear the scars of my wrath. But your life, I will be spare because you honor the God of All Gods," were the last words Jamel heard before he passed out.

#

The Old Man had run into his share of troublesome mortals and immortals.

Blood-suckers caused him the greatest difficulties. Vampires came after him because if they could drain his immortal blood, they would never have to drink the blood of another again. The rich rulers of the world, themselves mere mortals, sought him out for the same reason. In their case, a transfusion of his blood, even a pint, could bring everlasting life.

So, the Old Man had on his payroll an army of henchmen and modern weaponry to protect him from the undead blood-suckers, the live kind, criminal opportunists, and paranormal threats.

He paid them handsomely in gold and silver. The far North contained some of the richest untapped mineral fields for such treasures.

One day, instruments in the North Pole war room, which monitored law enforcement scanners from dozens of countries worldwide, drew the Old Man's attention.

Something was afoot in Peoria, Illinois. Law enforcement reported that nearly a dozen mall and special-event Santas had died under what they termed "mysterious acts of spontaneous combustion." While the authorities suspected foul play, they had been unable to find any link to the mayhem other than the Santa guise each victim wore before their incineration. The cases defied forensic science.

The Old Man, anxious to root out the truth, sent his most trusted associate, the Crimson Mage, aka Sigrillion the Bold, to find out what he could. He first taught the Old Man how to transmute his person into animals and inanimate objects.

#

Detective Ross Blanchard was familiar with setting traps. He had participated in many task forces and cooperative efforts between the Peoria County Sheriff's Department and the Greater Peoria Police Department. Such stings often netted felons, shut down gangs, or captured dangerous firebugs.

Taking their cue from the insane but strangely sober ramblings of Jamel Hernandez, the only survivor of the Mall Santas murders, Blanchard set up an elaborate trap.

He furnished it with a failsafe sprinkler system, an experimental design that utilized flame-retardants rather than water to eliminate potential chemical fires that burned hotter than normal blazes.

They built the trap by utilizing a mall corner, where the two entrances to the space could snap shut to prevent the perpetrator from escaping. Finally, they covered the area with hidden cameras to monitor the people approaching the Santa trap exhibiting odd behaviors or carrying flammables.

Otherwise, they camouflaged their handiwork under happy holiday decorations like giant candles, tall candy canes, snowflakes everywhere, a smattering of Xmas trees, garlanded, hung heavily with silver and gold ornaments, and buckets of tinsel.

Was it unusual for a smaller mall to have a Santa as its main holiday attraction?

Two officers, Sergeant Rod McMan and Jefferson Tang, manned a shut-down seller's kiosk near the Santa trap. They watched for suspicious activity among Mall stragglers, passersby, and parents with children.

#

After a few days, the routine became mind-numbing.

Xmas day was only a week away.

Officer Gerald Rasmussen, who originally volunteered to play Santa, soon grew tired of his role, between the constant crying children and demanding parents. He traded places with the habitually stoic Rod McMan, who became a quick study on what it took to be a Mall Santa.

Late one evening, as the mall was about to close, Rod McMan finished off with the last kid, Bradon, by name. That child had to have his picture taken with Santa.

Tired, the costumed McMan closed his eyes, sitting atop Santa's throne. He had a half hour before meeting with Ross Blanchard, the OIC (officer-in-charge), and Jefferson Tang for the daily after-action report.

Soon, McMan smelt something burning and felt heat like a furnace against his face and hands. He blinked twice, unsure of what he was seeing immediately before him. It arose as a burning gas pillar venting at an oil refinery.

He went to his waist, grabbed his gun, and fired at the apparition. The bullets struck the wall behind the flaming thing without affecting it.

"Guys, are you getting this?" he yelled as the ghostly flames intensified.

"In my head, what the hell? I hear a voice; it's like someone speaking near a raging waterfall."

McMan lost his mind as he became a channel through which the flaming thing spoke.

"Desecrator! Annihilator of the forest elders! Are you Old Man Nicholas?" McMan shouted out in an inhuman thunder.

Detective Tang arrived back at the kiosk station, saw the pillar of flame opposite McMan, and threw the sprinkler system switch.

Not far behind, the normally unflappable Officer Rasmussen choked out, "Almighty, protect thy lamb!"

McMan and the flaming pillar were doused with chemical retardants, causing the former to look around himself covered with the foam and say, "Where am I?"

Instead of dying out under the suffocating deluge, the latter conflagration formed an odd shape like a branching sapling, which shook violently.

"Where is Old Man Nicholas?" the thing shouted as flames began to spiral off its outline.

Dazed, Sergeant McMan said, "The North Pole…"

Immediately, the thing shook off the flame retardant like a dog shaking water from its coat. Its flames reignited, and it rose like a fiery phoenix. The blazing raptor struck at McMan's head, leaving a claw-shaped burn across the screaming man's face.

The flaming thing flew through the cage intended to trap mortal offenders, burning a raptor-shaped hole through its plexiglass ceiling.

Officers Tang and Rasmussen rushed out of the control kiosk to aid their fallen comrade. As Tang released a door to the capture cage, Officer Rasmussen called in on his police walkie-talkie, "Code 10:00, Code 10:00, Officer Down, Code 10:52, Code 10:52, Ambulance needed at Northwoods Mall!"

As the drama played out, and the blaring sirens of a paramedic vehicle approached the Mall, a mysterious figure stepped out of a wall where once, there had only been a wall.

Dressed in black from head to toe, the aged man wore a stunning stove-pipe top hat, dark suit, a flowing cape, whose metallic lining was emblazoned with magik glyphs and arcane sigils, a wide bow tie, and gold-tipped boots. He carried an odd cane, topped with a blazing stone in its bejeweled crown.

He stood quietly for a moment. A flash of recognition crossed his face as he sniffed the air like a bloodhound tracking a killer's scent.

"I must bring news to Nicholas before the beast arrives on his doorstep. Xmas itself is in peril!"

#

The North Pole was extremely busy. The last thing Old Man Nicholas needed was an interloper stalling the preparations.

One of the elves, Sniderinkoff, led the team in the war room that monitored incoming threats.

The Old Man watched a set of screens on a raised throne, the central node of the vast suite of surveillance devices that ensured the preservation of his immortal enterprise. The unmistakable psychic and radar signatures of mighty Sigrillion were fast approaching the North Pole. The Old Man stepped down from his throne and walked to the main audience hall, where several confederates gathered to receive the Crimson Mage.

Among those was Jack Frost, already seated, as Old Man Nicholas assumed the chief chair in the hall. Jack was an enigma, an ancient partner who at once was jovial, and in the next, he often grew as cold as a stone.

Sigrillion entered with a flourishing of trumpets, the thin, monotonous piping of unseen flutes, and the thunder of bongo drums, played by dozens of elves hidden off-stage. Their practice was to fuse their instruments to their persons, creating odd chimeras that troubled the eyes. With a short bow of deference to the Old Man, the man in black took a lone seat before the assembled dignitaries.

"Sire, the Flaming, Nameless Thing will soon be here," Sigrillion said, dispensing with the normal formalities. Since the Crimson Mage was his equal, the Old Man waived all the red tape, given the emergency.

"It has no name, Sigrillion? Surely, one as yourself has encountered a beast like this before, in your many aeons on the earth," replied the Old Man.

"There are things in this earth and the cold, outer spheres that are older than I. Such nameless things dwell in the roots of this world, going back before the dawn of time. My kind do not seek out direct knowledge of such elementals, for to do so would provoke their Guardians' wrath. I learned what I do know through whispers from the dead worlds devastated by their wrath. Cthugha, the living flame that imperils the universe, is their God. That Celestial's Name is found innumerable times among the immemorial ruins on the twelve known worlds."

Jack Frost considered the Mage's words as a look of puzzlement crossed Old Man Nicholas's face. Frost smiled cryptically. He was another Immortal whose motives were largely superficial to the North Poe's rank-and-file. In truth, his intentions were known only to himself.

"It is scant days until we lit the first Yule Log. The day of giving is almost upon us!" the Old Man said as a stumbling entourage, unaware of the grave words being exchanged between the Titans of the North, noisily entered the council chamber bearing two red and white fur suits, black boots, and brass buckled belts.

"Not now, Clydesberg," shouted the Old Man at his bumbling underlings.

"Can't you see we're busy on matters of state?"

Clydesberg looked up from his busy errant with the others from the weavers' guild. He spied the Crimson Mage and Jack Frost and uttered, "Oh dear!"

The knot of Clydesberg and his underlings quickly vacated the premises amid shouts of blame tossed among themselves.

"We have our preparations against the enemies of the North Pole," Jack Frost said, the head of the Old Man's security forces, "Also, we have many automatons and our varied occultic disciplines among the Masters who swear allegiance to you, Nicholas.'

"We will be ready for this Nameless Thing, an uninvited embassy of ancient Cthugha. No God of the Dark Ages past can best our Guilds!"

#

Hours later, alarm gongs sounded throughout the complex, punching out the first few stanzas of "Jingle Bells." Vast blast doors, several feet thick reinforced steel, slowly slid into place. The lights of the war room were dimmed so as not to distract the combat specialists who reviewed countless lines of data on their computer monitors.

The Old Man sat in his command chair as two armrests of weapons panels fell into place. Beside his lofty chair, two additional chairs ascended, one console for the Crimson Mage and the other for Jack Frost.

Frost entered the room unceremoniously while Sigrillion the Bold materialized beside his station, like a worker exiting a commuter train before its blurry departure.

"Jack, Sigrillion, take your seats, gentlemen; this is not a drill," the Old Man said, his eyes scanning two large screens suspended in midair.

Frost was the first to his station, "There, coming from the Southwest, it's emitting a strange conflagration of signatures. One of fire, one of the Redwood sempervirens genus, and one mimicking anthropomorphic emissions. Its trailing, psychic emanations are both localized yet diffuse, as if tethered to a vast consciousness in other dimensions. It defies classification by our systems," Frost said coldly.

"I'm cross-referencing its classification with data sources across the globe."

"And?" the Old Man cut his colleague short.

Frost went quiet as he gazed from one screen to another, surrounding his station.

"Nothing further, Sire. This One is an unknown quantity based on an incomplete analysis. I'm unsure which of our weapons will be most effective against it."

"Ok, let's hit it with a barrage of Scrooge missiles," the Old Man noted as the firing coordinates flashed into place.

5...4...3...2...1...

"Missiles away!" Frost said.

"Roger that," replied the nearby Sniderinkoff, the Elf-In-Charge (EIC) of the war room.

The trio of Scrooge missiles quickly reached the flaming raptor and exploded, sending a cloud of jagged shrapnel against it.

"Contact achieved," Frost shouted. "It's been blown apart!"

A shout erupted across the war room as the elves began to congratulate each other.

"No, wait a minute. The scattered fragments of the flaming thing are recombing into its original fiery form!" said Sniderinkoff as the elven joy that rocked the place faded.

"What next?" the Old Man asked Frost.

"It's covered half the distance to Sector 001."

"We've got four batteries of Phalanx CIWS (Close-In-

Weapons-System) that'll catch it in a crossfire of depleted uranium bullets," Frost said.

"Sigrillion? What say you and those automatons you've spent so much time and budget on?" the Old Man wondered aloud.

"Two of the Juggernauts guard the southwest side of the compound," the Crimson Mage said.

"They possess the means to stop the fiery elemental; I'm sure of it."

"Incoming," interrupted Sniderinkoff as the war room was rocked repeatedly.

"How could it?" shouted the Old Man.

Sigrillion acted as if he'd just come out of a trance.

"The thing's summoning psychic fireballs against us," he mumbled aloud.

"That's impossible; few guild masters have achieved that expertise out of thin air."

"The Phalanx are engaging the target," Sniderinkoff barked out.

The roar of Vulcan twenty-millimeter Gatling guns sounded in the war room loudspeakers. In monitors across a dozen workstations, the flaming raptor hovered in the crossfire of munitions, like a dandelion's cottony seedhead dancing in a crosswind.

Several concussions rocked the war room as conical spirals of looping flames traveled backward from the flaming raptor, enveloping and exploding the Phalanx units.

"Release the Frost Giants!" the Old Man boomed.

Two immense behemoths, metallic infernal machines encased in a flexible armor of congealed ice and reinforced carbon fiber, lumbered forward to meet the flaming raptor.

The compound, with its silver-gilded and black tourmaline walls, stood in dark contrast against the blowing snow drifts surrounding it.

Sigrillion's automatons stopped just outside the southwestern wall, extended their arms to a metallic grind, and fired weighted blankets of thermal-resistant carbon fiber at the thing. As the flaming beast fell to the earth, the swaying giants each shambled forward, firing a second round of nets, this time attached to cables.

Untold millions of volts poured from the Frost Giants into the glowing nests that clung to the flaming thing. The cables that carried the juice, as the twin behemoths tried to electrocute the nameless thing, melted as they were taxed beyond measure.

Sigrillion stood from his station and disappeared. Seconds later, the Crimson Mage appeared as a speck between the towering automatons.

"What's Sigrillion up to?" asked Sniderinkoff.

The Old Man leaned forward, watching the Crimson Mage.

"He has a mind of his own, that One does. Just watch; perhaps he knows something that we don't," said Old Man Nicholas.

#

Outside, surrounded by an invisible force blister, Sigrillion watched the flaming thing up close.

He didn't wait long, as the fiery beast burned through the carbon fiber net and stood apart from the trap.

The flaming pillar raised a ton of vapor as its heat turned the snow and ice surrounding it from a solid to its gaseous state.

"I figured as such," said Sigrillion as he raised his hands, wove cabalistic patterns into the air, and hurled a huge magic bolt at the flaming thing.

The thaumaturgic discharge electrified the air and split the flaming thing into several flaring fragments.

"Divide and conquer, I always say," quipped Sigrillion.

The Crimson Mage then struggled as the multiplied flaring fragments attempted to recombine. A resounding crash echoed across the compound as magical bolts, arising from his fingertips like several strands of a glistening spider's web, sizzled and spat between the thing's fiery splinters.

The sparking slivers recombined as Sigrillion's magical traplines broke, and he fell backward against the snow.

The Crimson Mage raised his right hand as he struggled to his feet, drawing further sigils into the air. He flung another bolt of magic at the flaming thing, now recombined in its original, hateful form.

"Desecrator of the ages! Murderer of the saplings and their elders! You who assassinated the Kings and Queens of the Sky! Where is Old Man Nicholas? Is he here?" thundered a Voice from the midst of the fire, one that all in the North Pole compound heard.

"Is this his, 'address unknown?'"

Some monitors, equipped with an "optic-encephalogram," designed by the late Dr. Matthew Roney, a renowned Canadian paleontologist, allowed select team members to view psychic visions inside the entity's thoughts.

What the Old Man saw made him sick.

Nicholas saw vast forests of towering redwoods and titanic sequoias filling the flaming thing's psychic horizon. At the feet of the huge bores, seedlings grew wild and free.

Then, armies of men swarmed one mighty forest, then another, like locusts descending on a cornfield. Soul-piercing shrieks filled the war room speakers as the men mindlessly fell the great behemoths, indiscriminately mowing down every one of them. The lumberjacks and jills behaved recklessly, like the Buffalo hunters of the old West, who killed off entire herds of the great beasts that once filled the great plains, driving them to the brink of extinction simply because they could. The ancient redwoods and sequoias retained shadows of sentient memory, unlike most trees that had lost that modicum of mental awareness and understanding over the ages.

"This thing thinks I'm somehow responsible for the ecological devastation rendered against the forests by mankind," the Old Man said.

"But, how can that be?"

#

Meanwhile, above ground, the Crimson Mage began to call down fire from the heavens against the flaming thing. In doing so, a fiery halo sprung up around his person, causing all the snow in his vicinity to vaporize.

The flaming thing brushed aside the fire shards, unphased by Sigrillion's assault. It then sent a flaming stream of fire toward him, like a flame thrower against an enemy bunker. The twin Frost Giant automatons simultaneously placed their lumbering bodies between the Crimson Mage and the flaming thing to protect their master.

Their sputtering, fiery remains fell haphazardly to the earth. The ground reeled and shuddered under their combined, immense bulks.

The flaming thing took to the air and fell like a burning raptor on its magical prey. Sigrillion struggled with the thing as dozens of flaming tentacles shot forth from his fiery opponent.

"I cannot match it flame to flame, kill it, kill it!" cried the Crimson Mage as his person merged with the flaming thing. Sigrillion lost his individuality as the fiery beast consumed him, absorbing him like a primordial Shoggoth enfolded its prey, as described in the ancient and forbidden Elder Things' pyramids discovered at the bottom of the world.

"Kill it!"

#

"It's all up to you, Jack," said Old Man Nicholas's voice into Frost's earpiece.

The Immortal rode in an elevator that soon broke the surface of the North Pole compound. He quickly stepped out onto the arctic tundra.

As the burnt head and blackened, flailing arms of the Crimson Mage sank into the flaming thing's maw, Jack began whistling a nameless tune. At the same time, his fingers wove cabalistic designs into the frosty air.

A thousand-fold army of skull-topped, many-shouldered, multi-armed, icy phantasms arose from the snowy plain and took flight.

They began encircling the flaming thing like a dipping funnel cloud in Midwest America. They sang ancient arias dripping with latent power, the secret songs the Valkyries sang before Odin showed up to work a powerful deed upon the olden earth.

Vast, primordial shadows arose in response to their summoning voices. One flew into the heavens, flowing to form a vast shade above the earth that blotted out the sun.

In turn, a palatable darkness fell across the face of the world.

Other shades formed a pentagram around the flaming thing, intoning powerful curses that sealed its power within the cabalistic symbol.

The flaming thing tried to extricate itself from the pentagram with its newfound powers; as it merged with the Crimson Mage, it gained its powers, though not understanding how to use them.

Jack became the incarnation, the hub of a new Ice Age, as temperatures across the globe fell and inland bodies of water and rivers suddenly froze over.

A great wailing of horror and pain arose psychically across the earth, causing Old Man Nicholas to bend over in pain as their multiplied voices threatened to submerge his personality amid the reeling chaos.

He fell off his throne in the war room as the air in the North Pole bunker grew frigid, and the elves and other races among the Old Man's crew panicked.

The flaming thing went solid, becoming a grotesque statue of dense permafrost.

Nicholas rose to his knees and shouted into his headset's mic.

"What have you done?"

Jack Frost smiled sardonically.

"You told me to stop the fiery demon," he said into his headset.

"But, this? Do you know what this means?" asked the Old Man.

"Yes, the only way to stop the flaming thing was to plunge the world into a new, exquisitely frigid Ice Age!" replied Jack, as a swirling mass of contradictions, at once a dragon, a gargoyle, a squid with flailing tentacles, and an ice storm unfolded from within the Immortal's diminutive form. The sound of great, pinioned wings flapping in place filled the snowscape.

"Now that the meddlesome Crimson Mage is eliminated, things will change around here. This world belongs to chaos. That I was a God during those ancient times, aeons before you walked the earth, that's a negligible consequence the world, and you will have to come to terms with, once again."

The Greed With In
Tiffany Vega

I was curled up on the couch with my book in hand. My mom was busy in the kitchen, and the banging of pots and pans was a familiar sound during the holidays. I peeked over my book to see my dad standing on the step stool wrapped halfway around the tree, trying to hang the tinsel on the tree. He and his mom could barely stand being in the same room this last year. It would have been a mix of yelling or silent treatment if they were in the same room. I just hoped that for dinner tonight, everything would go smoothly. Our tradition was to spend a night of pure blessing and joy together for my favorite holiday.

"You better watch out, Dad. You're not as young as you used to be, and if you fall, I am leaving you there for Santa to find." I lifted the book back to my eyesight to hide my grin. So far, this hasn't been the most joyful Christmas yet.

Dad turned to me, but the doorbell rang. I hoped that it was someone who would kidnap me and take me away from the horror that I knew tonight's dinner would bring.

"I will get it." I jumped up from the couch, keeping the train of thought of a kidnapper being at the door. But when I opened the door, there was no one there. I looked around, stepping outside to see if someone was running down the street. The boys my age loved playing ding dong ditch. As I stepped out, I tripped over something in front of the door. All I could think about was that it was going to be a flaming pile of shit. I landed on all fours, hoping no one was around to see me fall. It was bad enough that I was called Holly Jolly Jumbles. It's what happens when you dress like an elf and fall at school.

I stood, cleared the snow off my hands and knees, and looked back at the door. Sitting at the step was a present in a green and red box. A sense of joy overcame me. Did I have a real-life Santa that just dropped off a present?

"Holly, who is it." I heard my mother call out from the kitchen. "Is it your aunt Katie?" I knew she was talking to me, but I couldn't ignore the present. Something in me wanted to rip it open and see what was inside. But the voice next to me woke me out of my trance.

"Holly, who was it?" It was my dad standing at my side.

"I don't know, and I didn't see anyone but that gift." I pointed to the red and green box. Willing it to come to me.

"Hmm, I wonder who it's from," Dad said as he walked over to it and picked it up. It looked heavy; I could see his muscles tighten in his arms as he carried into the house. His eyes locked on the present; I could tell he thought the same thing I was thinking. Who sent it, and what was in it?

"What are you guys doing." Mom comes into the room with her Christmas apron on. She looks at the present, and her eyes light up; then something changes, and for a moment, she looks angry. "So, who is it for?"

My dad licked his lips like he was hungry for whatever was there. He pulled out the card. I could see hearts all around the card. Deep down, my heart stopped. I had been wanting Dean to give me a gift. I had been in love with him for five years. Could this be the year he noticed me?

"My darling, true love demands a cost. I was hoping you could give a little more of yourself, and I promise the rewards will be endless. What wouldn't you give for something so perfect?"

My mother's face turned red. "Who is that from?" Her voice was on the verge of yelling.

"There is no "to" or "from" on it." My dad said he held the box tighter.

"Just put the fucking thing down, "our" family dinner is done." My mom stomped her feet back to the kitchen. I could hear a pan hitting the wall.

"Dad, should we open it and see who it belongs to? I mean, it might be for me. I was hoping that Dean would bring me a gift." I crept closer to the present. It called to me to it.

"Let's go eat and see what your mom thinks." Dad pushed me towards the kitchen.

Dinner was quiet. Mom and Dad said nothing, and halfway through dinner, Aunt Katie called and said, and I quote, "The dumb ass doesn't want to stop playing his fucking video games."

"So are we going to open the gift after dinner and see what it is? What if Aunt Katie left it for all of us." I could tell Mom was about to blow her mind. Tears welled up in her ears.

"We can open it tomorrow morning with the other gifts." Mom managed to choke out. "Speaking of which, you know the drill; good little guys need to sleep so Santa can come and drop off your gifts."

I don't know why the thought made me smile, but it did. I was 15 years old and didn't believe in Santa anymore, but I loved spending it with my family and opening gifts.

"I know; I will shower and then go to bed."

****

I heard a shout, forcing me out of bed. I could hear my mother screaming.

"I thought you ended it with that home wrecker., and now you have her sending gifts to my house." I tipped toed towards the hallway, hoping they wouldn't hear or see me.

"I told you that I ended it. It was a mistake, and I love my family." Dad's voice was on the verge of screaming." "How do I know that this isn't from some man that you decided to fuck, and this is your way of rubbing it in my face."

I heard a slap. I knew that my mom had hit him. "How dare you compare me to that slut you had slept with. Unlike you and that whore I respect my marriage. "

"Open the fucking gift and see what it is. It's the only way we will figure this out."

My heart dropped; they were going to open the gift without me. What if it was mine to have? I peeked around the corner and watched as they both started to rip open the gift. I watched as they stopped once the box was open.

"It's so pretty. I need to hold it?" My dad demanded.

"Who would send a gem?" My mom reached out to touch it. My dad pulled the gem to his chest. "Let me see it." My mom's voice rose just a little.

"No!" He yelled, his hand turning red with how high he held the gem. "I think I should keep it until we figure out what it is... you know, for safety." He looked down at his hands. My mom's face was getting that look, her eyes getting small, her lips pushing together. I knew she was losing her temper.

"Give it to me; let me see it." I watched as my mother pushed my father with both of her hands. I had never seen my mother so upset.

My father took the impact without moving much. I could see a mix of hurt and anger grow on his face. He clenched the gem tighter in his hand. My father raised his right hand, the one holding the gem, and swung and hit my mother in the face. I stood frozen as my mother hit the floor, her hands covering her face.

I didn't know what to do, and I had never seen my parents fight like this. I took a few more steps into the room, my legs trembling with every step. "Mom, are you alright?"

Neither looked at me or said a word to me. My mother struggled to her feet. She picked up the glass vase on the table and threw it at my father. Then she took the lamp and ran at him with it in her hands, slamming it into his head. My dad flew backward, dropping to his knees. His hand flew to his head, dropping the jagged gem on the floor. My mother flew to the ground, tackling the gem.

"It's now mine." But before she could get up, my father was on top of her. Punches were thrown, bites were bitten, blood was spilled, and hair was pulled. So much blood was on the floor, I couldn't tell who it was from.

"Stop!" I yelled. For what seemed like a second, they looked at me, concerned, but like a switch, they went back to fighting over the gem.

They both grabbed at each other, unsure which one, but someone kicked the gem, and it slid across the floor to me. I hurried and picked it up. It took more muscle than I thought to pick up the gem. I wondered why it was so heavy. It was just a tiny quarter-size gem. I felt the weight in my hand. Its shape edges poked at my skin, but something told me to hold it tight and not let it leave my hand.

My parents were now standing up and looking at me. My mother's nose was broken and looked like it was crooked; blood was gushing down her mouth and her chin. My father looked like the side of his head was bleeding, and I could only imagine that there was a gash across it. I looked at them, waiting to see what they would do next. Something told me to run, but my legs wouldn't move. I tried to look at them in the eyes, but they were not looking at my face, but they were staring at my hands. I moved my hand to the side, and their eyes darted to where my hand with the gem was.

"Holly, please give Mommy the gem, " my mom pleaded with me. "Mommy needs it, " my mom screamed at me.

I squeezed the gem tighter in my hand. I could feel the edges cutting my palm, and a warm, sticky feeling oozed with it. Thoughts of taking a pan from the kitchen and hitting my mom flowed through my head. All I knew was that no one was taking the gem away from me.

"No, give it to me, sweetheart. That's Daddy's special jewel. " He took a few steps towards me. I could feel the gem warmth travel up my arm and into my chest. The need for its comfort, I knew I couldn't let it leave my hand.

I saw the candle leaving my dad's hand, but I didn't move; it hit me square in the nose, and the pain caused me to grab my nose with my empty hand. My vision blurred, and I felt the warm liquid run down my cheek as tears started to flow.

I must have been focused on the pain because I didn't see my mother come up to me, trying to pry open my hand.

"Mom, please don't." I wasn't sure why I was pleading with her. I knew I didn't want to give up the gem, but I also knew that it was what was causing all the fighting.

My dad ripped at my mother's hair, pulling chunks from her head. If it hurt her, she showed no signs of it; she kept bending and biting at my fingers, trying to get to the prize. Dad pulled my mother off of me and got on top of her. He put his hands around her throat, and I could see the whiteness in his hand as he squeezed tight. I watched, paralyzed, as my mother gasped for air. She lifted her hands to his face, cradling it as if she loved him, and begged him to stop. That thought quickly became a nightmare as I watched her drive her thumbs deep into his eye sockets, digging around as if her life depended on it, which was the case as my father's hands tightened around her neck.

I heard a pop and wasn't sure if it was my mother's neck or my father's eyes popping out. There was moaning, but I wasn't sure who it was coming from. Then my mother threw my father off her; there were bruises on her neck already. She gasped in and out. It looked like one side of her neck had collapsed. She struggled to get to her knees; she gasped for air every move. She crawled to me, blood oozing down her face. Her hand shook as she reached for my hand.

I didn't know what to do. I just watched my mother pluck out my father's eyes, and now she was coming for me. I heard a voice in my head. *It would be so easy to end her; look at her weakness.* The gem is all yours. I didn't want to hurt my mom; the gem meant nothing to me. It was just a piece of junk compared to my mother.

"Give me the gem." My mom crocked out. Blood spilled from her mouth with each word. I could only imagine the pain that she was in

"No!" I screamed, "What is wrong with you? Look at what you have done." I wanted to run, move from her, from what was before me. There in the background stood our Christmas tree, and one just hours ago, we finished as a family. The cookies were laid out for Santa, and my father lay on his back, his eyes hanging from their sockets. My mom was on her knees, bleeding. This is not what Christmas was supposed to be. We were supposed to be happy, singing songs by the fire. Talking about the things we wanted for the coming year.

No, this is not how I will let this end; I will not let this be my Christmas. I had to save my mom. She was all I had left. And I had to protect her from what was about to happen. The police couldn't find my dad's body like it was. There was something I had to do: fire; if his body were Burt enough, maybe they wouldn't know how he died. I stepped over my mother, pushed our Christmas tree over, and pushed it to the fireplace; it took only a second for the tree to blaze with fire. I waved the gem at my mom, and she crawled towards me. I opened the door and yelled for help.

A group of people caroling next door made their way towards us. I grabbed my mother and got her to her feet; she clawed at me.

"Where is it? Where is the gem." She grabbed my hand.

I put the gem in my pocket. I grabbed both of her shoulders and shook her. "Do you see what is going on? The house is on fire. Dad is in there."

For a brief moment, I thought I had gotten through to her. But then she looked into my eyes. "Give me the fucking gem."

I knew I could do nothing but burn the gem in the fire and hope that would break the spell my mother was under. I reached into my pocket and took out the shape-edge object. I raised my hand and tossed it into the flames. I watched as my mother's head followed the gem and then looked back at me like she was trying to figure out what I had just done.

"Mom, please, it's gone. It's in the fire. We need to get you help." I turned to wave someone over to help me. I felt my mom slip through my grip. I turned and watched her run into the fire.

"Mom!" I screamed. "Please come back."

The lady that I called over grabbed me by the shoulders. "We have to get you a safe distance from the house."

"I can't; my mother just ran into the house." I pushed her away. "I can leave her in there."

"We have to let the fire department do their job." The woman took me by the hand and led me to the street. The fire department sirens grew louder as they approached the burning house. I watched as they rushed with their firehose and equipment. Knocking down the wall of my family home.

One of the firemen came over, "The woman said that your mother ran back into the house?"

"Yes, my father was still there, and she returned to get him." I tipped at my eyes.

"We found two bodies in there. Was that everyone in the house.?" I nodded my head yes.

He walked away and yelled at the other firefighters. I put my hand in my pocket and pulled out the sharpened green gem.

There was a cold breeze, and then someone leaned in and whispered in my ear. "The greed within always wins." His voice was rough and low.

I turned to find a tiny old man, his hair the darkest black I had ever seen. "What did you say."

"The gift there is a present from me. See, I am a collector of sorts. I collect innocents, and you traded yours for that worthless rock."

"What are you talking about." I looked down at my hand. The once-green gem looked like a rock in my hand. There was no more need to protect the gem with my life.

"I hope it was worth it, my child." He let out a soft laugh; his eyes flashed red, and his eyes, for a moment, were different.

"What have I done?"

Home in a Box
Solomon Forse

I take a high step into the oversized box in the living room. My heavy tan boot compresses the cardboard against the pristine, white carpet. Around me, the house is dark except for the soft glow of the colored lights on the spruce tree, silent except for the gentle tick-tock from the mantlepiece clock.

"C'mon, Kevin, we don't have all night," says Rodrigo, poking me with a tube of wrapping paper.

"Shh." I poke him back. "You wanna ruin the surprise?"

I bring my other leg over the edge and ease into the box as if I am settling into a bathtub. As I slide to the bottom, knees tucked up to my chest, the container bulges at its sides.

I look up at Rodrigo, my camouflage patrol cap protruding just over the edge of the box.

"It looked a lot bigger in the store. I barely fit in this thing."

"And I can't believe I just broke into your house."

As Rodrigo kneels down, his hulking form blocks out the Christmas tree lights that twinkle through the numerous air holes I cut into the box hours before.

"Hey," I hiss. "*We* just broke into *my* house. And I wouldn't be cut out for Special Forces if I couldn't pull off a simple B&E."

Something smacks into the bill of my cap. As I reach up to reposition it, Rodrigo's fingers appear over one of the flaps of the box—and then his grin.

"We wouldn't be breaking in if you had a *key*, numbnuts!"

"Man, I swear I left a spare under that rock before I deployed. Anne must've moved it."

"Whatever you say, bro, but we gotta hustle. I've got my own gifts to wrap. Tuck your head in."

Rodrigo folds the flaps inward, dimming the interior of the box.

Before closing the final flap, he stops, hand resting on the edge.

"Real quick. Before I shut you in here, you gotta tell me— how exactly did you get *sixty* days of leave?"

I look down and sigh, then raise my eyes to Rodrigo's quizzical expression.

"Let's just say I had them saved up."

"Then what's everyone else in Iraq doing without you? I thought—"

"Don't worry about it." I reach a hand out of the box and blindly point to the floor. "And don't forget that card. Stick it to the outside when you're done."

"Oh, yeah. Let me find it."

Shadows cross over the tiny apertures as Rodrigo fishes among items on the floor. From outside the box comes the sound of unfolding paper.

"No way. You wrote this? 'Merry Christmas from Iraq'? Anne's gonna think there's a bomb in here, bro."

"Shut up, man. Just stick it on. And don't forget to punch the wrapping paper through the air holes. Unless you wanna go down for manslaughter."

"I'll think about it."

The lid seals over me. Everything goes dark.

Before I know what's happening, beads of sweat form across my forehead and along my temples.

Not again. Please, no. Not here. Not right now.

My stomach churns. The box presses my elbows, crams my feet, hugs my back, and pushes on my head.

A haunting memory flashes through my mind—a thunderous boom, my body crushed from all sides, voices screaming in agony, the acrid reek of smoke—

But I close my eyes, squeeze them shut as hard as I can, think of hugging my wife and children until the nausea subsides and I shove the darkness away.

I remember where I am when Rodrigo's hands rub back and forth across the lid, tapping the cardboard against the bill of my cap. When I open my eyes, shimmering lights cluster around me like multicolored stars.

Then hot breath comes whistling into the box.

"Hey, Kev, I can't figure out this wrapping paper. How am I gonna do the bottom?"

A moment passes before I realize what Rodrigo is asking—he's my most loyal friend, but not always the most intelligent. I chuckle, forgetting about the war for a moment.

"You serious? Just leave it," I rasp. "And hurry up—just don't be sloppy."

"All right, all right." A hand slaps the side of the box. "Hope you don't have to take a piss in there."

After a period of silence, the crinkling of wrapping paper surrounds me, and the space goes dark again. The t-shirt under my uniform clings to my chest with sweat, and the box starts to spin. I swallow, trying to focus on the sounds—anything to shut out the darkness.

I zero in on the tearing of scissors through paper, the squeaking of tape from the roll, the pressing of hands along the cardboard. But then I think of my wife upstairs—Anne sleeping peacefully in her bed, her eyes shooting open at the sounds from the living room. Would she call the police? Would she sneak out her door and peek down the stairs? What would she do if she saw the silhouette of my friend there in the house, huddled over all the presents?

I once wished I'd left a small pistol in the nightstand drawer before my deployment. Now I think better of it.

A sharp rip rattles me from my thoughts, and one of Rodrigo's fingers come poking through a hole. And then another, and another, until a dozen tiny sparkles adorn the walls of the interior, the dim light cascading across my arms and legs.

Knuckles rap against the box.

"Bro, can you breathe or what?"

I inhale. The air is already stagnant—that thick, dusty cardboard scent.

Almost... *smoky?*

The screaming echoes in my mind again, rubble piled on top of my chest, the darkness closing in—but I force my eyes shut, imagine a car ride in the family minivan, coasting through town, Ryan and Katie in the back, me and Anne in the front, the windows rolled up and the heat on full blast. My hands grip the steering wheel, Burl Ives' rich, resonant voice pouring through the—

"Kev, you hear me?"

"Sorry—uh, yeah. I can breathe... I'm fine, man."

"I'm just about done." A hand slides against the exterior. "Okay, and there's the card. Shit, Ryan and Katie are gonna go nuts! I can't compete with you, bro. I'm lucky if my kids get the video games they want."

"At least you spend time with them."

I recall the few times I'd accessed WiFi in between combat missions—the endless queue of videos from Anne awaiting me each time. All clips of Ryan and Katie. All the things I'd missed—tee-ball games, karate tournaments, dance competitions, and band concerts. As the queue grew longer, the messages from Anne grew shorter.

But I know she still loves me, that she isn't just holding out for the kids. Anne *wants* me. *Needs* me. Even during the few times I'd used the satellite phone—despite Anne's tinny, garbled voice from thousands of miles away—I could still hear it, a kind of silent yearning that filled the spaces in between the transmission delays, a desperate stillness that said, *I need you. Come home.*

And now I'm here. It's going to fix everything—the tears of joy streaming down Anne's face, the squeals of surprise from Ryan and Katie—everything will be right again.

"You're a great dad, Rod." I pause. "Listen, I couldn't have done this without you."

Rodrigo gives two gentle knocks.

"Thanks, bro. It means a lot."

"You're all set. Call me in the morning—I wish I could be here to see you pop outta this thing. I hope Anne takes a video."

"Shit. My phone's still in the truck down the street. Yeah, I'll call you tomorrow. Merry Christmas, man. Just be careful with the window on your way out."

"You won't hear a thing." A finger appears through one of the air holes. "Merry Christmas, Kev."

I latch my finger around Rodrigo's, clutches tight and then lets go.

Moments later, the living room window emits a hollow

squeak. The slightest draft of frigid air worms its way through the holes in the box. Then the window slides back into place with a cushioned click.

I never told Rodrigo.

It's better this way, or he probably wouldn't have shut me in the box. He would never have agreed to any of this. Not if he knew about the temporary discharge orders, the papers that read "unfit for duty," the scribbled signature from the psychiatric doctor. Not if I told him about the nightmares—about the darkness. Not if I told him about the bathroom mirror, the mirror that with each morning reflected new bruises, new contusions—

I won't tell Anne either. Not until she forces it out of me.

What I need now is my family.

And I'll be with them in a few hours.

Everything will be right again.

#

I hear a vehicle roaring in the distance, its engine thrumming at full throttle.

But I'm not in the box.

I'm bundled in my sleeping bag, halfway across the world, holed up in the corner of a mud-brick building, other sleeping soldiers scattered about the squalid hut that serves as a combat outpost.

The racing engine in the distance grows louder. Tires rip across a dirt road, swerving around obstacles. The vehicle's chassis strains and squeaks against the curves.

Something is wrong.

Who's on guard?

I try to move, struggle to free my arms, to find the zipper, to squirm free and grab my rifle. But my arms are stuck at my sides, legs crammed together—my whole body mummified in a swaddling death-grip.

The car sounds as if any second it's going to smash right into the other side of the wall.

My pounding heart beats within my chest, faster and faster.

I writhe and flounder, gritting my teeth and thrashing against the sides of my sleeping bag.

Then a blinding flash ignites the room.

A concussive force punches me in the chest and shoots out the bottoms of my feet.

Chunks of stone and dirt pelt my body. An enormous slab slams into my ribs. I cough and gag, sucking at the air choked with dust and smoke.

A darkness swirls around me, closes around my body, swallowing me whole as my ears drown in a high-pitched squeal.

The tone fades only to be replaced by screams. Voices I recognize.

But I can't move.

Then the screaming stops, and there is only an infinity of silence—hours of cold stillness broken only by strangled breaths as my chest heaves against the oppressive weight piled on my body. Even if I could call out to my friends, they wouldn't answer.

An eternity later, faint flashes of light dance at the corners of my vision.

Men shouting in guttural voices—Arabic.

Roving beams. Searching lights.

Twinkles all around me, speckles of light in the shards of shrapnel surrounding me.

Sparkles of all colors—red, yellow, green, blue.

But no.

They're Christmas lights.

Shining through the air holes.

I'm in the house.
In the box.
Right where Rodrigo left me.

#

In the wee hours of the morning, I jolt awake at the sound of a car.

My pulse races—I can't bear to experience the nightmare again.

But this time it isn't a dream. This time I'm not halfway across the world. I'm in the box, the revving engine of a sports car echoing through the still neighborhood and penetrating the cardboard walls that enclose me.

The vehicle sounds as if it will zoom past the house, but then it slows, engine reducing to a purr.

Tires climb up the driveway.

Doors open and slam.

Shoes click on concrete.

A key fumbles in the lock.

Who can it be? Not a robber—they wouldn't have a key. Then who?

I strain my neck, trying to twist around, but the box only pushes harder against my head, shoving my chin down to my sternum.

I can only listen.

And then comes the muffled but delicate notes of a female voice—unmistakably Anne's.

Has she purchased a new car? Made a withdrawal from our shared account? I remember seeing the family van in the driveway —why a second car?

The door creaks open. A whoosh of cold air shoots across the living room, swimming through the holes in the box along with the white luminescence of the kitchen light.

"Shh! Don't wake the kids."

Who's she talking to? And who's been watching the children?

Then heavy boots resound in the foyer. Another voice. A man's voice.

"Oh look, cookies! You don't think Santa will mind if I have a few bites?"

Anne's brother? He lives hundreds of miles away. Did she fly him in for the holidays? Perhaps she thought he might fill my absence—maybe Anne didn't want to suffer another Christmas alone.

I'll never forget last December—the way Anne's voice screamed through the earpiece of the satellite phone. *You promised you would be home.* The way her anger cut through the roaring winds of the dust storm. *It was another volunteer mission, wasn't it? Don't lie to me, Kevin.* The laughter of my friends as they threw rations at me and mocked my glum expression.

"Didn't I tell you to be quiet? Thank god they didn't wake up while we were out."

"Okay, okay. But I'm eating these. Santa already came, right?"

"Yes, but he might not come *next year*—I hear he doesn't like naughty boys . . . but lucky for you, I know someone who *does*. Get over here."

Then it's not her brother.

A vein rises on my forehead. Throbbing. Pulsating.

"Right here in the kitchen? On Christmas Eve? Who's naughty now?"

A poignant pang of jealousy wrenches my heart, squeezing it like a sponge before kicking it down to the pit of my stomach.

I tear against the box, flex my arms into the walls, shove my feet into the cardboard.

It refuses to budge.

I want to scream, but I can hardly manage to breathe.

No. Please, no.

A chill rolls down my body, from the top of my head to the soles of my feet.

The darkness must have followed.

And now it's found me.

As it grips me in steel bands, I feel it working on me. It fills my mouth with the concrete, the dirt, the grit of my untimely burial. It stings my nose with the burnt-liver stench of scorched flesh, the coppery tinge of the blood that oozed from my friends.

And there's no use in fighting it.

I'm fighting the unchangeable past, fighting the immutable fact that I had survived when my friends had not. And unlike my friends' children, Ryan and Katie would never have to hear those words—that "Daddy isn't coming home." And what did I learn from it? Nothing. I just picked myself up, continued my military career as if nothing had happened. Continued to leave my family behind while I chased my own aspirations.

And that was when the nightmares began. When the darkness came.

I can't do this anymore.

I fight even harder, grinding my teeth, pushing outward with all of my might. My muscles quiver, trembling with fatigue, but the walls only press closer. The darkness suffocates me as it crushes my shoulders inward, jamming my elbows against my ribs, thrusting my heels against my thighs.

I stop—slow my breathing, attempting to focus on the sounds around me.

Anne.

And that stranger.

There was something familiar about his voice, too.

And then it comes to me—the office party. Halloween. The guy in the vampire costume.

Anne's boss.

Brad.

White-hot jealousy roils inside of me, ready to burst, ready to push the darkness away.

"Wait—what the hell is that?"

"What?"

"In the living room."

Heels click across linoleum.

Get away from me.

"That was *not* here when I left. Are you behind this, Brad?" A switch flips, and a dozen thin streams of light pour into the box. "Oh my god, did you get the kids something for Christmas? Is there a puppy in there? We should have talked about this first. But damn it, I love you."

You bitch.

"No, no, it wasn't me!" Footsteps approach Anne's voice. "Well, I mean, I *did* get something for them—and something for you too . . . but I didn't put that box there."

"Oh, wait." Anne laughs. "It was the babysitter—Morgan. I gave her a key a few weeks ago after I changed the locks. She must have done something for Ryan and Katie. Or maybe she and the kids planned something for us?"

"There's a card on it. Should I—"

"No, no. Don't spoil their surprise. It might be for us, Brad."

Us?

My skin crawls with a searing spite, my whole body shaking with a trembling frenzy.

"Huh. Maybe. You don't think . . . Kevin . . . has anything to do with this, do you?"

"Oh, c'mon. How could he? He won't be back for two months. You're not still scared of him?"

"No, I just—"

"He's on a 'secret mission.' No contact. No communication."

An object drops to the floor, likely a purse, and then clothing rustles as Anne's tone softens.

"I promise, baby. The second he calls, I'll give him the talk. I have the papers ready. It's just you and me now. You're my whole world."

Her voice reduces to a near whisper. A voice she had once used with me in the most intimate of moments.

Everything inside me wants to burst through the lid and charge at the both of them in a rage of fury—but the darkness has only led me along, like a mouth gumming at my limbs, moving me further and further down an endless gullet.

"You're not just *my* whole world, either. You're my *children's* world. You're the father they deserve. They've needed someone who could be there for them . . . *we've* needed someone who could be there for *us*. Me, Ryan, Katie, and—"

"Damn it, I love you."

I pull my arms upward, struggling to at least cover my ears, to muffle the wet kissing, to deafen the tender moaning, but the constricting darkness clutches at my legs, creeping around my hands and arms so tightly that my fingers grow numb.

The harder I fight, the more it squeezes.

So I stop, and all I can do is clench my throat and close off the violent sobs threatening to spill out from me and explode in a primal wail of tortured pain.

#

A creak from the stairs jars me to consciousness.

I go to bring my hand to my face, attempting to rub away the salted crust from my eyes, but I find that I cannot move.

A heavy weight smashes my head downward, pushing it between my knees, arcs of pain shooting up my back and stinging the muscles in my neck. Everything else is numb—my limbs only suggestions, my extremities abstractions. I'm only conscious of the stifling air of the box as my muggy breath pools about my waist.

Then the stairs creak again. Playful whispering murmurs somewhere outside the box.

"Ry-ry, look. All the presents."

"Shh. What? Santa already came?"

"We missed him *again*."

The innocent voices of my children—voices I haven't heard in months. A new warmth courses through my veins, restoring feeling to my arms and legs. They'll get me out.

The soft hiss of socks upon carpet dances around the box.

"Quiet! Look—he ate some of the cookies."

"Whoa. Katie, come here. Look. What do you think this is?"

I try to speak, but the darkness crushes me. I strain to inhale, my chin pushed so far downward that my windpipe folds like a bent straw, my crumpled chest struggling to expand.

"You think it's a puppy?"

Ryan. Katie.

"They don't make puppies in the North Pole, stupid. Only toys."

"I'm not stupid. Doesn't Santa bring babies, though? Babies aren't toys."

Help me.

"But what if Santa brought us a puppy? Like the way the Stork's gonna bring Mommy a baby?"

"What? Who said that?"

"The bump on Mommy's belly. It means the Stork's gonna come."

No. Please, no. Anne...

"What're you—"

I battle for air, my heart pounding against my rib cage as I contract my abdominal muscles, squeezing them against my lungs. Finally, I gasp, a bit of air rushing down my windpipe.

"Shh. Ry-ry. I hear something!"

My mouth opens, lips trembling, the words almost spilling out—but the darkness forces them back down my throat.

One of them crouches in front of the box, blocking the faint flight trickling in from the glow of the living room.

"Look! Holes. For breathing, like at the pet store. It has to be a puppy!"

Something scratches at the exterior, and then a hand slaps against skin.

"Katie, no. Don't touch it—you'll make it bark or something."

Footsteps shuffle away from the box.

No—don't leave.

"But if it wasn't Santa, who brought it?"

"Hey, there's a card. Maybe it says."

"Ry-ry, you said *don't touch it*."

"All right, fine. But I think I know who it was . . . it was Brad."

No.

"Yeah! It was Brad. I don't think Daddy would let us get a puppy."

"Nope. He doesn't love us anymore. Like Mom said. He just loves his Army friends."

"You really think Daddy doesn't love us, Ry-ry?"

"He changed."

I didn't change. I just made a mistake.

"I wish he was here. He could see the puppy. Maybe he would let us have it."

I'm here. I'm right here.

"Stop thinking about him. Like Mom said. We'll get used to Brad."

No. You don't have to do that—please, my darlings.

"I like Brad."

"Me too. I think this is gonna be the best Christmas ever."

"I can't wait to see the puppy. I'm gonna pet him all over."

No. I'm here. You still have me. I'm right here.

I clench my jaw, squeeze my eyes shut, focus all my energy on drawing air into my lungs. I have to say something. Anything. Even if it kills me.

"We'll open it in the morning. C'mon, let's go before Mom wakes up."

The stairs creak again.

A wheeze gushes from my throat, my mouth forming around the words as I push the remainder of the air from my body.

"*I'm sorry.*"

But my sweet, innocent children are already in their rooms.

Only the darkness hears me.

With the emptying of my breath, the darkness constricts with a frightening force, squeezing with an inexorable, irrepressible power.

My lungs collapse, ribs splintering and organs flattening. A lightning bolt of pain shoots through my body, and the walls continue pressing against me from all sides. My tendons rip, muscles tearing as bones fracture.

My skull cracks between my knees, eyes bulging from their sockets. Blood pours from my broken nose, spilling from my crushed mouth and shattered jaw, a motley of bodily fluids commingling at the bottom of the container.

#

In the living room, a dark pool spreads like an oil slick across the pristine, white carpet. Its surface reflects the twinkling lights of the tree.

Falling from the box, a card flutters through the air, unfolding and landing in the pool, sticking face-up.

The dark fluid quickly soaks through the bottom of the thick paper, a crimson red stain bleeding into the parchment.

Within seconds, it obscures the scrawled words written in black ink across the card:

Merry Christmas from Iraq.

Holly Jolly
Alexander Jose Martinez

"Have a holly jolly Christmas, and when you walk down the street, say hello to friends you know and everyone you meet."

The radio played in the background as the Martins, clad in matching flannel coats and lumberjack hats, drove through a light snow. It had started falling before dinner and had laid pretty thick before easing up. It had come just in time for their yearly "ritual."

"OH-HO, THE MISTLETOE," belted the father and son as they drove through the winter wonderland of northern Vermont.

They couldn't be happier to make their annual pilgrimage from their home in South Burlington to the largest Christmas tree farm in the state. An hour north, just outside of the Jay State Forest, set amongst New England's most pristine, untouched wilderness was "Jolly Old Nic's Christmas Tree Farm." In actuality, it was more of a preserve than a farm, with hundreds of acres of property that butted right up to the state forest; it could be challenging to navigate the two if it weren't for the fluorescent blazes marking the trees on the border. The same family had owned the land for generations and used the tree sales proceeds to ensure the area's beauty was maintained and respected. They were good people and had gotten to know the Martin boys well over the years.

"Hung, where you can see, somebody is waiting for you. We interrupt this holiday classic to report that the Vermont State Police are still searching for the Phillips family. The family was reported missing on the first of December and were last seen at their home in Richford. Anyone with information should contact the Vermont State Police at 802-"

"Let's find something a little more spirited," Jack Martin told his son as he searched the local radio stations.

It had been the main news story in Vermont for the last two weeks. A small-town family vanishes without a trace. Loved ones suspected foul play, but nothing conclusive. It had put a damper on the holiday spirit of those living in the timber-clad regions of the Northland. Jack knew that when you live in the more remote places in the world, people are unfortunately missing out. With their proximity to the Canadian border, it was surprisingly easy for people to pick up and start anew in the "True North." That is what Jack had hoped the Phillips family had done. Considering the idea of a family of three, including a young girl, meeting an untimely end didn't sit well with him. He wouldn't let those intrusive thoughts distract him from an otherwise excellent birthday thus far.

"Hey, Dad, can we roll the windows down? I know it's still snowing, but I need some fresh air." Thomas Martin asked his father.

"Well, Tommy," Jack said as he leaned closer to his son. "You know the Taco here is getting up there in years; let's just hope the power windows still work," he said as he tapped the dash of his 2007 Toyota Tacoma and flashed a wry smile.

This night was Jack's and his son's favorite tradition. They started shortly after Thomas had learned how to walk. Each year around Jack's birthday in mid-December, the two of them, father and son, would drive the hour or so north to "Jolly Old Nic's" and pick out the perfect white pine to serve as their family Christmas tree. The Martin boys would leave after dinner, typically staying up all night, driving, hiking through a couple of snowy miles to the white pine section of the "farm," cutting down a beauty, hauling it back to the Tacoma, driving back and set the tree up in time for Jack's wife and young daughter to wake up to it first thing in the morning. Thomas loved all of it. He loved singing Christmas carols with his dad on the ride up, hiking to find their tree, and sometimes through the snow. He loved using the axe and handsaw to cut down the tree, though his dad typically did most of the cutting; as he had gotten older, he had gotten more responsibility. He even loved the corny lumberjack outfits he and his dad sported yearly. However, he had already grown out of three different jackets. The part he particularly loved was sneaking back into the house in the wee hours of the night to set up and decorate the tree. Seeing his sister's eyes sparkle with joy when she got her first glimpse of the tree each year was better than any other Christmas present he could ever get. He loved this tradition and would not trade it for the world.

"You having a good birthday?" Thomas asked his father.

"Best one so far," Jack replied—a running joke since he said the same thing every year.

The temperature in the Tacoma dropped rapidly, and when Jack noticed his breath had turned to foggy white mist, he decided it was time to put the windows back up. Their headlights pierced through the soft veil of falling snow, casting long beams that shimmered and cut through the darkness. They were closing in on their destination when their right headlight began to flicker, clinging to life for a moment but eventually fizzing out. Father and son looked at each other and started to laugh.

"I have heard it is pretty bad luck to drive around as a padiddle," said Jack. "Guess we should turn around, huh? What do you think, Tommy Boy?"

Thomas cracked a smile, "Not a chance, Dad."

"That's my boy. We better call your mom before we lose service, and she will send the state troopers out after us."

Thomas laughed, and Jack called his wife. They continued driving into the night as it grew ever darker around them, unaware of how unlucky they were and the terror awaiting them at "Jolly Old Nic's Christmas Tree Farm."

***

The faint glow of neon lights cut through the light snow to reveal the sign the Martins had been waiting to see. Strewn between two towering eastern cottonwoods read "Jolly Old Nic's" in alternating red and white letters. It always reminded Thomas of a giant of a giant candy cane. It was the most symbolic welcoming of the Christmas season he could imagine. They had replaced the sign in recent years, but Jack still thought it had that old-school neon vibe he remembered, even as a kid coming out with his dad.

"Come on, Hammer, let's go pick a winner," he could hear his father say in his long-ago memories.

This place was special to Jack and his family and was now a third-generation tradition. The annual trip "up north" always marked the official start to the Christmas season for the Martins, and this year was no different. As they pulled up to the gate, they were greeted by none other than "Old Nic" himself. Dressed head to toe as Santa Claus, fake beard, wig and all. This was, of course, not the original "Old Nic," but Nicolas Bunting IV, keeping the tradition alive for a fourth generation. Amazingly, he still had his great-grandfather's original hat and coat. Though rather worn through the years, it had been refurbished to the best of his grandmother's and mother's abilities. The original pants, however, did not fit this "skinny Nic" the way they had with some of his predecessors. His smile showed through the fake beard, and the genuine pleasure to see the Martin boys was evident.

"Hey there, Hammer! I was wondering when you guys would be making it up," Nic greeted them as he approached the driver-side door.

He poked his head inside the window, "Good evening, Tommy. Have you been a good boy this year?"

"Hey, Nic!" Thomas lit up like a...well, like a Christmas tree.

His joy could not be contained in the Tacoma as he quickly opened his door, dashed around the front of the truck, and gave Nic a big bear hug.

"Haha, I missed you too, buddy."

Thomas felt something odd on the hip of "Old Nic" during their embrace. "What's that?" he said, pointing to a pistol holstered at Nic's side.

"I didn't know you carried," said Jack.

"I normally don't, but I've had a few customers report suspicious movement and track up on the mountain the last couple of weeks, stuff that had them pretty scared."

Jack and Thomas looked at each other, a little perplexed.

"What do you mean *suspicious*?" asked Jack.

Nic leaned back into the window as Thomas returned to the passenger seat. He looked around, worried that someone might be listening to their conversation.

"I don't know exactly, but when people are up there alone at night, especially the ones who go all the way to the white pines, they say they feel like someone is watching them. They said they thought they may have seen footprints in the snow that hadn't been there when they had gone up. I also have had a few reports of coyotes on the north ridge, so maybe it is just them. Still, this time of year, they can become desperate, and since they are shooting on sight, I figured why to take any chances."

The coyote explanation was plausible, but Nic seemed worried about something else. The Martin boys could sense his anxiety about the whole thing.

"Do you guys want to come inside for coffee or cocoa? Warm them bones before trekking out."

"No thanks, we're good." The Martin boys held up matching thermoses and clanked them together.

"Very good. I am just glad the snow seemed to stop. You guys should have a beautiful night for a hike. I know you guys know how clear it is up here, but after a light snow, the air and sky are always the most crisp. Enjoy your solitude. You guys are the only ones out there tonight. My last customer came back down about an hour ago."

Nic sauntered back to his "lodge," a cosy little wooden outhouse adjacent to the parking lot, equipped with a space heater and old antenna TV. On the outside was an old painted wooden sign; it read, "NIC'S PLACE" in a beautiful old script, complete with vintage reindeer paintings done by his great-grandmother. It was just another one of the things Jack Martin loved about this place. As Nic was getting comfortable and flipping his antique television between the few channels his antennas picked up, the Martins began loading their "tools." Jack took a large axe, slinging the leather strap over his shoulder, and brought a smaller hand saw in a backpack. Thomas had his version of his father's ax, but he fastened a much smaller hatchet to his belt. They both had their thermos in hand as they began the trek into the dense Vermont forest, giving a two-finger salute to Nic as they ventured into the darkness, leaving only their footprints in the snow behind them.

***

As the Martins made their way into the furthest reaches of the farm, Jack quizzed Thomas whether he remembered how to find what they were looking for. This was their seventh trip together, and he hoped his son may be getting old enough to take the lead. They were quite the outdoorsmen, and over the years, Jack had taught his son some basic survival skills, including setting up a makeshift shelter, starting a fire, and some simple first aid. They had also taken a foraging class together earlier in the fall, and Thomas was a top shot with the 30-06, though his dad had yet to take him out hunting. Jack told him that when he was old enough to butcher the deer, he would bring him, though Jack didn't enjoy hunting as much as he did in his youth. He thought that for a 10-year-old, Thomas was well beyond his peers in terms of his ability to survive.

"Dad, why do people call you Hammer?" Thomas asked his dad as they reached the top of the first major ridge.

The lights of "Old Nic's" were long gone, and there was nothing around them but snow and the majesty of the forest.

"Well, Tommy, you know I used to wrestle and box when I was younger, and when I got pretty good at both, people started calling me Jackhammer. My friends and family shortened that to Hammer".

He was being modest. Jack Martin had won the New England Golden Gloves from ages 14 to 17 before winning state wrestling titles in his junior and senior high school. He had considered pursuing a career in mixed martial arts while in college before a series of bad knee injuries cut his athletic career short. It was then that he had found his love for the outdoors.

"Oh, uncle Joe said it was because you were a brick shit house," Thomas giggled.

"Hey, watch your mouth, young man," Jack said with a smile to his son. "And what do you mean *were*?"

He flexed an arm to the amusement of his son, and they both laughed. As they moved higher up in elevation, they were both in awe of the beauty of the Vermont sky around them. As Nic had said, the air was crisp and clear, and the stars had come out in full. From the top of the ridge, I could see the beginning of the old-growth white pines, and the area designated for Christmas trees was not far ahead. It was as if the moon itself was guiding them to their destination, full and bright, casting a soft light directly over a small patch of pristine white pines, the likes of which could adorn the fireplaces of royalty. No one would bat an eye at them.

"Alright, Thomas Martin," Jack said, feigning seriousness, "Where to now?"

A grin began to spread across Thomas's face; he thought it was hilarious when his dad called him Thomas. He looked across the ravine in front of them and pointed to a series of trees marked with fluorescent blazes, marking the end of the farm and the start of the state forest.

"There!" he said excitedly. "At the very edge, right next to the state forest, we'll find our tree!"

They were nearly two miles from the farm entrance and had been hiking for a solid hour through the snow. Still, the excitement of finding that perfect tree propelled them further into the night. The snow had layered thick at their elevation, silencing the world around them and turning it into a silent, white abyss. They breathed a little heavier, each breath fogging the cold mountain air. To get to the white pine grove, they had to traverse a thick section of forest, navigating each step carefully through the snow. As they moved into the most densely populated section of the forest, Jack thought he heard a low murmur from off to the west. He stopped in his tracks and asked Thomas if he heard anything. His son shook his head from side to side, still glowing with excitement. They continued, but Jack had an uneasy feeling growing in his stomach. The crunch of his son excitedly plowing through the snow seemed to carry in the stillness of the woods, but Jack felt something was off.

There was a second sound, softer and almost imperceptible at first, a faint echo of their footsteps. Jack paused as he felt a prickling sensation creep up the back of his neck. He scanned the trees around them with his flashlight, expecting to see coyotes or maybe a black bear, but all he saw were suspicious shadows and the twisting shapes of the forest.

"Thomas," he snapped at his son, who immediately recognized his dad's tone meant business. "Listen."

The feeling that they were being watched was undeniable. Thomas, matching his father, began scanning their surroundings with his flashlight. Now, they both heard a soft crunch, snow compressing underfoot. Then again, only now it was closer. The Martins looked at each other as panic ran across Thomas's face.

"Let's keep moving," Jack said, thermos now stored, one hand on his flashlight and the other slowly sliding the ax from his shoulder.

They quickened their pace, and the snow was no longer a novelty but an impediment to their progress. The sound followed as they closed in on the white pine grove. A shadow in the snow, unseen but always there, keeping pace just out of sight. Jack knew they were not alone and that someone or something was stalking them, hidden in the white silence, ready to make their move. His instincts began to take over, and he readied himself for a fight.

They continued to march through the snow, and all at once, there it was, right in front of them. Standing brilliantly in the moon's light was the most perfect white pine they had ever seen, and then they heard a voice from behind them.

"Howdy, neighbor!"

***

The voice had startled the Martins, who the magnificent tree had momentarily transfixed before them. It had come from behind them, and they immediately turned to face their foe.

"She's quite a beaut, ain't she?" said a skinny middle-aged man with a graying comb-over and light mustache.

"You gentlemen have exquisite taste. You need any assistance getting her back to the lot?" the stranger continued, wiping the fog from his spectacles and dusting some snow off his shoulders.

"We came prepared," Jack said, showing the stranger the ax, much like a rattlesnake shaking its tail when it felt threatened.

"No worries, I meant with the transportation. I am not much help when it comes to cutting down the trees, but sometimes, the bigger ones need the help of the snowmobile. I parked her not too far back if you want a lift back down the mountain."

"Who exactly might you be, friend?" Jack asked ax still firmly between his hands.

"Oh geez," said the stranger as he removed his hand from his glove and held it out to Jack. "The name's Todd; sometimes Nic sends me up to help with the trees."

Jack looked a little puzzled, but this twig of a man didn't strike much fear in him; he was far less threatening than some of the scenarios Jack had been playing out in his head moments before. He shook his hand and introduced himself and his son.

"Jack Martin, this is my son Tommy."

Thomas shook the stranger's hand.

"Hey, little neighbor, are you staying warm out here?"

Thomas pulled his hat down and tightened his scarf.

"Umm, yeah, I guess so," he replied uneasily.

The stranger paced around the tree, and the Martins began to unpack their gear.

"I've only seen a handful of people make it up this far in the last few days. Many looked at this tree, but no one committed to it. If you guys hadn't found it, I would have considered taking her home to surprise my wife and daughter. Imagine their faces waking up to see this beautiful girl lit up for the holidays."

Jack took a swig of his thermos and began prepping the tree. Todd was a little fidgety as Jack started swinging away with the ax. After a few minutes, he made a pretty good dent in the trunk and called Thomas over with his hatchet. As Thomas took a turn, Jack decided to warm up with a hit from the thermos.

"Are you new? I have been coming here for years and never seen you before?" Jack asked the mysterious man.

Todd seemed a bit off-put by the question, squirming in his jacket as he answered.

"Well, ugh, wouldn't ya know it, but I got laid off a couple weeks back,"

He put his hands behind his back and rocked back and forth a bit. Sweat started to glisten on his forehead.

"So, ugh, I decided to offer my services to Nic, try and make a little extra money before the holidays, at least until I could find another job."

Jack was becoming increasingly suspicious of this strange little man, especially because ever since he was a kid, a big part of the tradition at Nic's was that you cut and pulled your trees; never before had they used a snowmobile. It was why he knew the further they went into the farm, the better the trees would be since most people didn't want to haul a tree out over two miles. As Jack was getting ready to point this out, Thomas called him.

"Dad! I think it's ready."

Jack, forgetting about the stranger, motioned to Thomas with his hands.

"Alright, Tommy, give it a push and watch yourself when it falls," he called to his son.

Thomas leaned into the tree, its bark scraping against his chin as he thrust it with all his might. A loud cracking reverberated as the trunk split and the tree fell. As it did, Jack looked at Thomas, who was calling to him.

"DAD! LOOK OUT!"

Jack instinctively thought the tree was falling in his direction, but then he heard the rest of Thomas's warning.

"HE'S RIGHT BEHIND YOU!"

Jack turned just as the stranger was wrapping his arms around his head. They struggled and fell to the ground, with Todd landing on Jack. He had a wet rag in his hand that he was forcing towards Jack's face, and all he could do before fading to black was yell.

"THOMAS! RUN!"

As his father went limp beneath the stranger, Thomas grabbed his hatchet and took off for the thicker part of the forest. He could hear his pursuer in the snow not far behind him. He ran as fast as he could into the darkness, hiding behind the largest tree. He could hear Todd crunching through the snow as he tried to prepare to defend himself. His heart was thumping in his ears, almost drowning out the sound of Todd's steps. He clutched his hatchet tightly, ready to use it if he had to, but the stranger's voice was the last thing he heard before fading to blackness. "Hey there, little neighbor."

***

Jack's first sense to return to him was his sense of smell. The distinct smell of burning pine was warm and pleasant. As his eyes adjusted to the low light, he realized he was in a cabin. He tried to reach for his phone but quickly realized he was bound to a wooden chair. As he acclimated to his surroundings, Jack saw that his son was bound to a chair a few feet away, closer to a fire raging in an old fireplace. There, stoking the flames, was their attacker, the stranger they had met in the forest. Todd turned to greet his captives as if he could sense that Jack had woken up.

"Hey there, neighbor; sorry about that fuss back there, but it couldn't be helped."

Jack struggled in his chair as the stranger strode toward him with a fire poker, aglow with heat. Sweat was streaming down his head, and his glasses fogged a bit, reflecting the light of the fire, flashing red and orange. The closer he got to Jack, the more he struggled in his chair, but his restraints were done with care to make sure he wouldn't be going anywhere.

"What the hell are we doing here?" Jack asked his captor.

"Why are you doing this to us?"

"Well, neighbor, like I said, it couldn't be helped."

It was about this time that Thomas began to shake the effects of the chloroform and began to show signs of life. This was a bit of a relief to Jack, albeit small, as they were obviously in a very dangerous situation. Todd paced between the Martins, contemplating how to explain how they had gotten to this point.

"You see, neighbor, it hasn't been a merry Christmas season for me. A few weeks back, I lost my job at the paper mill at Johnson. Twenty years of loyal service didn't mean much to them; they only care about their bottom line, and good ol' Todd was an unnecessary expense."

Todd was pacing maniacally, wringing his hands together as sweat accumulated on his forehead.

"After the *layoff*, as they called it, I knew we would lose the house, so I brought us here. My dad had built this place when I was a kid before there was much of anything up here. I figured we could squat here, and I could look for work, but that idea didn't sit too well with the wife. She's always nagging me, but what the hell does she know? She hasn't worked a day in her life, yet she expects all the bills to be taken care of. Sometimes, I wonder why I even married her."

Jack suddenly realized he recognized this man: Todd Phillips, the father of the family who had gone missing. At this point, he remembered how this seemingly harmless man could incapacitate someone much stronger than himself.

"Todd, did you chloroform me?"

Todd flashed a wry smile.

"One of the benefits of working in a paper mill is they don't lock up the chemicals; maybe that's why they let me go."

"Why the hell did you bring us here?" Jack coughed as he started to regain a bit more of his senses.

"I couldn't let you make off with *my* tree now, could I? That would've been the cherry on top of this awful Christmas season. Maggie may have even left me if I didn't bring back this beauty."

Todd gestured with the fire poker to the tree, now standing in all its glory at the far end of the cabin. Something else was moving slightly behind the tree, something Jack couldn't quite make out. As his eyes adjusted, he focused on the object swaying behind the tree, and when he realized what it was, his blood ran cold, as he knew both he and his son were in mortal danger. There, behind the tree, swinging from a rafter, was the corpse of a middle-aged woman, her hands bound behind her back and her mouth gagged. Jack starred in terror, and Todd took notice.

"Oh, I see you've met my wife, Maggie. She hasn't been very chatty lately. Still upset about losing my job, but we are making the best of it. Isn't that right, honey?"

He gave a light tap on her bound feet, and she swayed with a bit more force, causing the beam holding her up to creek and moan. It was clear that Todd had become unhinged and that if he and his son were going to survive this ordeal, Jack would have to think of something quickly. Now was not the time to panic, but another horrifying thought had entered his mind.

Where is his daughter?

***

As Jack was surveying the cabin, trying to figure out a way out of their mess, Thomas was also beginning to come out of his haze. He hadn't been hit with quite the dose of chloroform as his father and was a bit quicker to regain his acumen. He studied his captor as the thin, fidgety man spoke to his father. Thomas looked around to see if there was anything he could use to free himself. As he peered around the dimly lit room, he noticed the beautiful white pine he had helped cut down only a few hours before, and just beneath its canopy of lush, emerald needles was his hatchet. It was only a few feet away, but it might as well have been a mile in his current condition. He extended his feet toward it, but it was still out of reach. He tried maneuvering his body to extend his reach, but the hatchet remained beyond grasp. As Thomas struggled with his constraints, Todd noticed he had come out of his slumber.

"Well, hey there, little neighbor. I'm so glad you could join us!"

Todd now focused on Thomas, pacing around the cabin, staring the boy down, contemplating what he would do with him.

Todd worked his way behind Thomas until he stood directly behind the young man, peering across the room at his father. Jack was looking back at this stranger who had upended their family tradition, throwing them into a nightmare before Christmas. Jack felt helpless as the deranged man stood behind his son, glaring at him. He could feel himself losing control and struggled against his restraints to no avail. A mix of dread, hatred, and helplessness raged in his chest like wildfire. His head was spinning, and he wasn't sure if it was the rush of emotions or the after-effects of the chloroform, but he thought he might pass out at any moment.

As he struggled, every muscle in his body strained against his restraints, his wrists raw from the effort, but no amount of force could free him. During his struggle, he noticed that the expression on Todd's face had changed from nervous and anxious to almost joyful. The sick bastard smiled from ear to ear as he genuinely enjoyed his newfound power over the Martin boys. As if they had not suffered enough, the dangerous stranger did something that threw Jack into a frenzy. Calmly and cooly, Todd reached into his pocket and removed a large pocket knife, opening the blade and touching it to the cheek of the younger Martin.

"Such a shame, only a couple years younger than my daughter," he taunted Jack.

Fear choked at Jack's throat, tightening like a vice as he ran through all the horrible possibilities. The helplessness was suffocating, a dark, crushing weight that made breathing hard. He wanted to scream, to plead, to do anything to stop what was happening, but his voice was caught in his throat, choked by the terror of what he couldn't control.

"Leave...him...alone!" Jack managed to choke out.

Todd loved it, drinking in Jack's fear and hate like a fine wine, savoring every sip. Jack's blood boiled as he strained, but he could do nothing besides watch. Watch as this toothpick of a man destroyed his family. He locked eyes with Thomas, trying to convey as much strength and love as he could, silently praying for some miracle, some way to protect his son. It was then that he noticed something. Behind Thomas, behind Todd, behind the corpse of Maggie Phillips. Behind all of them was a window, partially covered in frost but still revealing a small view of the outside world, and peering in through that frosted window was something Jack couldn't believe.

Is that? I must be dreaming, is that Santa Claus?

Low and behold, Jack was not dreaming. There, on the other side of the silvery glass, was Santa Claus staring back at him, white beard, red hat and all. The moment's shock was *almost* enough to make him forget his current situation. He was about to say something until the bearded man put his index finger to his mouth and motioned for Jack to remain quiet. Jack almost heard him whispering, "Shhh!" in his ear. He listened and watched as Santa moved away from the window, making his way towards a back door to the cabin. Jack could see the door slowly opening, and the faintest "creak" could be heard from the door. Todd must have heard it because he began to turn towards the door, and Jack realized he needed to regain his captor's attention.

"You're pathetic! You know that?" Jack barked at the lunatic, still holding a blade to his son.

Todd turned back to Jack, red-faced with disgust. Jack knew it was a risk, but Santa may be his only chance at a Christmas miracle. He had to distract Todd, though.

"WHAT did you call me?" Todd hissed at him.

"Real tough, holding a knife to a child. You are too much of a pussy to try that shit with a real man."

Thomas was floored; he rarely heard his father use language like this, and it was typically light-hearted and comical, but this was something different.

"You heard me. You're pathetic. It's no surprise you lost your job, and I can't see how a string bean like you could do any kind of *real* work. The kind of man who picks on kids and probably women too, hell I bet your wife said the same thing before you–"

"SHUT YOUR FUCKING MOUTH! YOU SHUT IT OR I'LL, I'LL–"

"You'll what? You don't have the balls to stab me, and you're a pathetic *little* man who couldn't even take care of himself, let alone his family."

Todd moved away from Thomas and strode over to his father to show him he wasn't afraid of him, though he was visibly shaking. He clutched the blade in his hand, fire reflecting in his glasses, making him look even more crazed. He pressed the edge against Jack's throat.

"Well, tough guy? Not much to say with the knife at your throat, huh?"

Jack held his breath as he saw Santa coming up behind his son. Santa placed a hand over Thomas's mouth so he wouldn't alert Todd to his presence in the cabin.

"I'm gonna get you out of here, buddy; just sit tight." whispered the familiar voice of Nic.

Nic worked to try to free Thomas from his restraints, but Thomas, recognizing that they didn't have a lot of time, had a different plan.

"Nic," he whispered, "My hatchet."

Thomas motioned with his head to the small ax sitting underneath the Christmas tree. As Nic tried his best to quietly maneuver to the tree without alerting the man with the knife at Jack's throat, he caught the gaze of Jack, who nodded at him to make his move. Todd, satisfied with Jack's silence, pulled the knife from his captive and began to turn away before Jack, in desperation, spit on him, hitting Todd directly on the right lens of his glasses. Jack laughed as Todd reached up to wipe away the saliva from his glasses. This was the final straw for Todd as he tackled Jack through the chair, burying the blade in his abdomen. As they hit the floor, the force of their combined weight broke the chair. Jack's hands were still bound as Todd began plunging the knife into him, over and over. By now, Nic had freed Thomas and instinctively form-tackled Todd from his father. Though not much physical specimen, Todd was still a full-grown man and could throw Thomas off without much effort. He then turned his sights on finishing off the younger Martin as he stepped over the top of the child, knife in hand. He raised the blade in the air, preparing to bring down a fatal blow, when a rope and two muscular hands were around his throat from behind. Jack, covered in blood, still bound at the hand, had broken free from the chair and was now choking the life out of Todd with the restraints on his hands. In a frenzy, Todd began bringing the knife down behind him, landing a blow to Jack's ribs and his upper leg, but Jack just tightened his grip until he heard a loud "THUNK!".

Nic, who had just cut Thomas Martin free, buried the hatchet square in the middle of Todd's forehead. Todd's eyes crossed slightly as a trickle of blood made its way down the crown of his nose. His facial muscles twitched and pulsed as the life began to fade from his eyes.

"THWUMP!"

Nic pulled the hatchet from Todd's head, splattering blood across the floor of the cabin. At this, Todd's knees buckled, and he fell to the floor, convulsing a bit as the blood pooled around his head. Thomas ran to his father and hugged him hard.

"Oh geez, bud, maybe not so hard," Jack said, clutching his bloodied abdomen.

"Oh my god, dad! We have to get you to a hospital."

"I'll be ok, but I may need some help getting down the mountain," Jack said, throwing an arm over Thomas. Nic followed suit on his other side, and they started towards the door.

"Nic, my man, you are a legitimate Christmas miracle. How the heck did you find us?"

Nic smiled, his fake beard barely hanging in his face.

"Well, Hammer, I became a little worried when you boys didn't return after a few hours. Not once have you stiffed me for the bill in all the years I've known you. Maybe the snow was too much, and you guys decided to pack it in. Still, when I was about ready to close everything up for the night, I noticed your old Tacoma still sitting in the lot. I knew something was wrong when I saw that, so I started high-tailing it up the mountain after you. Your tracks were still pretty clear in the snow, but then I came across snowmobile tracks next to yours by the white pines. Your tracks eventually disappeared, but then there were the snowmobile tracks, and they were fresh. I followed them; it looked like whoever it was had a tree in tow. After about a mile, I saw the lights from the cabin and cautiously approached. When I saw that psycho holding the knife to Thomas, I knew I had to do something."

"You saved us, Nic," Thomas said.

"You're our guardian angel, buddy," Jack added.

They had almost reached the door when they heard a commotion from behind them. They froze on the spot, still reeling from the trauma they had just endured; none of them knew if they could handle anything more.

***

They turned back to see where the noise could be coming from. The cabin only contained three rooms, if you could call it that. The main room had a fireplace, their beautiful white pine, a couple of chairs and a small couch, a small, and a few rotted-out cabinets rotted-out. A tiny bathroom with a toilet in what looked to be the remains of a shower but no tub. And a small loft with a twin bed, accessible only by a ladder. There was nowhere they couldn't see; at least, that's what they thought.

"Where the hell is that coming from?" Nic asked as they scanned the cabin.

The noise had become more focused on pounding and seemed to move the Christmas tree.

"Look at the rug, it's shaking!" Thomas said as he pointed beneath the tree.

"I'm gonna set you down on the couch, Hammer; think you'll be alright?"

"I'll be fine, Tommy; help Nic with the tree."

Thomas and Nic slid the tree off the rug and watched as the braided wool jumped off the floor each time there was a pounding. Nic pulled back the rug to reveal a trap door. The pounding continued, and the door reverberated. Nic grabbed the hatchet firmly in his hand and motioned for Thomas to grab the latch.

"On three, Thomas, you open it up and stay behind the door, Hammer catch!"

He tossed him a flashlight.

"Keep a light on the opening, Thomas. If I say "close," you shut that thing as if your life depends on it."

Thomas nodded and prepared to open the hatch. Jack had the light on the spot, and Nic, still in full Santa gear, clutched the hatchet, ready to bear down on whoever or whatever might be hiding below.

"One"

Nic tightened his grip, and his knuckles whitened.

"Two"

A bead of cold sweat was running down Thomas's back.

"THREE!"

Thomas pulled the hatch door up with authority, and the light shone down to a crawl space. Nothing was visible at first; had there been, Nic likely would have buried the hatchet for a second time. After a few seconds, a figure emerged, and Nic lowered the hatchet. A teenage girl was walking out of the dimly lit cellar door, blocking the fireplace's light with her hand.

"Dad? Can I come out? Is it Christmas yet?"

***

As Nic and the Martins studied this nearly emaciated young girl with long, curly red hair and nearly translucent skin, she took in the scene in the cabin. She was wrapped in a knit blanket and barefoot and struggled to adjust to the light. This child had been spending a lot of time in the crawlspace; whether by her own accord or if she was held against her will was yet to be determined. When she saw her father's body, she screamed and ran to him.

"DAD! Oh my god, what happened to him?"

Nic and the Martins were speechless. How do you explain to a young girl that they had killed their homicidal father to save themselves? Could she even comprehend the horrors her father had committed? She huddled next to him and wept.

"Miss Phillips, you should come with us. We have to get to a hospital, and you may also need to see a doctor." Jack said in a low, calm voice, trying not to set the young lady off.

"I can't leave him, and I have to stay."

At this point, she noticed her mother swinging from the other side of the cabin but was seemingly unfazed by this development.

"He's my dad, and I won't leave him," she said through tears.

Nic and the Martins conferred about how to handle the situation.

"We can't all fit on the snowmobile, and we need to get you to a hospital ASAP," Nic whispered to the Martins. "We can send the cops up for her after we ensure you are alright."

"It feels wrong leaving her here, but to be honest, I am getting a little woozy, so we may want to get moving," Jack replied.

"Apart from the obvious trauma, I think she will be ok for a couple of hours until we can get some emergency personnel up here," Nic added, "And once we get a little further down the mountain, I should get service. Otherwise, I have been paying an extra $10 monthly to boost my signal for nothing."

They all chuckled. It was decided that the three of them would go down the mountain and get help but that they would return with the police and medical personnel as soon as they could. The girl agreed but didn't budge from her spot beside her father on the floor. Nic and Thomas helped Jack onto the snowmobile and descend to Nic's place. About halfway down, as promised, Nic got cell service and called in the report to the Vermont State Police. By the time they got down to the lodge, the sun was starting to rise, creating a sprawling array of cyan and marigolds on the snow-covered landscape. It would almost be beautiful if they had not just endured the night they had. They were greeted by two cruisers and an ambulance waiting for them in the parking lot. Nic insisted on helping Jack into the ambulance before giving full statements to the police and leading them back to the cabin. After a quick examination, it was determined that Jack hadn't suffered any life-threatening wounds but that they wanted him to get a full examination at North Country Hospital in Newport. Before he and his son embarked on the journey to the hospital, Thomas embraced Nic. He hugged him tighter than he had ever hugged anyone in his short life.

"Nic, I love you, but we will probably get a fake tree next year."

They all laughed; there was nothing else they could do. Jack laughed so hard he burst out of the bandages that were being applied to his torso, but it was worth it to feel that small ounce of joy after such a trying night. On the drive to NCH, Thomas couldn't help but fall asleep on his father's shoulder. Even in his awkward position in the back of the ambulance, the warmth and safety of his father's embrace was all he needed to drift off. While Thomas slept, Jack called his wife to update her on what had happened. While she was relieved they were alright, she couldn't believe they had been in such an ordeal with the missing Phillips family. A couple of hours later, Thomas passed out on a chair in the hospital room, and Jack was about to close his eyes. As he was preparing for a well-earned sleep, his phone buzzed. It was Nic.

"Hammer, you won't believe this...she's *gone*."

"What do you mean she's gone?"

"The Phillips girl, gone, no trace of her, and it gets weirder."

"Are you messing with me, Nic? Because I really can't handle that right now."

"Hammer, I swear I'm not; I wouldn't dream of it after last night."

"How does it get *weirder*?"

"Get this, she burned down the cabin."

"Holy shit...why?"

"I don't know, man, but dig this, they put out the blaze and only found her parent's bodies, no trace of her anywhere, no tracks in the snow, nothing. Vanished without a trace."

"Geeze, Nic, that's crazy. What do the police think?"

"Honestly, I get the feeling they suspect we had something to do with this, so don't be surprised if you get grilled about it. Anyway, I just wanted to call and check in and let you know what's going on out here. They still want me to give my official statement. If I don't see you, have a great Christmas."

"You too, Nic, thanks again for saving my ass."

After Nic hung up, Jack stared at his phone momentarily, absorbing the news he had just received. As he sat there in the dark of his hospital room, recovering from multiple stab wounds, as well as a myriad of bumps and bruises, Jack couldn't help but think of a line from his favorite Christmas carol, *"Somebody waits for you." H*e couldn't help but wonder if it would indeed be a Holly Jolly Christmas this year.

The Abominable Foeman
Mark Daponte

Christmas Eve, 1989, New York, NY

After Joe Angulio twisted open a can of "Pringles," he said to Judy Clowery, "Now that you finally got a VCR, instead of us self-absorbed film students having to go to 42nd Street theaters to watch Grade Z movies, we can study their 'nuances' from the safety of our crime-ridden neighborhood."

Judy brushed her dyed black bangs away from her eyebrows, paused the videotape, and said with a smirk, "At least at those theaters, I'd just have to hear junkies snorting and snoring behind me instead of one certain guy blah and blahing before me."

"Give me a break! You can barely hear what these actors are saying here! Just...proceed with the not-so-chilling conclusion of 'The Abominable Foeman' maestro."

Judy pressed the remote's "PLAY" button and watched the 1932 Christmas horror movie unfold, straining to hear the clichéd dialogue that blended with the soundtrack's hisses caused by the film's advanced age. Both laughed at chunky character actor Billy Gilbert staggering through a forest, gasping and glancing back in wide-eyed terror as snowflakes and tears slid down his cheeks.

"Back, you beast. Back!" he cried.

"What the hell is *that*?" Judy asked after seeing the film's first appearance of "The Abominable Foeman."

"Stop blah and blahing! I'm trying to watch. But, yeah. Just what the hell is *that*?"

The beast looked as if its poor-excuse-for-a-costume would have been deemed unworthy to use by Ed Wood. It loosely resembled a diminutive albino gorilla with hands that were on closer, still-frame inspection. It appeared to be oversized white gloves with black paint splashed on its fingertips. Two ill-fitting unicorn-like horns sprouted from each side of its furry head, and four jagged fangs obscured most of its black lips. A close-up of its face revealed it to be Rondo Hatton, who Joe noted was "an actor afflicted with Acromegaly and his worst movie role ever here."

"This hackneyed plot is too complicated," Judy chided. "Let me get this straight. So what that woman at the Christmas party thought was egg nog laced with brandy, was egg nog laced with Satan's blood?"

"Correct. And once she drank it, she turned into an extension of Satan—a beast that only appears on Christ's birthday. Christmas. Guess it's Satan's idea of a tie-in Christmas gift. Got it?"

"That darn Satan! Such a trickster. Did he come up with the dumb title of the movie too?"

"Don't blame him. You know a movie's going to suck if its title sucks and--Hey. Wait a second. Do you recognize the set?"

"Don't tell me—it was used on a Universal Film—um—'The Ghost of Frankenstein,' 1932?" Joe guessed.

"Close. 'The House of Frankenstein,' 1931," she corrected him.

"You're right. God, am I slipping—and so is Billy boy."

They watched a sobbing Billy Gilbert continuously slip and fall on wet leaves and patches of snow. He stopped running to snap a branch from a tree and held it high over his right shoulder like an axe. The beast half-growled and half-chuckled, then showed Billy that its once non-existent fingernails now resembled ten rusty tent spikes.

"Hey! I think Freddy Krueger wants his fingers back," said Joe.

"Shhhhhhh!"

The beast wiggled its fingers as if they were playing a piano's keyboard, then ripped the branch out of Billy's hands.

"I said back, beast! Just let me live!" pleaded an exhausted Billy as he fell to his knees.

The beast mocked his plea and the Christmas season by growling, "Ho Ho Ho!"

A close-up of the beast's bushy eyebrows bobbing up and down was abruptly replaced by a placard that read:

> **"Last reel of 'The Abominable Foeman' lost**
> **The Abominable Foeman**
> **Directed by**
> **F.W. Murnau**
> **Alan Penrod**
> **And**
> **Franklin Pingborn"**

"That's it? We don't know if the beast did in Billy. And why did it take three directors to direct one crappy Christmas movie?" Joe asked.

"Because two of them died of heart attacks while filming most of the film. And the third one died after he filmed the last reel," Judy said as she ejected the videotape. She placed it on one of the many stacks of punk records positioned under posters of the "Ramones'" album covers that filled her studio apartment's walls.

"So what happened to that last reel?"

"I read that 53% of movies made in the U.S. before 1950 no longer exist. And I read that one of 'The Abominable Foeman's' directors, F.W. Murnau—after he finished filming the last reel, he told the producer that filming the movie killed him."

"A lot of directors say that after a tough shoot."

"Yeah, but do many directors die in a car crash on the same day after filming the last reel—like what happened to F.W.?"

"Not that I know of. Jeez, *now* I'd like to see how that crappy movie ended."

"For the last 57 years, no one has seen that reel. But for the next billions of years, everyone will get to make fun of this Christmas classic because—hold on."

She entered her bedroom and returned holding a round, dust-covered metal film canister. Handwritten in faded black magic marker on frayed yellow masking tape covering the canister's sides were:

"The Abominable Foeman, Reel 13, 1932."

"I hold in my self-absorbed hands *the* last reel!" Judy announced.

"Where did you get that?"

"Remember how I told you my grandfather owned a film lab and was selling it in a month?"

"What about it?"

"When cleaning that lab out, they found a storage room full of old canisters. And one of those film cans—is that!"

"And what are you going to do with *that*? God, the film is just as filthy as its canister."

"I bet it is. That's why I'm gonna clean it up, then give it to the American Film Institute for eternal safekeeping."

"Please. You know about as much as cleaning film as your boy Johnny Ramone knows about playing Beethoven."

"I'll show you. Step into my laboratory, Igor."

She grabbed his right hand and led him to her bathroom. Nine empty, pint-sized brown medicine bottles and an aluminum paint roller tray filled with a liquid that looked like watered-down ginger ale sat in her bathtub.

"The tray's filled with Isopropyl alcohol. It cleans film," Judy said.

"Who doesn't know that?" Joe laughed.

"Okay. Ready for the unveiling—for richer, for poorer, in sickness and health, until death do us part?"

Judy removed a pair of white cotton gloves from her back pocket, slipped them on, and then twisted open the film canister, unleashing an eye-watering odor.

"Whew. That smells kinda like—"

"Vinegar, right?" Judy finished. "I read that's because when old film decays, its acetate releases a chemical that smells like vinegar."

"And I bet you read how to get rid of that smell, huh?"

"How did you know, Joseph?"

"And I know you're venturing into unknown territory here. What does a 19-year-old video store clerk slash film geek know about cleaning a 57-year-old film?"

"Who better to take care of film than someone who loves film and knows how to treat it right? Starting now."

She carefully removed the film from the canister and unspooled two feet of it to show that it was red.

"Uh, since when is a black and white movie red?" asked Judy.

"I don't know. Maybe the reel was tinted red or something."

"Looks that way Pew! Someone hasn't taken a bath in 57 years. In the tub, ya go."

She submerged two feet of film in the tray and gasped when it instantly dissolved, leaving behind a liquid that was the color and viscosity of blood.

"Did you read why that film just did that?" Joe warily asked.

Judy removed her gloves, dipped her right index finger in the tray, placed it under her nose, and noted that it "even smells like blood. How could that be? It's just film."

"Wrong. It's not *just* a film. It's a *cursed* film!"

"And who cursed it?"

"Since it's called 'The Abominable Foeman,' and Satan's a subplot in it, I'd say Mr. Satan did a curse on the film too. And the curse and the beast live in that red gunk—which is Satan's blood! So unless you want to be *the* beast, don't you dare drink it like it's laced egg nog like that actress did in the movie. You hear?"

"I hear someone here has been watching too many Grade Z horror flicks," Judy nervously laughed.

"Why couldn't Satan curse it? I bet he cursed those three directors for making a crappy movie about him, and they all died."

"You're beginning to kind of make scary sense. And it's scaring me."

"Is it?"

"No! But isn't it time for you to get to work at our favorite video store tonight?"

"It sure is," Joe said, looking at his wristwatch. "God. It must be the only video store open on Christmas Eve."

"Guess people need to do something other than fight on Christmas Eve."

"Yeah. Hey. Maybe you should just mail that reel to the American Film Institute. Let them clean it and get cursed."

"I think you're right."

He grabbed his knapsack filled with textbooks and walked with Judy toward the apartment's door. After Joe stepped into the building's hallway, he reopened the door to warn in a Boris Karloff-like voice: "But remember. She who even touches the Foeman's blood dies...or even worse!"

She faked a hearty laugh and retreated to her "Cocoon Room." Her bedroom was a place where, with the help of the "Ramones," she shielded herself from the outside world and her place in it. Judy much preferred having Joey Ramone's voice fill her head than her questions:

"Why won't Joe ever ask me for a date? Or just try to kiss me? Is it because we work at that same video store, and if we break up, we'd still have to see each other? No, that shouldn't be *the* reason. We have way more in common than just our workplace. We're both majoring in film, both gangly, gawky, and socially awkward, and him kissing me might be too weird for him. It'd be like him kissing himself, I guess. Should I change my major from Film Studies to another career that involves non-money-making, like being a social worker? Oh, enough of me!"

Judy put an end to mulling her future plans by opening her Walkman, slipping on her headphones, and plopping in the Ramones' album, *Brain Drain*. She fast-forwarded the tape to the beginning of "Merry Christmas (I Don't Wanna Fight)." Just as she was about to press "PLAY," she noticed something strange on the tip of her right index finger.

Hairs.

A patch of half-inch high white hairs was at the end of the finger.

"How did these get here?" she thought as she chewed the hairs off. "Wait. Did that happen because it touched the blood of that 'cursed' film? And I'm turning into a 'Foeman...huh, Foewoman?'"

The hairs unnerved her so much that Judy went into her small kitchen to make a Bloody Mary to calm her nerves and played the "Ramones" tape at such an eardrum-shattering volume that she did not hear a stolen credit card slip in and jiggle by her front door's lock, the door creaks open, and two burglars creep into her foyer. Gary Lipmein and his slim, dim-witted criminal partner, John Benza, looked like a mutant version of Laurel and Hardy. That is, the old comedy team, if they were unkempt, perpetually sweaty, had pockmarked skin, wore torn white Converse sneakers and t-shirts, rarely bathed, and were junkies in their mid-30s; constantly looking for their next fix and an apartment to raid. Gary, the chunky Oliver Hardy of the pair who loosely wore a stained red tie, accurately surmised that: "This place looks like a student or some kind of artist lives here. They have fewer coins to rub together than we do. We'll see." He ordered John to look into the kitchen while he went into the bedroom to see if there were any signs of jewelry.

John walked into the kitchen to see Judy pouring vodka into a glass of tomato juice on a rickety table. As Judy sang along to the Ramones, she did not hear John creep behind her or see him wrap his right arm around her shoulders to secure her arms and place his opened left hand on her mouth. She shook the bulky headphones off of her head but wished she still wore them after hearing approaching footsteps and Gary's voice snarl behind her:

"Merry Christmas. Try to escape or scream, and I'll kill you. Do you understand?"

She nodded. As John released her then gulped down her drink, Gary demanded:

"Take us to your money, bitch."

"Look, guys. I'm worth nothing. I work at 'Louie's.' It's a

lame mom-and-pop video slash book store down the street that will likely close soon. How much money do you think I have from working there?"

"Yeah. By the looks of this place, we're even doing better, man," John said, then laughed to show that he desperately needed caps on most of his yellowed teeth.

"Shut up you!" Gary ordered. "As for you—"

Gary grabbed Judy by her black t-shirt and slammed her against a wall.

"Tell us where you have cash, or we'll tear this place apart and look for some—starting by breaking every album you have. Beginning with Richard Hell and ending with—"

"Don't do that! Okay," Judy surrendered. "I got a couple of hundred hidden under my bed."

"Now you're talking. Take us there," Gary snapped. She led them to her bedroom, got down on her hands and knees, and looked under her bed. Balancing on two ten-pound dumbbells was her cardboard safe: The Dead Boys' "Loud, Young and Snotty" album. She handed it to Gary, who ripped it apart. Ten twenty-dollar bills floated to the floor. As John picked them up and Gary "admired" the album cover, Judy grabbed a dumbbell and stood.

"Does your mother know what music you listen to, sister? What crap!"

He looked up from the album to see her hurl a dumbbell barely missing his head. Judy then went for Gary's face with her black fingernails, three of them leaving deep bloody scratch marks on his right cheek. John tackled her to the floor.

"Bitch, you got some balls," Gary roared as Judy's right heel thudded into John's groin. She made a break for the door, but Gary grabbed her by her right wrist.

"No! Don't kill this one!" John pleaded. Gary backhanded

Judy across her face and then landed an uppercut to her chin, knocking her unconscious.

"Is she d-d-d-dead?" John asked.

"N-n-n-no. But I don't see her waking up soon, which will give us time to live here temporarily. Rent free."

"What do you mean?"

Gary pointed to the $200 in John's hand and roared, "Go get the junk from Leroy around the corner on Avenue D and bring it back here."

"Yeah. Maybe he'll give us a better count because it's almost Christmas."

"And maybe he won't. Maybe he'll give us a wrapped Christmas present with a green and red tie that we can use for our arms. Just--Just get it, and we'll shoot up safely and sound here, man. Capiche?"

John rapidly nodded and replied, "Si. Muy capiche!"

He ran out of the apartment, leaving Gary to wipe a smattering of blood off of his face, then remove from his "Strand Bookstore" tote bag a spoon with black burn marks tarnishing its bottom, a batch of cotton balls, and two hypodermic needles. He went to the bathroom to half-fill his spoon with water, where he noticed the "The Abominable Foeman" canister in the sink and the paint tray filled with what looked like a small pool of blood.

"What's with her and this blood?" he thought. "Is she a vampire? Hell, she's pale and dresses all in black like one. Maybe she is."

Gary saw the "1932" date on the masking tape and reasoned, "That makes this an antique. Which could be worth something to the right film nerd." He picked up the canister, reentered the bedroom, stepped over Judy's prone body, and sat on the bed.

"You messed with the wrong junkie, sister," he chuckled, then kicked her in the stomach.

***

Judy awoke to a splitting headache. She wondered why she was lying on the floor and who had badly bruised her jaw. Her memory was jarred when she heard Gary cackle:

"Well, gabba-gabba-hey-oh-let's go! Josephine Ramone awakens!"

Judy looked up to see Gary wobbly standing in her bedroom's doorway, his stained red tie now wrapped around his left bicep. She instantly recognized the "junkie chic look" he had been cultivating for years: the heavy-lidded eyes, the head half-bowing, then suddenly standing at attention as limp hands wiped away droplets of forehead sweat.

"Where are you, man? I said bring it in here now!" Gary barked.

An uneasy John entered the bedroom, his shaky hands holding the tray filled with blood. He placed it on the floor and then left so he wouldn't see Gary dip his hypodermic needle in the tray and pull up its plunger until it was filled with blood. He brought the needle closer and closer to Judy's throat.

"What—what are you going to do with that?" Judy whispered.

Gary pointed at the three angular cuts her fingernails had left on his face and hissed, "Since you withdrew my blood, I'm giving you some of yours."

He jammed the needle into a purple vein running along her left forearm, shot the fluid into her, and sang the first stanza of "I Wanna Be Sedated." Judy's eyelids slowly closed but creaked open to see John return, holding a stack of her albums and "The Abominable Foeman" reel.

"No...Don't take that film. It's cursed," Judy said before she passed out, the needle half-protruding from her arm.

"Curses to you too! Foiled again, eh?" Gary laughed.

After Gary had packed as much of Judy's belongings of value as he could fit into his tote bag and left the bedroom, he returned to mock her labored breathing with: "Tsk tsk. Look at you. Just another soon-to-be dead junkie who never knew when enough was enough."

****

"Judy? Are you there? If you are, pick up!" Joe's voice pleaded through her phone's answering machine.

But Judy was no longer in her apartment. Her form was now the one of a white beast that had haunted and hunted down three men who thought they could offend Satan by creating a sordid film without receiving any repercussions. In 1932, two of these fabulists were stopped from completing the film when they were scared to death by encountering the beast and succumbed to heart attacks, while the third, who had finished the film for them, had swerved his Packard one night to avoid its shadowy form standing in his car's path and crashed into a telephone pole. Now, two miscreants who dared to treat a deadly curse lightly will be duly punished for mockingly injecting Satan's blood, blood that turned Judy into a beast and filled her body.

The beast could only see in black and white and hear mostly hisses, as if living in a scratch-filled print of a long-forgotten 1932 movie. It could barely make out hearing Joe saying through the answering machine, "Right before I started my shift here, these two lowlifes came in and tried to sell Louie your 'Abominable Foeman's' reel. Louie told them we just deal in videotapes. Thank God one of those morons registered for membership here and put down his home address in Brooklyn. I'm going there now to get your film back, then have them arrested. See you and Merry Christmas!"

The beast's instinctive thirst for revenge sent it out of the apartment's front window, down its fire escape, and dashing down sidewalks (causing passerby to either step aside and laugh or remark, "Cool white gorilla costume, man!"), until it stood softly growling outside a run-down apartment building in a part of Brooklyn called Prospect Heights. It could hear the start of a thunderstorm, and John wondered aloud in his living room, "How could a fifty-year-old film not even be worth fifty cents?"

"I guess video stores don't buy films, idiot. We'll shop it around more tomorrow," Gary replied.

"I bet we'll have better luck selling her records, man."

"We will. Yeah, in honor of Josie Ramone, let's hear her big brother Joey sing," Gary scoffed.

John flipped through Judy's records in Gary's tote bag, found a Ramones album, placed it on his record player's turntable, and dropped the needle in the middle of its second side.

"C'mon, stooge. You can play it louder than that!" Gary said.

John twisted the "VOLUME" knob until the walls vibrated because of Joey Ramone singing "Animal Boy." As both badly sang along to the "Ramones," neither heard a tent spike-sized fingernail jiggle by their front door's lock; the door creaked open, and two fur-covered feet creep into their foyer and then entered the dark living room.

"What the...?" John gasped as a flash of lightning burst through their living room window and half-revealed the beast, its hands looking like white gloves with black paint splashed on its fingertips.

Gary menacingly approached their intruder and said, "If you and your piss-poor Halloween costume don't get out of here on the count of three, I'm going to kick your ass right out of your monkey suit. One—two—"

The beast, a foot shorter than Gary, wiggled its fingers as if it was playing a piano's keyboard and then growled, "Ho Ho Ho!" John and Gary looked at each other and laughed.

"Ho ho ho to you, too! Wait. I get it. Ho-ho-ho means it's Santa Claus Christmas time. And you're no monkey. You're an evil snowman! Are you the abominable kind or the little 'Frosty' kind? But that's neither here nor there," mocked Gary. "Now, where was I? Oh yeah. I will ruin your face after I count to one-two—*What the hell?*"

Gary stopped counting when he realized that what was once the beast's non-existent fingernails had been replaced by fingernails resembling ten rusty tent spikes. Five of the spikes grabbed then slashed through John's throat, exposing arteries spurting blood and Gary to be a simpering coward. As John took one last breath and then toppled to the floor, Gary cried, "Who—what are you?"

The beast's pupils and unicorn-like horns turned from black to bright red, sending Gary screaming for help, running to the bedroom's window, opening it, and then stepping outside to the fire escape.

Joe approached the apartment's opened door and walked inside, noticing the last reel of "The Abominable Foeman" on the couch and John's blood-drenched body lying in front of it. Joe followed the sound of Gary's faint cries to the bedroom window, where he watched the Foeman chase him into a rainstorm and the forests in nearby Prospect Park.

"Just what the hell is *that*? Is that—it is!"

Joe grabbed the reel, ran out of the apartment, and sprinted towards the park. He zig-zagged through dirt paths dotted with snow and towards Gary's hoarse voice, which grew louder with each step Joe took. He stopped running when he heard Gary repeatedly cry:

"Back, beast! Back!"

Joe hid behind a faux nineteenth-century gas lamppost on a path, where he watched a sobbing Gary continuously slip and fall on wet leaves and patches of snow between thunder crashing and lightning flashing on his face. Seeing that the beast was gaining on him, Gary stopped to snap a branch from a tree and held it high over his right shoulder like an axe.

"Jesus. I'm watching 'The Abominable Foeman' again, except now it's live and in color," Joe realized. "And that guy's Billy Gilbert, and is the beast some other woman who's filled with Satan's blood? Can it be—Judy?"

The beast half-growled and half-chuckled, then ripped the branch out of Gary's hands.

"I said back, beast! Just let me live!" pleaded an exhausted Gary as he fell to his knees.

The beast's bushy eyebrows bobbed up and down as it backhanded Gary across the face, then landed an uppercut to his chin, knocking him unconscious. Joe watched the beast repeatedly slash Gary's neck and face with its ten nails, leaving a bloody corpse. The throat slashing stopped when the beast noticed a stunned Joe staring at the gory scene. The beast loudly growled, took a step towards him, then slowly spread its arms wide as if it wanted a hug.

"Judy? Is that you?" Joe asked.

The beast looked up at the sky and pointed at the full moon emerging from the black clouds.

"Ho-ho—Joe...Help...me," Judy's voice meekly begged as she collapsed. As Joe approached, the beast physically transformed from a white, furry creature to Judy dressed in black. Blood oozed from the sides of Judy's mouth as her eyes slowly closed. Joe kneeled, placed his right ear to her chest, and screamed:

"No! You're not going to die! I'll—I'll save you! But—how? I know!"

He ran to a streetlamp, removed the reel from its canister, unwound the film until its conclusion, and held it up to the fluorescent light.

"Such a cliché movie. You're supposed to turn into some monster when you see a full moon, not turn into a human like Judy, but how do I get her to stop dying? Is the answer in here? I think…There it is? No, there *we* are?"

The last frames of the movie unnerved him so much that it caused his hands to shake and goosebumps to form on his arms. They showed an actor and actress who were the spitting images of himself and Judy, as if both had time traveled back to a 1932 soundstage forest but were wearing clothes from 1989, which included Judy's "Ramones" t-shirt.

"Just who the hell directed this reel?" he whispered.

Joe shook the inexplicable image out of his head and searched for film frames to show how to save Judy.

"There it is! That's how I'll do it!"

Joe ran back to her and mimicked the film's conclusion. He gently lifted her left index finger, then her right one, positioned them to form a cross, and then kissed her, only to see that her eyes remained closed.

"C'mon, Judy. It's the end of the movie! Be the movie! You can do it…Please?"

He kissed her again, longer and lovingly. This time, her eyelids fluttered and then shot up.

"At last!" she gasped, realizing that Joe was finally kissing her.

Judy threw her arms around his neck and asked, "But—how did I, we get here? What happened?"

He laughed, helped her to her feet, and replied:

"We just had a happy ending—and now a happy Christmas!"

Yuletide Bonfire
Sam C. Tumminello Jr.

Tardiness is an unbecoming habit. It conveys a certain degree of callousness or disdain for the other party's time. Layered upon that, it also indicates a lack of forethought or a failure of planning for the tardy party. Those things were well known to Malcolm Cole why he was bitterly cursing himself for the latter and hoping the indication of the former could be forestalled. In the future, he would wonder if things would have been much better if he had been at the party even later.

It was December 21, early evening or late afternoon. However you wanted to frame it. The weather was chilled, having dropped somewhat rapidly the upper thirties Fahrenheit with mild humidity, leaving a mist in the air illuminated by a spectacular full moon. The mist was surprisingly thicker in the mountains where he was driving up a two-lane road. He wanted to go faster but dared not. These forested low crags were unfamiliar to him, but what happened when you hit a deer that was going 50 mph was not. Checking the estimated arrival time on the GPS array of his car, his jaw clenched. There was simply no way he would get to the Seher home in time for the festivities to start. Squeezing the steering wheel and his jaw tightening further, he made a decision. Trying not to divide his attention too much from the road, he queued up "Henry Seher-Home" on the car's hands-free phone and hit "call." He was going to be late, so the least he could do was be considerate of being late.

Henry Seher was a well-polished man. Tall with sandy blond hair and hazel eyes, he radiated a patrician-like grace. Only a year after the dreaded fortieth birthday, he was doing well. A few years prior, he had taken over the family business, Seher Exploration and Surveying. He maintained the company's reputation of being fast and precise in finding or measuring whatever the contract specified. So, of course, the contracts remained steady in occurrence and lucrative in nature. More to himself than his guests, he flashed a ten-thousand-watt smile and took another sip of his whiskey. He was standing on his back patio, tending the considerable fire in the pit and keeping an eye on his numerous guests milling around the patio. It was the annual company yuletide party, and though attendance was on the low side, everyone seemed to be enjoying themselves. The cordless phone he habitually kept in his pocket rang, catching his ear despite the general murmur of the party and Bing Crosby crooning about Christmas. Depositing his whiskey glass on a table with a half-empty finger food platter, he hurried away from the noise. Standing some yards away under an oak tree, he didn't recognize the number on the phone's caller ID screen but answered anyway.

"Hello?"

"Hello? Mr. Seher? This is Malcom Cole. I just wanted to apologize. I'm going to be a few minutes late."

Seher glanced at his watch, and the toast was to start soon

"I got a little turned around on these roads."

"Please call me Henry, Malcolm. And don't sweat it; neither Taika nor I will be mortified if you get here a little late. Better than finding out you ran off the road or hit a deer."

"Thank you, sir. I'll be there as soon and safely as possible."

"I'll see you then."

Malcolm Cole had been an unusual resume to come across Henry Seher's desk for a job that effectively was his assistant. His hiring might even be seen as political; the Cole family was relatively new to this range of mountains, and he was not yet thirty. But the appeal had been fair and the tidings quite good for him, so Henry hired him. As an employee, he was extended an invitation to the annual yuletide party even if he had not technically started working for him. But back to the festivities, Henry thought, as he returned the phone to his pocket and walked back to the patio.

Malcolm exhaled a breath he didn't realize he was holding and forced himself to relax his grip on the steering wheel. Glancing up to his rear-view mirror, he caught his gaze. His nut-brown hair was not styled and would probably need another combing when he got to the Seher home. His allergies had flared up red, rimming his unremarkable brown eyes. He returned his full attention to the road but nervously scratched his face where his beard had been. He had fretted over how to trim it. Indecision led him to shave it off for lack of an answer. He swore he now had tan lines on his face from the beard. He sped up a little more and adjusted his hands on the wheel. Pointless to switch on music, he was barely getting enough signal to make calls, and none of the radio stations were much to his taste. To break the tedium, he began tapping his fingers across the steering wheel in a simple tattoo. Within a few minutes, he got the first of many frights that night.

"Malcolm?! Malcolm? Can you hear me? Are you alright?" urged Henry again on the cordless phone. Malcolm called him again in the middle of the toast and quickly hung up. He called a third time and hung up again. He hurried through the toast as fast as he could and returned the call. Without thinking about it, Henry began walking toward the patio of his home, dreading that Malcolm had had an accident and needed rescue.

"Mr. Seher?" replied Malcolm, sounding more startled than in danger.

"Call me Henry. But yes, *are you alright?*" Seher replied, stressing the final three words.

"Yes...yes, sir. I won't be much longer. Is everything okay there?"

"Of course. Did you mean to call those last two times?"

"I called you again?" Malcolm glanced down and, to his horror, realized he had been tapping his fingers on the steering wheel's phone controls. Seher started to say more when Malcolm interrupted him.

"I think I may have butt-dialed you, sir."

Seher chuckled in relief.

"It happens; I'm just glad something dreadful did not happen. I'll see you when you get here."

With that, Henry Seher hung up and noticed his wife, Taika, gesturing to him from inside. Dark brown hair with cobalt blue eyes, she was a little taller than most with shoulders that declared motherhood had not invalidated her athleticism. But she only had two hands, so she probably needed help bringing out another round of hors d'oueuvres. Putting the phone on the table beside the backdoor, he smiled back at her. But unexpectedly, her gaze focused on something behind him, and shock flooded across her face. He turned only to see his guests recoiling from the fire. It had flared greatly and turned a bizarre bruise-like purple. This had never happened before. The fire then grew even greater, giving the firepit a giant-sized blowtorch appearance. This was bad, bordering on apocalyptic.

"Come inside, everybody! Inside the house, everybody!" Henry shouted, waving them in from the patio. He glanced back to see Taika dashing from window to window, unfurling then securing the drapes. Turning back to the patio, only a few had heeded him and were hurrying inside. Most seemed transfixed by the unworldly indigo flames. With shock, he sensed something moving in the flames.

Now Malcolm was in a mild panic. Not only was he late, but his iterant phone calls had interrupted the festivities. There was some great tradition and symbolism to these parties, a great toast and prayer led by whichever Seher oversaw the company. Unwittingly, he almost certainly disrupted it. The remaining minutes of the drive seemed to inch by until his GPS finally announced he had reached his destination. He swore there was something of a smug "tsk-tsk" in the GPS's voice. Driving into the Seher's home driveway, he was confronted by an imposing eight-foot brick wall with a sliding electric gate. Rolling down his window to punch the code into the gate's control. The gate opened achingly slowly, but once it opened enough for him to drive through, he zipped in and parked in one of the spots left. Shoving it into the park, he turned the car off, found the emergency comb, and tried to smooth out the defects of his hair. Opening the car door, he zipped up his jacket, and he stepped out into the misty night. The grounds were impressive. The house was a relatively plain three-story house with a sloped roof built upon a sharp swell of earth. The brick wall and a copse of trees on either side garlanded it. It conveyed a stately prominence standing out in the mist at that moment. A simple castle built upon a hill, unpretentious in appearance but majestic in spirit. He started walking up the curved gravel driveway when a car nearly struck him.

With a metallic CRUNCH, the white sedan slid into the closed gate and nearly ripped it out of its tracks. Malcolm Cole stood there for a moment, stunned. It had come within inches of hitting him. Realizing that cars typically do not slide down driveways by themselves, anxiously, he ran over to the car and checked the driver's seat. Someone was inside, slumped over the steering wheel. Thankfully, the impact had not rendered the door useless, and he could pull it open. The metallic stench of blood rushed out at him in the chilled air. The driver, an older man with a goatee and shaved head, had injuries inconsistent with his car crash. His head was at an angle not seen in the living. More ominous was that the man's left arm had been filleted nearly from his biceps to just short of his wrist. The bleeding may not have been fast, but it was prodigious. The blood had soaked through his shirt and khakis and left his car reeking of a slaughterhouse. The shock of the scene made him oddly calm. "Okay, Malcolm, this is something you cannot handle yourself. Time to get help," he thought. Turning toward the house, he began to run up the driveway into the mist. With sudden prescience, he decided to run into the trees to make his way to the house. There was a non-zero chance of another car coming bowling down the driveway.

The hill was steeper than it seemed from below, or he was far more out of shape than he would have hazarded. A sound caught his attention, and he paused to step into the lee of a tree. What was that? It sounded like someone was running down the driveway, and the fast rhythm of the crunch of gravel with every step seemed off. He started to call out when he heard a deep huffing, snorting like a draft animal. That was...not right. As the sounds passed him going farther down the driveway, he concluded it was time to get moving. He had hardly taken a few more steps when a bestial roar blared out near the gate, wrecked car, and his parking spot. Time to pick up the pace. Resuming the hike up the hill, he glanced back only to see a shape flickering through the moonlit shadows the of the trees. Run, run, run, run... He was near to the peak when a bright light shined into his face. Malcolm was so surprised that he nearly fell on his face as he stopped to shield his eyes. Another roar erupted from behind him amongst the trees but much closer. *Much* closer. The light left his face, tracing a route toward the closest corner of the house. Then it did it again. Regaining his stride, Malcolm needed no more urging. Angling from the front patio, where a few cars were still parked, to the corner, he misjudged the terrain. In the last few yards, nearing where the light had urged, he missed the barren raised flower bed and fell into a head-over-heels tumble. Before he could recover, the light blinded him again, something grabbed him by the collar of his jacket and half threw him into the side of the house.

"Stay behind me." uttered the loudest whisper he ever heard. Another roar split the air nearly beside them. The light flicked away again, illuminating what had been chasing him up the hill in the trees. No taller than an average man with two arms, two legs, and a head, but from there no resemblance to a human. It was a greasy, deep blue green like the color of bread mold. Without hair of any kind, burning coal-red eyes glared out from below a sloped brow on a gaunt, noseless, and earless face partially shielded by its long, wiry fingers. One hand clutched a large vicious-looking flint knife. Recuperating from the blinding light, it brandished its stone knife. It took a half step forward toward them, baring its ivory teeth and bellowing a feral challenge to what pricked its eyes with brightness. Somewhere deep in Malcolm's mind, the creature was recognized simply as a "ghoul".

A flash and thunderclap sounded out, heralding an eruption of blood on the ghoul's lower abdomen. Another flash and thunderclap pealed forth, and a second hole appeared in the ghoul's upper chest. A third explosion bullseyes it squarely where its sternum should be located, and its legs collapse in on it. Reaching its hands out to catch itself, the fourth shot bangs ineffectually.

On hands (still clutching that knife Malcolm distantly noted) and limp knees, the ghoul raises its head to remind the others of its aggression and tenacity. A fifth shot centered on the gaping nasal cavities tears its head inside out. The ghoul slumps face-first into the flower bed. The light flicks off. Eyes adjusting to the half-light of the night and ears' ringing subsiding, he finally registers who the loudest whisperer was.

"Malcolm Cole? I'm Henry Seher. Glad you could make it." while racking his shotgun.

"To here. Beside the house, not the party. It probably would have been best if you would have skipped it. The party, that is." his boss explained with that ten-thousand-watt smile. A less intense light shone down from a second-story window above them.

"That's my wife Taika, Malcolm," Henry explained.

"It's Malcolm, everything is fine. We'll be in a few minutes," he shouted up to the light.

Unsure of what else to do, Malcolm waved at the light as friendly as he could. Vaguely, he could see someone wave back. Still trying to grasp what exactly had just happened, Malcolm blurted out the first thing that crossed his mind.

"That must be the nicest ugly Christmas sweater I have ever seen."

The sweater was a baby blue alpine scene with Santa Claus and a half dozen elves snowboarding down the mountain, giving the viewers exaggerated winks behind their snow goggles and thumbs up.

"Really?" Henry replied. "I know it's a touch uncomfortable and juvenile. But I would not call it 'ugly'."

Malcolm just stared back with the expression of a landed fish. "Everybody's critic," Seher thought as he placed a hand on a hand on Malcolm's shoulder to usher him to the back of the house and said

"Let's get inside. I can't speak for you, but I could go for a couple of our little tiny quiches."

"*What* was that?" Malcolm asked, but the shock still had not passed.

"12 gauge 'buck and ball', it's a slug with a couple pieces of buckshot stacked on top. They pack a hell of a punch, huh? Winchester loads them, I think."

Henry replied, mistaking what Malcolm was referencing. Malcolm didn't feel the need to correct him. Mostly because as they came around the house to the back patio, the scene of the party, Malcolm reckoned calling it worse than an open-air abattoir, was a gross understatement.

Blood by the gallons congealed on the smooth concrete of the patio. Entrails were strewn about, and strips of skin littered the patio like a confetto of undercooked pasta. Blood had even overwhelmed the smell of the woodfire. Henry answered Malcolm's unspoken question.

"It was fast, nimble even. And whatever that 'knife' is. It's stupendously sharp. That thing just kind of came out of the fire. Like just crawled out of the flames and just started...was just a whirlwind of violence. Cutting and stabbing at them. Them...Jesus Christ...they aren't a 'them'. They are people. People I've known for years, seen nearly daily."

Seher's voice wobbled, then choked. His aura of smiling, aloof, unflappable confidence crumbled. He cradled the shotgun and covered his face with his free hand. Malcolm gave him a moment.

"Who else survived?" he asked as gently as he could.

Clamping down on the horror and fending off guilt, Henry replied

"Taika, a couple of others, and myself for sure. A few made a run for the woods in the chaos. Maybe they got to their cars? Did you see anyone else on the road?" Henry inquired with embers of hope.

"No, well, I nearly got flattened by a white sedan once I got here. Uh, the car crashed into the gate. I checked the driver. Older guy with a goatee. He...didn't make it."

Henry's face dimmed even more, and he tilted his face back to stare into the bright moonlit sky. He took a deep breath and then looked back at Malcolm.

"That accounts for Doug, then. We'll have to go to the barn and get the tractor to clear the gate. Ahhhhhh, fuck, I got a lot of people killed today. Christ, am I glad the kids are at their grandmother's?"

"How did you all "make out" in the house?" Malcolm asked.

Henry broke eye contact again and replied

"We hid. Taika had already closed the drapes. So we just cut the lights off and made as little noise as possible. It worked. Once we got a plan figured out, Taika, I, and somebody else, it was largely over. I think." the older man answered.

Malcolm craned his neck away from the carnage and inspected the rear of the house. The house was dark, with drapes drawn across all the glass on the 1st floor. Couldn't tell about the 2nd and 3rd floors. The backside of the house had been modestly decorated Christmas-y for the yuletide party. Lots of outdoor faux garlands and inflatable characters. A bundle of mistletoe was tacked in beneath a horseshoe over the back door. He turned back to the horror and his haunted employer.

"It didn't go into the house? Didn't even try?"

"No. No. It didn't. Taika hit the lights and drew the drapes fast. It seemed to prioritize everyone on the patio over the few that ran." Seher explained. "I guess the house confused it, or it knew we weren't going anywhere, so it took its time with the others," he gulped.

"But you came up with a plan. Draw it in close, spotlight it, then blast it into mince?" Malcolm asked.

"Yeah. Taika ran the million-candle spotlight."

"All right then, boss. Your plan worked. You saved me and everybody else you could. And you had said something about quiches?"

Malcom's last question shook his boss out of his despair, and the smile and aura flicked back into place.

"You got ice in your blood there, Mr. Cole. Focused on the matter at hand. I knew you were a good choice." he intoned.

Malcolm wanted to correct him. He was no "ice blood". He simply was so scared that he had been pushed over the edge that he came out on the other side. But he didn't. His boss seemed to be just hanging on, and having someone else who seemed steady was, in turn, steadying him. There was no need to ruin that.

Then, one of the victims of the ghoul caught flame. A deep, foreboding bruise with colored flame. The victim burned startingly fast, crumbling into a cindered husk in moments. Then another caught a flame and burnt down nearly to nothing. Then, a third. And a fourth. If there had been any doubt as to what fresh hell was unraveling before Henry Seher and Malcolm Cole's eyes, a howling snarl sounded from beside the house from where they had come removed all doubt. Malcolm moved to bolt when Seher grabbed onto his shoulder.

"Wait. We need to draw it away from the house. And I have a plan. When we run, follow me." The spotlight illuminated them from a second-story window again, and Henry looked up and gestured to the effect of "We know. Hold on." It winked off.

Henry ignored the palpable fear radiating from Malcolm and returned his gaze to the corner where the ghoul would emerge. There. Staggering like a foal trying to find its gait, the ghoul turned the corner rather widely. But more to the point, it saw them and hissed, redoubling its efforts to break into a full gallop.

"RUN! RUN! RUN NOW!"

The two of them broke into a dead run into the misty woods. Following their weaving around the trees, the ghoul gave chase. All three hurtling further from the blacked-out home and its patio massacre.

The large tractor barn loomed suddenly from the darkness and not too soon for a flagging Malcolm. It hadn't been the hill; he was that out of shape. Henry got to the side door before him, which was adorned with a horseshoe, and opened it in time for both of them to duck in and slam the door shut again. Leaning against the door and trying to get his heart rate down to something that did not feel like it was on the verge of exploding, Malcolm inquired.

"How safe [heaving breath] are we [heaving breath] in here?"

"Not especially, but that's part of the plan," Henry replied honestly, if distantly.

The boss found the light switch, and a large overhead bank of LEDs appeared. The interior of the tractor barn was expectably dominated by the presence of an orange Kubota utility tractor and all the various tools and supplies to maintain it. Tucked into the farther side was a rack of various hand tools, woodworking tools, and many labeled stacked plastic crates. A tractor-sized rolling door is on the other. Henry stepped over to the hand tools, started searching, and then asked,

"Where is it?"

"Where's what?" responded a now breathing normal Malcolm.

"It. The thing. The monster."

"Oh," Malcolm said, stepping away from the door and staring at it with suspicion.

"It *was* following us?" pressed Seher.

"Yeah. Yeah. It sounded like it was nearly on us, me, right before we got to the barn."

Both men found themselves staring at the door with dread.

"WHAM!"

Malcolm nearly leaped out of his shoes when another "WHAM" came from the door.

"Is it throwing things at the door?" he inquired incredulously.

"But why?" replied Henry as something else struck the door.

The next impact sounded different instead of just a flat "WHAM" of an impact on the hollow metal door. This "WHAM" also had a "CLANG" mixed in. Followed by a mute roar. Two and two became four in Henry's mind as he darted away from the tools toward the storage bins.

"Brace the door!" he shouted as he began to tear through the plastic crates. Malcolm stood dumbfounded, looking around for something that could brace the door. A nearby rolling tool cabinet looked promising. It protested being used as such as Malcolm struggled to roll it into position to block the door. Only partially pressed against the door, the knob turned. Malcolm turned to scramble away when something with a grip as strong as fate grabbed his jacket collar and jerked him backward on his heels.

It couldn't get the door open all the way, thanks to the obstinate tool cabinet. But the ghoul had enough space to thrust an arm through to try to drag him back. Suddenly, he was shoved forward, and the wheels of the tool cabinet squealed in protest at being pushed in a direction it disfavored. Before Malcolm could react, he was wrenched backward into a much wider gap. Wide enough for the ghoul to thrust its other hand through with its flint knife grasped. The primeval blade flipped into position to carve his throat open. He was going to die at a work Christmas party. A fucking work Christmas party. Malcolm Cole closed his eyes and hoped that the hunk of flint was as sharp as it looked.

"HEARTS, STARS, AND HORSESHOES, MOTHER-FUCKER!" bellowed Henry Seher bringing a large rusty horseshoe down hatchet-like onto the ghoul's knife-hand. The horseshoe impacted with a taser-like buzz, and the ghoul uttered a shriek of pain. It jerked back, releasing Malcolm's collar. Seher grabbed the wrist of the ghoul's knife and barked.

"MALCOLM, DRAG IT BACK!"

Despite the belated realization that getting closer to that knife was a bad idea, Malcolm did as he was told grabbed the ghoul's arm, and threw himself forward. Pushing his heels off against the door and doorframe, Malcolm could pull its arm far enough in to bring the ghoul's face into the door's gap. Plan in action, Henry did his part by pummeling the ghoul's face with the horseshoe. Each impact yielded that tooth-itching electrical buzz and the slap of iron against flesh. Spasming in pain and desperation, the ghoul flicked its wrist unexpectedly, and the knife's point clipped Malcolm's scalp above his ear. Producing a yelp of his own, Malcolm let go of the ghoul's wrist, and it was gone. The sudden release of tension left him sprawled on the floor.

"Here." Seher offered his hand to Malcolm. The younger man went back onto his feet, and Seher pushed the door back closed. Turning back to him, Henry hefted the now ichor-gummed horseshoe in one hand and a rusty but not sticky one in his other.

"So. I know how to kill it," he stated flatly.

Anticipating Malcolm's bewilderment, he continued.

"It's a draugr. They are Norse undead. Nasty, nasty bastards. Very difficult to put down. I must have botched the ritual for Woden or Hel to send one of those to clear accounts."

"I'm sorry, Mr. Seher. Did you say *ritual?*"

"Please call me Henry. But yes, *ritual*. It's rather benign when you get down to it.

On Yuletide. With the special Yuletide log. With a special Yuletide drink. Then, it's the community or family feasting initiated by a special ritualized toast. The toast is to honor...the powers beyond, ancestors, kings, jarls, whomever. Then, a thanksgiving for the passing year and good fortunes for the approaching year. That's it. My family has been doing it forever, and it works like the other rituals. The years are inevitably better if you do it as the traditions instruct. Maybe not wonderful, but never as bad as they could be. Anyway, I was in the middle of it when you butt-dialed me. I lost my place and must have made a bastard of a mistake."

Henry paused to gauge how credulous Malcolm was. He had not objected beyond "ritual," so Henry continued.

"The relevant point is that such fay, magical, or otherworld things are tricky to deal with conventionally. If not impossible. So, you must combat them with other ritualistic or mystical methods. I hit that draugr with a quarter pound of supersonic lead, and it got back up. The shotgun is not cutting it. I left it in the corner. But bashing it with a horseshoe made it recoil in pain. Horseshoes are good luck tokens because they are traditionally wards against spirits or magic or whatever. That's why it threw things at the barn. It had to knock down the warding horseshoe before it could even try to come in. That's why it didn't follow me, the wife, and the others into the house. So, I plan that we go out there and run the damn thing down and finish it off."

"Have we got more than two horseshoes to use?" Malcolm asked wearily.

"No."

"Great."

Henry snapped his fingers

"We need to alert Taika. Have you got your cell?"

Malcolm handed it over.

"You already have my numbers in your contacts?" Henry asked, surprised.

"It seemed prudent."

As his house phone rang, Henry uncomfortably remembered that the sagas were not infallible. Some inevitably had their details eroded by time. Suppose its entirety was not lost. He had figured the burning was just an inevitability from being killed by a magic entity, but clearly, it did draw upon its victims to mend itself. Was he sure it was a Draugr? What if he was missing something else? Or did not know what he did not know. Taika picked up. Second-guessing himself could not help. Any plan is better than no plan.

"When we come up on this thing," Henry said between pants

"I'll go to the left, and you take the right. Try to stay behind it and aim to hit something important. Don't just bonk it; break bones."

They had left the barn with horseshoes in hand and were jogging down the path back to the house rather than trying to navigate the woods again. Malcolm nodded a grim reply. A little bit further they were back to the house. It was as they suspected and feared. The draugr stood just surprisingly far away from the back porch. Judging by the residue accumulating on the back porch, it had been hurling anything at hand to try and dislodge the wards tacked over the backdoor. The lights were back on. And even from the distance they stood, Malcolm could see movement behind the concealment of the window blinds.

"It does not like mistletoe either. Seems like it could get closer to the barn to knock off just the horseshoe," Henry noted.

The duo had slowed from a jog to a quick walk. No point in trying to fight the thing while gasping from a headlong sprint. Henry snorted with bitter mirth.

"Dual threat, mistletoe is. Obligate your better half for a kiss and repel monsters."

"Noted, boss," Malcolm answered.

As their steps crossed from mist-topped frosty sod to pressed concrete, the draugr turned around to face them. Henry had done a real number on it back at the barn, Malcolm realized. The right side of its face was mangled. Scrambled facial bones hung in a drooping swollen flesh over a shattered jaw drooling ichor. How its right eye stayed in position, Malcolm dared not guess. Regardless, it was like its uninjured left eye, scowling with the heat of a rage that could rival a well-stoked furnace. It had been hefting a purloined bolt of firewood, let go of it, and with a flourish of its right hand, the stone knife was conjured into its hands. A clever feint.

Before either of them could react, the draugr dropped into a crouch and shot put style threw the bolt of firewood at Henry, then moved left to meet Malcolm in full stride. Maybe Henry had not fully alienated the powers beyond as he could turn his body and take the firewood on the shoulder rather than the face. Most of it, anyway; he still dropped like a sack of potatoes and made no immediate attempt to get back up. Malcolm turned back to the imminent problem. The Draugr was hurting. That much was clear. It was not moving as fast as it had earlier. Nor was its footing anywhere as sound. It had to step around or over the mess of its earlier slaughter. Overturned chairs, tumbled standing tables, scatterings of hors d'oeuvres, not to mention any blood, viscera, or husks of its previous victims. Hesitating to a near-lethal level, Malcolm Cole did the first thing that came to mind. He hurled his horseshoe with all his might at the draugr.

And missed it by more than a foot as the lump of iron tumbled through a window on the backside of the Seher home. The draugr stopped in its approach and turned back to see where

Malcolm's last best chance had gone. It turned back to him as the movement within the house reached a feverish pitch. If the mangled face of a netherworld-spawned monster could contemptuously sneer at someone, the draugr was doing so to Malcolm. He was going to die at a work Christmas party. "Fine," he thought. "Let it come". And with that, he locked eyes with Draugr. Then, he experienced his final fright of the night.

It was a spine-chilling outpouring of pure berserker fury. Piercing and pitiless, it was a near-feral sound, one that even stunned the draugr. "PERKELE!" shredded the night as an incandescent Taika Seher bounded across the porch and patio with a power and grace that a tiger would approve of. The Norse ghoul did not even have the time to turn and face her properly before she drove her weapon into its back with her full momentum. The sound of impact reminded Malcolm of when he saw a powerline transformer catastrophically short with the CRUNCH of the draugr's vertebrae being pulverized and nearly lost beneath it. Slumping onto its face, the draugr had hardly time to try to crawl away before Mrs Seher moved in to finish it. Standing over the monster, she lifted her weapon above her head and drove it down to crush the draugr's skull like an egg. With that, the blue-green revenant flared out of existence with a peal of thunder. Taika stood there momentarily, looking a touch disappointed that there were no remains of the slain creature she could fashion into a trophy or a macabre notice of "No Trespassing." Her gaze swiveled to Malcolm Cole, and he made a silent oath never to do anything that might rouse this formidable woman's ire.

"Excellent timing, my Viking queen." Henry declared in a pained voice. He had finally roused, and aside from holding the shoulder that had taken the firewood awkwardly, he looked no worse for wear. Taika, wearing a sweater matching her husband's, Malcolm noted, relinquished her weapon, flew to his side, and locked him in a tight embrace. Henry failed to suppress an obvious wince, something she noticed. "That's for calling me a Viking. I'm not a Viking; I'm Finnish." she rebuked him endearingly.

"I know, my dear not-a-Viking queen," Henry replied. The two looked at one another for a silent moment before tears welled up in their eyes, and they embraced tightly again. Shoulder be damned. Malcolm stood there, still not having moved from when he had hurled the horseshoe, but turned about conspicuously looking everywhere but where Henry and Taika were having a tender moment. Bringing his gaze back to the Seher home, he tried to pick out which window he had smashed. A small handful of people were standing on the back porch, most simply stunned, but a few were also crying. Struck by a need to do something, Malcolm noticed the large steel lid that fits over the still merrily burning bonfire. With careful steps, he retrieved it and placed it over the fire, snuffing it out.

"Ah, uh, thank you. Malcolm." Henry paused again, then gently broke his wife's embrace and gestured to her.

"This is Taika, my wife.

"Cole?" she asked with a minute accent.

"Yes, Ms. Taika. I sincerely appreciate your intervention. Now and earlier. Though if I may inquire," gesturing at her discarded weapon, "why a cast iron skillet?"

Henry started to answer, but she got the words out before him.

"It was the only iron thing I could find." Then she added to preempt his follow-up question.

"Iron has magical qualities. Not steel, iron. Cold iron slays daemons and repels the fell. Cast iron is like cold iron. The skillet was the only thing I could lay hands on."

Malcolm nodded, his confusion only lessened, not dispelled.

Then Henry noticed the people out on the porch. The ten-thousand-watt smiled flicked on.

"Come along, Malcolm. I need to introduce you to, uh, who's left." He said while he and Taika started to walk back to the porch. Malcolm,, still rooted in the spot, glanced around once more, resurving the scene he found himself in.

"Mr. Seher-"

"Henry. It is 'Henry,' Malcolm. You have earned the right to call me by my first name,," his boss cut him off.

"...okay, 'Henry,' but what the fuck are we going to tell the cops?"

Henry Seher's aura dropped again as even his wife flashed revelatory concern to him. What the *fuck* were they going to tell the cops?

"Ah, well, Malcolm, we'll just have to figure that out. It can't be the hardest we've done tonight. We banished an otherworldly monster with farrier's kit and cookware, after all."

GENERATION DEAD: I'M DREADING OF A NAZI CHRISTMAS SPECIAL #1 (DECEMBER 1996)

Jude DeLuca

STORY THUS FAR: Five college students were the sole survivors of inhuman experiments at the now-destroyed Area 52. Alice Vane, Gina Vivaldi, Salli-Ann Maza, Maximillion Thibodeaux, and Bridger Warren were shocked to discover they'd been killed and resurrected via alien technology. Now wielding extraordinary powers, these five banded together as GENERATION DEAD.

Operating out of a small Nevada state university under the watchful eye of their alien-cyborg housemother, POSE, RAINBOW, WINTER, AIRGUN, and SEATLLE are navigating the start of their 20s while fighting to save the world from the otherworldly horrors bent on controlling or destroying the Earth.

Or they might just kill each other. It wouldn't be the first time!

BRIDGER'S DOS AND DON'TS ABOUT CHRISTMAS

Hey buds! We're at that part of the calendar, which can be the happiest or the most miserable time of the year, depending on who you ask. That's right, we're in the last stretch, folks. Final page of the calendar. The big 1-2. Starts with a D and ends with an -mber. December. And you know what that means...

Boxing Day!

And the day BEFORE Boxing Day!

Real talk. In my experience, I've learned Christmas can potentially be the most frightening day of the year. I've read enough comics, seen enough TV shows, and sat through enough movies to know the slightest thing can turn the holiday season into a living nightmare. And I'm not just saying that because I've seen *Christmas on Elm Street* 500 times. This year.

Don't get me wrong, I love Christmas as much as the next genetically enhanced Spokane college student superhero. And so do all my buds in Generation Dead. Me, Al, Gina, Salli-Ann, and Max go all out once Thanksgiving's over. But that's because they know how to take Christmas seriously, thanks to yours truly.

Hey, once you've been murdered by a bunch of solipsistic alien super geniuses and brought back with the power to turn into a living tidal wave, you can't take any chances!

This is why I and my vast expanse of knowledge on the holiday season gleaned from a meticulous career as a connoisseur of mind-rotting entertainment, put together this helpful little guide to make sure we make it through the winter in one piece.

1. DON'T BE A GRINCH: Many people don't celebrate Christmas, and that's cool. No reason they need it shoved down their throats if it's not their bag or their religion. Or maybe they don't need a reason. The important thing is you do NOT make people feel bad for not being gung-ho about Christmas. Maybe they have a good reason. Like their dad got stuck in a chimney playing Santa Claus, or their grandma got run over by a reindeer walking home from their house on Christmas Eve. Maybe they got chased by a psycho who was hiding in her sorority house. She killed her boyfriend by mistake, so now the guy's still inside the attic with her dead sorority sister and house mother hanging from a hook, and the police just left her alone-! *A-hem*. Likewise, if you're not feeling the X-Mas vibe, you do you but don't make it everyone else's problem. Holiday burnout's a real thing, and it's nothing to feel bad about, bro! Just because you're not having fun doesn't mean we all gotta pay for it. And if you're not feeling it, TALK ABOUT IT.

2. **DON'T BE A SPOILED BRAT**: There's nothing wrong with wanting gifts on Christmas. It's natural. It's been a long year, so we want a little reward for making it through another spin 'round the sun. But don't go overboard. People don't automatically owe you a Red Ryder BB Gun or a copy of *Bonestorm* or that new Turboman doll. There's always a fine line between being unhappy when your parents didn't show you consideration towards your wants and needs and being a little monster because they got you 38 out of 39 of the things you wanted. Recognize when they, your siblings, or your buds are and aren't trying their best. However...

3. **DON'T BE A MARTYR**: The holidays are stressful. You've got a right to be pissed about it. But here's the thing. If your only reason for buying the perfect gift or, throwing the perfect party, or hosting the perfect Christmas is because you're chasing that sense of moral superiority, don't be surprised when Santa starts shoving coal in places where the sun doesn't shine. When buying a present, you're thinking about what makes someone else happy, not what makes YOU happy. You ain't fooling nobody when she opens that box under the tree and finds a bowling ball with HOMER engraved. Christmas is supposed to be about other people. Yeah, doing good feels good, but you gotta

be mindful about WHY you're doing it. There's no greater gift to give to yourself than self-awareness.

With those big guns out of the way, here are some more helpful holiday tips.

1. DO NOT WISH IT WERE CHRISTMAS EVERY DAY BECAUSE YOU HAVE NO IDEA HOW THAT CAN PLAY OUT

2. DO NOT WISH YOU WERE NEVER BORN BECAUSE THEN YOU END UP TRAPPED IN ANOTHER UNIVERSE WHERE EVERYTHING SUCKS, AND IT'S BLACK AND WHITE AND WHY THE HELL DIDN'T THEY BEAT THE SHIT OUT OF THAT OLD GUY AT THE END OF THE MOVIE???

3. DO NOT BUY GIFTS IN A WEIRD LITTLE STORE YOU SWEAR WASN'T THERE THE OTHER DAY, ESPECIALLY IF THE OWNER TELLS YOU NOT TO GET IT WET AND NOT TO FEED IT AFTER MIDNIGHT (Although technically the guy stole Gizmo but my point remains)

4. DO NOT TELL KIDS SANTA CLAUS ISN'T REAL BECAUSE HOW THE HELL DO YOU KNOW HE'S NOT WHEN WAS THE LAST TIME YOU WERE AT THE NORTH POLE?

5. DO NOT GIVE MALL SANTAS CRAP; THEY'RE JUST DOING THEIR JOB, AND THEY'RE LIKE THE UBER EXAMPLE OF THE DISGRUNTLED POSTMAN. YOU HAVE NO IDEA IF THEY'RE GONNA SNAP AS SOON AS LITTLE JOHNNY PEES ON HIS LAP

6. DO NOT DONATE TO THE SALVATION ARMY. Look, I'm talking seriously here now. Those people are homophobic, transphobic, EVERYTHING-phobic creeps, and don't let anyone make you feel bad about ignoring them and their stupid little bells. However, don't assault or harass the people who collect

for the Salvation Army. For a lot of them, it's not a choice. It's not their fault. They don't deserve to be treated like crap.

7. DO NOT USE MISTLETOE AS AN EXCUSE TO BE A CREEP. It shouldn't have to be said that "No" means "BACK THE FUCK OFF." You're not being cute trying to force people to kiss you because it's Christmastime. That goes double for New Year's Eve.

8. DO NOT GIVE SHIT TO THE CREEPY RELATIVE YOU NEVER MET BEFORE WHEN THEY STAY OVER FOR THE HOLIDAYS, OR THEY WILL END YOU. Unless they start it, in which case, show no mercy. Just cuz it's Christmas doesn't mean you have to be a pushover.

9. DON'T BE A DICK IF SOMEONE PUTS ON A FEW POUNDS DURING THE HOLIDAYS; IT'S NONE OF YOUR BUSINESS, AND NO ONE ASKED YOU ANYWAY

Now, that last one was a bit personal. I to admit I tend to overindulge just a little during the holidays. Well, more than usual. With all the Christmas cookies and gingerbread men and plum puddings and angel wings and mince pies, it's hard to avoid putting on a little weight. Or maybe more than a little. But I'm fine with getting nice and Rubenesque for the winter, especially with the way Mrs. Z, our housemother, bakes. For a cyborg wasp woman, she makes a mean pumpkin pie.

"Al, put the Christmas tree down," I begged during the commercial break for "The One Where The Gang Saves Christmas." "You're missing the best part."

"*Could I* be *any jollier?*" Matthew Perry inquired.

"What do you think? Does this look better?" Alice asked.

"It's fine, Al, you're worrying too much," I said as she picked up the tree in one hand with her superstrength and moved it to the other side of the living room. "You know Gina's gonna kill you if you break one of her ornaments."

Alice put the tree back in the corner where it originally was. Then she picked it up and put it on the other side of the living room. "This is going to drive me crazy."

"You're such a perfectionist," I sighed. "But it's okay because that's why we love you."

"Look what I got!" We turned to see Gina enter the room alongside Salli-Ann and Max. She eagerly held up a couple of purple plastic decorations while Salli-Ann and Max took off their coats. "Purple mice!" Gina cheered as she held up her newest ornaments. "Aren't they cute? As soon as I saw them, I knew they'd be perfect. I've never owned purple mice before." That surprised all of us. Gina's the original Lisa Frank Punk, so if she didn't own purple mice Christmas ornaments already, she needed to up her game. I thought she owned every kitschy, cutesy Christmas ornament ever made.

"Alice moved the tree again, I see," Max shook his head.

"Bridger, how can you stomach this crap?" Salli-Ann said as she plopped down on the couch.

"It's not crap," I said. "Look, Ross's trying to get them to fit Santa's sack of gifts down the chimney.

"*Pivot!*" David Schwimmer shouted on the screen. "*PIVOT!*"

"It's the same thing every year, on every show," my Hopi compadre continued to criticize as she picked up the TV Guide and flipped through the pages. "*Roseanne* Saves Christmas. *Sabrina the Teenage Witch* Saves Christmas. *Murder She Wrote* Saves Christmas. *The Nanny* Saves Christmas."

"Don't forget the *Spice Girls Save Christmas* tomorrow night," Max added. "Bet they save it with Girl Power!"

"I'll bet I'm gonna hurl," Salli-Ann threw the guide away.

"This is the only time of year you can watch this stuff. You can't do it once January 6th comes around and Christmas ends for real," I pointed out. "Well, I mean, you *can* watch them, but that'd make you look like a big weirdo."

"Bridger," Alice gently put her hands on my shoulders and looked me square in the eye. Concern was written all over her face as she gravely told me, "Look at me, honey."

"What is it, Alice? Whatever is the matter?" I asked in a formal speaking voice.

"Here it comes," Salli-Ann muttered. I could see Gina giggling while Max tried to shush her.

"I don't know how to tell you this, but..." Alice paused for effect. "You *are* a weirdo."

"NO!" I dramatically gasped.

"Yes!" She nodded her blonde head.

"Wha, w-why didn't anyone *tell* me?!" I cried, feigning horror and swooning. "Was it that obvious the whole time?! I don't believe it! How could I have been so blind?!"

"It's okay, Bridger, because we love you!" Alice held me tightly as I pretended to sob in her arms. "We'll always love you even though you're weird!"

"But I'm a w-weirdo, Alice!" I blubbered.

"Yes, but you're OUR weirdo!" She grandly declared.

"Oh my *GOD,* you're both freaks!" Salli-Ann groaned while Max and Gina laughed their butts off.

DING-DONG

"Oh, the pizza's here," Alice said as she headed for the front door.

"God bless Mama Simone," I sighed as I followed Alice. "Her pizzas are the real reason for the season."

"Stop, please." Salli-Ann half-jokingly begged. "I implore you."

Alice handed me the two pies, and I savored the smell of mozzarella and tomato sauce. While my back was turned, I overheard Alice ask, "Is something wrong? I paid the right amount, didn't I?" Turning around, I saw the delivery boy hadn't left our doorstep. He looked a little weirded out about something, so I returned to Al's side to see the problem. Maybe he wanted a bigger tip or something.

The pizza boy finally said, "Look, it's probably not any of my business, but I think your decorations are in poor taste. Is it supposed to be some wacky frat boy joke or something?"

"Poor taste?" Alice and I exchanged confused looks before she returned to the delivery boy. "I admit Gina might've gone a bit overboard this year, but I wouldn't exactly call it poor taste."

The delivery boy's face went from apprehensive to appalled as he shouted, "You don't think a swastika's in poor taste?!"

"A swastika?!" Alice and I cried out in unison.

"Dude, what swastika?!" I said.

"Uh, right there!"

Alice and I turned our heads to the left and gasped as we saw what was now on the front of the door.

Gone was the plastic wreath covered in twinkly fairy lights and figurines of animated movie princesses Gina hung up the day after Thanksgiving. In its place was a simple pine wreath with cones and red berries. A red ribbon was placed on the bottom half.

The hole in the middle was filled by a silver snowflake ornament resembling a sun symbol, with what was a Nazi swastika in the center.

"The fuck did that come from?!" I demanded as Alice ripped the wreath off the door, looking just as pissed as I was. Gina, Salli-Ann, and Max heard our loud voices and came up to see the trouble.

"What's all the shouting?" Max wondered before he caught sight of the wreath in Alice's hands.

"Alice, what the hell is that thing you're holding?" Salli-Ann wanted to know.

"What happened to my princess wreath?!" Gina shouted.

"So, you guys didn't put the-hey!" The pizza boy stumbled back as Alice marched past him into the street. She looked up and down the block before running down the street. Alice ignored our calls, and we followed her as she ran from house to house until she stopped dead in her tracks.

"It wasn't just us," she said.

The four of us gaped in mute horror while Alice scowled in disgust.

Every house in the area sported an identical-looking wreath on its front door. Same shape. Same color ribbon. Same swastika in the middle.

We must've spent an hour going door to door, alerting everyone to what happened. None of our neighbors knew where those wreaths came from, and no one was happy to see them. There's no telling how long they must've been up there before the pizza guy brought it to our attention. Someone called the cops, but I wasn't sure who. I doubt they would've been able to do much anyway.

"That wasn't there when I came home, I swear!" Gina pleaded as we returned to our house. She hadn't even said anything about her missing princess wreath, which meant she was seriously rattled. None of us could blame her. Our pizza was stone cold when we got back, but we didn't feel like eating anymore. "If I'd seen it, I would've told you all. I would've never left it on our door!"

"I know Gina, it's okay," Alice gently assured her. She tossed the offending wreath on the kitchen table. We didn't dare get any closer. I'm surprised Al didn't trash the thing as soon as she got her hands on it.

"Oh God, what if I could've caught the fucker who put it up before he got away?" Gina sobbed. "I screwed up, didn't I?"

"Gina, calm down; it's not your fault. Max and I didn't see it either." Salli-Ann told her.

"Max? You okay, bud?" I noticed he was lost in thought and hadn't spoken in a while.

"I knew it!" Max suddenly announced. "I know where I've seen that thing before!"

"What?!" The girls and I cried out as Max ripped the ornament off the wreath for closer inspection.

"God damn, I knew it," he muttered as he scrutinized the offending silver trinket. "Arctic Sun."

"Wait, I've heard that name before," Salli-Ann spoke.

"I did, too, but I can't remember where," Gina added. She asked herself, "Was it on TV, maybe?" Alice said nothing, but I could tell she was deep in thought. Even I thought the name sounded familiar.

"They've been leaving flyers around campus," Max revealed as he held the ornament out. We crowded around it while Max covered the swastika in the center. With its center blocked, the sun symbol became a lot more recognizable.

"You're right! I've been seeing that all over town!" Gina declared.

"What the hell are they?" Salli-Ann asked.

"Ain't it obvious?" I replied.

"That's called a Black Sun," Alice explained. We turned to her as she said, "I took a criminology course that discussed domestic terrorism like the Ku Klux Klan and other hate groups in America. A Black Sun's a modified swastika worn by Neo Nazis. Bikers, skinheads, whatever. It's a recent thing, though. Not many people know about it."

"Jesus!" Max scowled as he tossed the ornament back on the

table near the wreath. He shook his hand like there might've been residue on it. "I don't know who runs Arctic Sun, but I've been hearing in the queer alliance that their people keep bumping up at parties and fundraisers," Max told us. "I've seen 'em running little bake sales and rummage sales. I thought they were just another charity group helping the homeless. Some of the guys in the alliance have had run-ins with 'em, but nothing more obnoxious than the usual 'God loves you even though you *choose* to be gay' crap. Figured they were a new church."

"And you didn't think to mention this because WHY?" I asked.

"Well, I sure as Hell didn't know that's supposed to be the New Swastika, or I would have said something!" Max yelled.

"Is that all you know?" Alice interjected.

"Yeah, do they have a headquarters or something we should check out?" Salli-Ann inquired.

"I have no idea, but it's like they're everywhere," Max answered.

"So then, who put those wreaths up?" Gina hugged herself. "I still can't believe no one noticed anything."

"Let's go see if that's true," Alice declared.

The five of us spent the rest of the night canvassing the neighborhood, talking to everyone even after they'd spoken to the cops. Unfortunately, our trip turned up Jack. Everyone swore they hadn't seen or heard anything. Most had been more focused on decorating their trees or having dinner.

Neither the sorority house nor the frat house across from it knew who was responsible. Still, the sisters of Lambda Sigma Eta and brothers of Chi Mu Nu were already heavily into their seasonal prank war and got the idea the other was responsible. We had to hightail it out of there when they started tossing water balloons at each other. Which, I gotta admit, were not filled with water. Alice had to drag Salli-Ann away before she froze both houses into ice blocks.

Nobody had any weird dealings with the group even when we asked about Arctic Sun. Some thought it was a church like Max figured; others said it was like the Salvation Army. One guy called them a pyramid scheme. We returned home feeling miserable and exhausted.

By then, our pizzas had congealed into an ugly, unrecognizable mess. It was far too late to put them in the oven to reheat them, and none of us (even me) had the strength to eat. Into the garbage, it went. I shed a single tear over such a waste of a perfectly good pie.

The following Saturday morning, we were all feeling miserable, wondering what the fuck was going on. Not even three stacks of Mrs. Z's gingerbread pancakes with homemade maple syrup were enough to lighten my mood.

"Sorry, Mrs. Z, but I'm not up for a fourth," I said as I pushed my plate forward.

"Oh, Lord almighty, you're sick!" She cried as she checked my forehead. That didn't even get a chuckle out of Gina as she absentmindedly spun her spoon around in her coffee.

"Where's Alice?" Salli-Ann asked before yawning particularly loudly.

"I don't think she ever actually went to bed," Max said as he rubbed his eyes.

"Al didn't go out again without telling us, did she?" I asked while assuring Mrs. Z I was fine.

"She musta been up all night on her computer lookin' for info on Arctic Sun," Max explained.

"You think she found anything?" Gina sounded hopeful.

"I hope so," Salli-Ann scowled. "I wanna catch these fuckers. Who the hell puts a swastika on a Christmas wreath?" Gina, Max, and I shared equally dark expressions, while Mrs. Z looked confused before Alice burst into the kitchen. She carried with her a bundle of papers and printouts.

"Alice, sweetheart, there you are," Mrs. Z tittered. "You look exhausted, dear! Is there some sort of Earth bug I should know about?"

"I'm fine, Mrs. Z," Alice replied. Lucky her, Alice's genetically enhanced body meant she was more durable than the rest of us and could go for longer periods without needing to eat or sleep.

"Did you get any shuteye at all, fearless leader?" I wondered.

"Nope, I was too busy chatting with the other teams out there," Alice revealed as she started handing out papers to us.

"Man, I hate getting weekend homework," I tried to joke. Hey, *someone* needed to lighten the mood, even if Salli-Ann was glaring at me.

"Oh, thank God," Gina sighed. Turning to Max, she said, "If he had gone another minute without making a bad quip, I would've been seriously worried."

"Whoever or whatever the Arctic Sun is, they're bigger than I thought," Alice stated. "I was curious if this group caused problems for other heroes, but apparently, they've been *very* busy this past month. I spoke with everyone."

"Who's 'everyone?'" Max replied.

"EVERYONE," Alice emphasized as we reviewed the information she gathered. "Wombat Woman. Sweetheart and the Jersey Devil. America's Adjudicators. The staff at Miss Merriweather's school. The Guts team AND the Glory team. The Steel-Suited Magnolia Squadron. Generation Undead. The guys in Xtreme Genes. I spent hours speaking through message boards, chat rooms, and video calls. I even spent about 30 minutes receiving telepathic communication from Sol Sister in the Justice Nuns. She told me that the Power Paladins recently had an Arctic Sun encounter."

"Aren't those guys from, like, a thousand years in the future?" Gina asked.

"That's what I said!" Alice threw her hands up.

"Shit," I whistled as I read a newspaper article with some emails attached to it. Over in Sheperd Falls, the Halloween Girls had to go back on duty to deal with some psycho dressed up like an old fairy tale demoness. After unmasking the killer, the Girls learned she was an Arctic Sun volunteer. Emails from the Halloween Girls exclaimed how pissed they were at dealing with this crap when it wasn't October.

(EDITOR'S NOTE: SEE THE HALLOWEEN GIRLS TIE-IN ISSUE FOR MORE OF PERCHTA'S WILD JAG)

"The original Purple Tigress said she might've had an encounter with a prototype of Arctic Sun back in the 40s, so they've been around for a while," Alice told us. "They're some American knock-off of the Nazi Party she said. A loose organization of double agent villains stationed in the States but never caught by the authorities."

"If they've been around this long, why hasn't one of those other teams taken them down already?" Salli-Ann angrily asked.

"There's always a splinter group that starts up when the rest are wiped out," Alice frowned. "They're like cockroaches. That's what the Ruby Scimitar said. They tried to get a foothold in his daughter's elementary school, but he wasn't having any of that."

"Oh shit!" I cried.

"What is it?" Max inquired, looking up from a report of the Magnolia Squadron fighting an Icelandic giantess. **(EDITOR'S NOTE: YOU CAN READ ALL ABOUT THAT WHEN THE MAGNOLIA SQUADRON FIGHTS THE IRON-COATED YULE LADS)**

"I just remembered I gotta get to the mall!" I shouted as I hurried to get my jacket and skateboard. "Verdona Klemp's supposed to be doing an in-store signing for the new holiday *Chillblaines* book! I shoulda left forever ago!"

"This is more important than a stupid kids' book, Bridger!" Salli-Ann yelled at me from across the table.

"This can allow us to ask around about Arctic Sun," Alice reasoned. "Who knows how far into town they've infiltrated?"

"We should swing by school too," Max added as he scratched his goatee. "I'll stop by the queer alliance and ask some more questions."

"And I need to find my princess wreath," Gina sighed.

Realizing we would all head out anyway, Salli-Ann rubbed the bridge between her eyes and said, "Okay. Let's go to the mall."

With that settled, the five of us made our way to the Roswell Falls Shopping Plaza. We kept our eyes open for more of those goddamn wreaths or flyers with the Arctic Sun's symbol. Alice and the rest would sometimes stop to ask if anyone had seen strange activity or people hanging up wreaths on doors. Whoever these guys were, they were surprisingly good at being sneaky.

Meanwhile, I was getting antsy, as I could only imagine the line at the mall's bookstore. From a distance, we heard Christmas carols being blasted out over the mall's speakers until we finally reached that haven of consumerism.

"Let's hurry up, get your book signed, and then we'll go," Salli-Ann ordered as we walked towards the glass doors. Red and green lights were wrapped around the plaza's name above. "The longer we take to figure this thing out, the worse it'll get."

"Man, the line's gonna be a nightmare," I feared. "What if she doesn't have time to sign a copy for me?"

"Are you for real?" Salli-Ann asked.

"Uh, yeah!" I said. "This is *Chillblaines*, Sal! The scariest kids book series of all time!"

"Exactly, for *children!*" Salli-Ann specified. "You're 20!"

"Great literature isn't bound by something as petty as 'age groups,'" I argued as I picked up my board and shoved it into my backpack.

"Y'know, Sal, you're not exactly one to judge," Max chuckled. "Don't you watch every episode of that *Beautiful Moons* show?"

"That's completely different!" Salli-Ann looked offended. "*Beautiful Moons* touches on serious topics like gender discrimination, body shaming, and racial persecution."

"I'm sure the fact you're crushing on the goth clown girl has nothing to do with it," Gina giggled with a catlike grin.

"Salli-Ann! Really!" Max gasped as he took his Stetson off to fan himself. "I never took you for a clown girl!"

"Her name is Grunge Trinculo, and I am not crushing on her!" Salli-Ann proclaimed. "I'm just very invested in her emotional arc!"

"Man, I can't wait to see how Verdona made a horror story out of the Navajo string game," I said to myself while Salli-Ann argued anime with Gina and Max. "'All Tied Up'" is gonna be so sick. And then I gotta pick up the new *Heart Attack* holiday book, the new *Death Rattle* book, and *Lung Buster*, and *Stomach Churner*, and…"

As I realized the young adult horror market was becoming saturated, I noticed someone was missing.

"Where's Alice?" I asked.

"She must've gone in already," Max figured.

"Wait, there she is," Gina pointed. We saw Alice standing on the other side of the doors, her back to us.

"Why is she standing there?" Salli-Ann asked.

"Maybe she was waiting for you guys to wrap it up," I shrugged. "Yo, Al!"

The four of us entered the mall to where our fearless leader stood...

And then we all felt like someone had punched us in the gut.

<u>ARCTIC SUN IS PROUD TO BRING YOU A WHITE CHRISTMAS!</u>

It was as if we stepped into a nightmare. The mall was decked out in banners and signs with the same Black Sun snowflake symbol we'd seen the other night. The only difference is that these lacked the center swastika.

Something bubbled up in my stomach. I thought I was gonna puke as I watched little elves dressed in red and green prancing around on all the levels, ringing bells, handing out peppermints and gingerbread cookies to shoppers.

All of them wore armbands with the snowflake on them.

The big Christmas tree in the center of the building was covered in snowflakes and tinsel. Elves at the base handed out gifts to little kids. There were signs directing people to visit Santa's village. A choo-choo train was set up, being conducted by an elf, and the cars filled with cheering kids. I shuddered at the mental image of where I figured the train was heading.

"This is real, right?" Gina choked out. "You're all seeing this, right? I'm not having a stroke?"

"I think I'd prefer a stroke right now," Max gulped.

Salli-Ann's left eye was twitching up a storm.

Alice's face was completely blank, which I knew better than anyone, which meant she was beyond enraged.

"Guys." We all jumped back as Alice spoke. "Let's visit Santa."

We followed the arrows to Santa's village in silence. All around us, people shopped and laughed as if the mall hadn't been practically remade in Hitler's version of the perfect Christmas. Out of all the weird shit I've seen in the last few years, this managed to top it all.

The little elves repeatedly tried to offer Alice and Max baked goodies, which were promptly ignored. They did not attempt to approach me, Gina, or Salli-Ann. Likewise, the elves only gave out candy and gifts to white kids while ignoring all the rest. Gee, I wonder why.

We finally reached the entrance to Santa's village, formerly the food court. The tables and chairs had been moved to create a makeshift toy maker's town. Kids lined up to speak to the supposedly jolly fat man as he sat on a throne of candy canes and gumdrops. By his side was Mrs. Claus with her grey curls and little glasses on her rosy cheeks. I couldn't help but notice how tall she was. Almost as tall as Alice.

Over to the side, we saw Mayor Blanche Hannigan eagerly speaking with a reporter for the local news. Her signature beehive of blonde curls was decorated with little ornaments that shook whenever she moved her head.

"Naturally, the holidays are the busiest time of year for the Roswell Falls Shopping Plaza, but it's thanks to our friends at Arctic Sun that we've seen a business boom like never before!" Hannigan clapped. "Thanks to their philanthropic efforts, at no cost from my constituents, I might add, they've graciously set up this lovely little display for all the kids of Roswell Falls to meet the one and only Saint Nick! Arctic Sun's helpers are stationed on every floor handing out presents to the needy without cutting into profits for our fine storefronts and establishments."

"Oh, of course," Salli-Ann snarled, her hatred for the mayor revitalized with a passion. "Of fucking *course,* Hannigan helped set this up!" She began marching to the mayor before Gina and Max pulled her back. "Hannigan! *I'm gonna freeze your ass and shatter it with a sledgehammer, you hear me, you gutless Nazi loving-!*"

"Now, now, Salli-Ann," Alice calmly said as she touched Salli-Ann's shoulder. Gina and Max instinctively backed up. They knew how scary Alice could be when she was steamed. "Act like that, and you won't get to see Santa."

"Fuck Santa!" Salli-Ann snarled. Several parents and kids gasped. "Yeah, that's right, I said it!"

"Alice, you are disturbingly calm right now, and I figure that's because you're either gonna kill someone or you have a plan," I said. "Or you have a plan TO kill someone."

Alice closed her eyes and smiled in response.

I've seen that smile before, and it meant two words.

No mercy.

Sometime later, I watched from the sideline as Alice and Max reached the front of the line to see Santa Claus. I was no longer worried about getting to the Verdona Klemp signing. Well, maybe a little worried.

"Ho ho ho!" I heard the man in the red suit cheer as a little pigtailed girl jumped off his lap. "And who do we have here?"

"You see, Sister dear, I told you we would meet Mr. Santa," Max said.

"Brother dear, I hoped to see him but feared it impossible!" Alice clapped.

"Excuse me," Mrs. Claus said. "There's an age limit to speak with Santa."

"We are big for our age," Max replied. "I am only 10."

"And I am 9 and a half," Alice giggled.

"Uh-"

"Oof!" Santa cried out as Alice and Max quickly sat on his lap. Santa was a big guy from where I could see him, but there was barely enough room for the two. "Well, now, you two certainly are big."

"Mother always said to drink our milk," Max replied.

"We always listen to Mother," Alice explained.

"We LOVE Mother," they spoke in unison.

"What are your names, children?" Santa asked.

"I am Greto," Max spoke.

"And I am Hansela," Alice spoke.

"What... unique names," Santa chuckled. "What can Santa bring you for Christmas?"

"Sister dearest and I are both red-blooded, blonde-haired, blue-eyed children, and we have been very good all year," Max implored.

"We have waited for Christmastime so Brother dearest and I could tell you our secret wish," Alice pleaded. "Only you can give us what we want, Santa."

"Santa will do what he can," the old man laughed. Meanwhile, Mrs. Claus was struggling to make sense of the situation.

Max announced, "What we desire is for all the children in the world-"

"Every race-"

"Every creed-"

"Every religion-"

"Every gender-"

"Every sexual orientation-"

"To join hands and sing a song of tolerance and racial harmony."

Santa and Mrs. Claus looked like they were gonna burst a blood vessel.

"We LOVE racial harmony!" Max and Alice cheered.

"That's our cue," I whispered. I grabbed Gina's and Salli-Ann's hands, and the three of us swayed to and fro as we sang "*Feliz Navidad*" with huge smiles on our faces. Gina's light manipulation power created a rainbow above our heads. At the same time, Salli-Ann's cold abilities generated light snow to fall as we sang. We ensured Santa and Mrs. Claus got a good view of us while Max and Alice clapped ecstatically at their Christmas wish coming true.

"C'mon everybody, it's Christmas!" I cheered. Kids started lining up next to us, holding hands and singing along. Some parents pulled disposable cameras out to take photos. All the elves stopped prancing around, glaring at us with utter hatred. Mayor Hannigan saw the display of human togetherness and looked like she was about to keel over from joy at the good press she could reap.

And then Santa blew up.

"*NOOOOOOOOOOOOOOOOOOO!!!!!*"

Max and Alice were tossed off the fat man's lap into a presents display. Santa stood and yanked out a syringe from his pocket, jammed it in his neck! His face contorted as he ripped the beard off his head. Kids cried and ran away as Santa's body bulged and grew, his teeth sharpening into fangs, his costume splitting at the seams.

"ENOUGH OF THIS!" Santa growled as he ripped at the skin on his face. "OF THIS GODDAMN CHRISTMAS FARCE! WE SHOULD'VE BURNED THIS PLACE TO THE GROUND FROM THE START! ENOUGH! **ENOUGH!**"

"Did Alice know that would happen?!" Gina cried out as people ran away from Santa's village.

"I don't think any of us saw that coming," I groaned.

"Who cares?!" Salli-Ann shouted as ice grew over her knuckles, forming spiked gauntlets.

Santa wasn't the only one going through the change. The multitude of elves were shuddering and twitching as their skin bubbled. Their ears grew into points as their skin turned an ugly shade of red. Claws grew through their gloved hands.

"Alice, I think you made Santa unhappy," Max deadpanned.

"No negotiating with Nazis!" Alice leaped up into a fighting pose.

"The little race traitor bitch wishes to fight!" Mrs. Claus threw off her glasses and tore off her hair, revealing a wig hiding short blonde hair. She tore at her dress to reveal a tight leather corset and thigh-high boots with stiletto heels. A gloved hand dug under her chin, ripping off latex to expose a coldly beautiful face with piercing, ice-colored eyes.

Standing by her side, Santa finished his transformation into a vaguely lupine monstrosity covered in tatters of red and white.

"Santa's not only a Nazi, he's a WEREWOLF Nazi!" I shouted. "That's even worse!"

"SCHWARZE LOVING WHORE!" Nazi Claus (Santa Klaus?) growled as the five of us grouped. "RIP YOU APART!"

"Bring it, Wolf Man!" Salli-Ann dared.

The mall descended into chaos. Shoppers and employees ran for their lives as all the little elves finished transforming into demonic little beasts. *Do They Know It Christmas* played on the speakers over shrieks and screams? The elves tore through stores and stands, demolishing whatever their grimy little hands touched. Gina, Max, and I went after the elves while Salli-Ann personally tangled with Santa. Alice wrestled with Mrs. Claus, who disturbingly seemed to have the same strength level as Al.

"What was the end goal for this?!" Alice yelled as she put Mrs. Claus in a headlock.

"You have no idea how long this all took! Months of planning gone to waste because of you!" Mrs. Claus slammed Alice into the floor on her back. She lifted a stiletto heel and tried to slam it into Alice's head. Al caught the heel with one hand and swung Mrs. Claus back and forth, beating the Aryan bride against the toy village. Mrs. Claus broke loose and charged at Alice with both fists. When Alice managed to grab Mrs. Claus's wrists, the statuesque Nazi headbutted her in the face!

"What the fuck?!" I screamed when Mrs. Claus tried it again, only for Alice to SINK HER TEETH INTO CLAUS'S NOSE! The woman screamed, and I could see Alice bit down harder!

"Bridger, focus!" Max shouted at me as he pointed his finger and fired an air bullet through an elf's head, splattering his brains over a Styrofoam snowman. "Al's a big girl. She can handle herself!"

"Right, my bad!" I nodded and brought forth twin geysers to sweep up a group of snarling elves. I directed the geysers into each other, and SPLAT! Elf pancakes.

"How many of these freaks are there?!" Gina sliced through elves with shocking pink and sky blue beams from her hands, now speckled with blood red as they carved through the onslaught of elves. "What even are they?!"

"Put 'em down and make sure they stay down!" Max ordered as he sniped elf after elf on different levels. It wasn't long before we got the attention of the elves, who'd been more focused on destroying other parts of the mall, and they converged on our location.

"Why doesn't Salli-Ann just freeze them solid?!" Gina asked as she vertically sliced up an elf in half. The two halves fell in clumps, giving a good look at its organs.

"Sal's hands are full!" Max bellowed as he pumped bullet after bullet into an elf that wouldn't stop coming at him. Indeed, I turned around to see Salli-Ann duking it out with Nazi Claus himself. I wouldn't think to repeat the string of curse words the Winter Queen uttered for those of you with delicate constitutions, but she was almost as pissed as Alice. Nazi Claus slashed at her with his claws but kept hitting the ice. Salli-Ann roared as she shoved her gauntlets into the ground, summoning worth a barrage of ice spikes shooting upwards, trying to skewer the furry Nazi.

"There's too many!" Gina said as her rainbows carved up more elves. "We can't let them get out!"

"Right, I'm on it!" I grabbed out my trusty board, created a geyser beneath me, and rode off into the mall on a wave. Atop the waterway I fashioned, I could see how badly the rest of the mall was being ravaged. The little freaks weren't going to stop until nothing was left. I guided the water with my hands and mind, sweeping up elves left and right in the deluge. I could feel them struggling to break free from my grip, so I had to increase the pressure. Needed to make it bigger so they couldn't escape. This was the hardest thing I ever had to do, the hardest I ever pushed the limit of my power. I sucked up all the rampaging elves into the water, plucked them up, and into the ever-growing mass beneath me.

I hopped off with my board and stopped to assess my handiwork. A globe of water full of struggling, writhing little monsters trying to get loose. I held on, wouldn't stop, straining to keep them trapped.

I raised my open hand.

Then, I clenched my fist tight.

CRUNCH!

The increased water pressure crushed all the elves together into a clump of bone and guts.

I opened my hand.

The cage of water broke and drenched the stores. Chunks fell to the ground everywhere. I gasped and almost fell to my knees but grabbed a nearby bench to steady myself. God, I felt exhausted but needed to get back and help my friends. I maneuvered over dead elves on my board, trying to pick up the pace as I heard more angry snarling.

Santa's village was drenched in blood as I skated through body parts and organs. An elf with half its head blown away twitched on the floor. Everyone had converged on Nazi Claus. Max fired barrage after barrage of bullets into his hairy flesh while Salli-Ann and Gina tagged teamed with swords made of ice and light shoved into his sides. Nazi Claus seemed more determined to go after Alice, who hadn't slowed down at all, even after the beating she exchanged with Mrs. Claus.

Alice flipped onto Nazi Claus's back and rode him like a mechanical bull from Hell.

"Heel!" Alice shouted. "Heel, boy! *I SAID HEEL YOU NAZI SON OF A BITCH!*"

"I got a clear shot. Let me take him down!" Max begged as he fired a bullet into the werewolf's eye, bursting it open.

"This is for stealing my wreath, asshole!" Gina jumped forward and skewered Nazi Claus's knees with her rainbow blade. The wolf fell and tried to howl as Alice grabbed his jaws and wrenched them open. Salli-Ann pulled back her fist, generated a brand-new spiked ice glove over her knuckles, and SHOVED IT INTO HIS MOUTH!

"ALICE JUMP!" Salli-Ann screamed as Nazi Claus's body was torn apart by icy spikes exploding out of his body. Just before the spikes broke through the skin, Alice somersaulted off at the last second.

Alice still managed to stick the landing as the five of us were splattered in blood from the exploded Nazi.

"Oh God, it got in my mouth!" Gina moaned. "Ew ew ew!"

"I told you I had a clear shot, Salli-Ann," Max groaned as he tried to wipe blood off his face.

"Yeah, well, he's dead, so whatever," Salli-Ann bluntly said.

"Is everyone okay?" Alice inquired. "What happened to the rest of the elves?"

"Took care of it, Boss Lady," I said. We stood in the devastation, surveying all the carnage. The loudspeakers were now playing *Grandma Got Run Over By A Reindeer*. "So, um, is this a win?"

"I guess?" Alice asked.

"We could've planned this better," Max said.

"I think I got fur in my teeth," Gina spat.

"We killed a bunch of Nazis. That's always a win," Salli-Ann said. We all had to agree to that. "If Hannigan hadn't let them-"

"Uh, Sal, not to interrupt, but Alice?" I asked.

"Yes, Bridger?"

"What happened to Mrs. Claus?"

"*YOU THINK I WAS GOING TO RUN?!*"

The five of us turned to see the now noseless Mrs. Claus, blood flowing from her mutilated face, holding the Christmas tree from the front of the mall over her head.

"*FUCK Y-*"

Salli-Ann didn't even allow her to finish before encasing Mrs. Claus in solid ice where she stood.

Alice casually strode over to the ice block and shattered it with one punch. Turning to me, she said, "Bridger, you wanna see if you can still get your book signed?"

"Oh shit, I forgot! Thanks, Al!" I boarded my way to the bookstore in the hopes Verdona Klemp was still there. And also, y'know, alive.

NEXT ISSUE: NO NEED FOR JAI ALAI!

MERRY CHRISTMAS AND HAPPY HOLIDAYS FROM GENERATION DEAD AND ALL OF US AT DNA COMICS!

<u>FUCK NAZIS!</u>

Baby Its Cold
Nate Walton

A red 2022 Honda Accord with a Grinch sticker on the side of it pulls up in front of a large rural home. Its occupants are two twenty-something young office workers; they are currently on their first date on Christmas Eve, having only just left the office Christmas party less than an hour ago, and sang Christmas tunes to her all the way to the young man's home.

"You want to come up for a coffee? Maybe some hot chocolate," the warm invitation poured out of the young man's smiling face. Nic hoped beyond hope that his Christmas Angel would agree.

"I really can't stay." Noel hoped the lie didn't show on her face; she liked Nic a lot; he was a real solid guy and honestly deserved better than what he was getting himself into. If only he understood that which he had asked for without asking, would he truly want it if he did?

"Baby, it's cold out here, at least if I have to send you home; please let me do so knowing I warmed you up as much as you warm up my heart," Nic half pleaded, half-joked. Not sure rather she should laugh at the desperation or just give in to the cuteness of it,. Noel finally smiles and nods, letting Nic have his way this time. At this point, he's in charge; she's along for the ride, but does he know that?

"Okay, but soon I've got to go away," Noel stated bluntly, feeling the need to quickly reestablish control of the situation, knowing that she had not lost it. However, she still feels the need to correct the situation. There, let him have his way but set limits; give a little till they try to take a lot.

"I know, Noel, but right now Its cold outside" Nic popped the car door open right on cue."And we got a few hundred steps to the door." Nic felt the rush of anticipation like never before; here was the most amazing, kind, beautiful woman he had ever met, spoken to, let alone been lucky enough to take on a date, about to enter his home, by her own choice even! He just hoped she didn't sense his childlike inner nerd excitement. But he knew inside he knew that he wore his heart on his sleeve, no way to hide who he was. Fortunately, he could delay the discovery a bit.

Noel opened her car door before Nic could reach the handle, robbing him of the chance, and began to step out. "This evening has been great; I'm so glad you agreed to accompany me to the LogiCorp Christmas party. I was dreading having to hang out with the accounting crew all by myself" Laughter echoed, blurring even further the intent of the half-joke between them as they struggled and battled on the ice-covered Slip N Slide that doubled as the sidewalk; they reached the door the laughter between them going from a giggle to a riotous laughter as they grasped for balance with the door frame.

"I gotta be honest, I was hoping you would stop by. I mean, the party was fun, but hanging out with other LogiCorp suits can only be so much fun; we cant really get to know each other when we got a bunch of old number-crunching codgers talking about profit and loss and overhead asset equity sheets or something the entire time. I mean don't get me wrong, they are fine for the 8 hours a day you gotta be around them, but not my idea of a fun time." Nic hoping his honesty about work wouldn't offend his company, even if he thought it wouldn't matter at this point. They entered the front door, out of the freezing grasp of the night's darkness and into the warm green and red embracing glow of the season.

"So...very...nice." Noel had to struggle to stifle her laughter as she had never seen so much Christmas spirit in one room. The tree was enormous, music notes in white and gold, green and red lights glowing everywhere, enough heat coming off them to warm you across the room, the beautiful angel topping it, older than both the wide-eyed twenty-somethings staring at it combined. Still, the rest of the decorations covered every visible inch of the room. Every surface is in service of the season. It was almost as if your third-grade teacher had poured the entire class budget into decorating a living room instead. "Wow, reminds me of the mall when I was a kid..." she trailed off, realizing how condescending she must sound, wishing she had gone with the third-grade teacher comment instead; she turned to see him smiling, standing next to the tree and some glass angels, the reflection in his ice blue eyes catching Noel's eye. Like ice in the night sky.

"Oh wow, are they real crystal?" Noel hopefully inquired

Nic motions for her to come over. "Yeah, they were my moms; she had collected them for years. Every year, we would receive a new one at Christmas, became the unofficial start to our Christmas season. We would get dressed in our warmest, most Christmas clothes and go down to the local Ames Department store, my brother, my mom and me, every year till she passed. Would you like to check them out?"

"May I?" Noel hopefully inquired while stepping closer to

Nic, erasing the distance between them in an instance. He stood in awe as she glided across the room, feet barely touching the ground. Magic would be his guess, Christmas Magic, perhaps?

"Of course." As Nick lifts one of the crystal angels into Noel's delicate angelic hand, their skin meeting in a shock, the kind you only get from two opposite charges uniting for just the briefest of moments; it causes the angel to nearly fall from her grasp, slipping from her hands much like her control of her emotions are flowing away like the ebbing tide. She gasps in horror at the moment, in fear of the Angel breaking yes but fear of hurting her newfound kindred spirit that much more, but due to Nic's incredible cat-like reflexes, he manages to catch the Angel mere inches from the tabletop, and its once inevitable fall from grace.

"I'm so sorry; I did not mean to; I'm so clumsy," Noel urged forgiveness, the words shaking out of her mouth more than they were spoken, like a scolded child begging to be loved again.

"No harm, no foul," Nic assured her none was needed, "I'll hold your hands; they're just like ice" As smooth as they were, the Angels were just as slick as the melting ice, waxed and shined to a perfect finish, Noel had never seen such art such simple beauty, it warmed her heart in the way only a cold winter night can. The way only a night like this can. A perfect night. A Night that makes you feel 'that' feeling. 'That' feeling. Knowing that feeling was taking over, as it always had, Noel forced the first words she could think of out of her mouth, desperately trying to cover it with whatever she could. "My mother will start to worry." She herself almost caught off guard by the absurdity of her own words.

She glanced at the Santa Clock, "I mean, look, it is already a quarter till Rudolph." There, that will remove any sense of strangeness from the situation.

Sitting the angel back on its shelf, doing all he could to stifle a laugh, but losing the struggle, perfecting the angel's position and place, "Beautiful.." he slowly turns his head to Noel with that smile and those eyes"...Whats your hurry? If you are uncomfortable, I understand," Nic motions towards the door, only to continue his motion towards the kitchen ", but I was going to switch the coffee pot on and grab us some Christmas cookies?" With that, he clicked a button, and the fireplace fired up behind her. Causing the flames to roar to life illuminating the room in warmth and mood lighting. The overwhelming comfort instantly deleting any objections before they could even be offered. Noel gave a nod telling Nic to continue.

Nic grabbed them two cups of coffee, basic dark roast for him (the bitterness means it's working, just like the nine to fivers), sugar, and pumpkin spice creamer for Noel. He poured both cups in front of her and allowed her to mix her own cup, just so she wouldn't think him capable of anything underhanded. As expected, she was a two-sugar shot of creamer kinda woman, and Nic could respect that; he preferred the bitter, warm morning embrace of black coffee but to each their own. At the same time, she appreciated the gesture, as she had lived the college life up until just recently and had woken up after a roofie in college on a night out a few years back. Every day, she thanked God her roommates had decided to Den Mother her to safety that night. Good friends were worth their weight in gold. Chills still ran up her spine with the cold, harsh fear of what could have been that night, how bad things could have gone if that gross, manipulative bastard had gotten his way. How close she was to almost being a statistic, a victim. Never again. With a forced smile, she lifted the coffee cup to her lips and leaned back into the warmth of the fire in a single motion so smooth it took Nic's breath away. Unnatural yet perfectly pulled off, the type of thing you can't describe but never forget.

"My father will be pacing," it came out as a giggle, intentionally so; the implication intended to be her father worried about everything all the time. Knowing that he would be concerned how things went tonight, it just made her feel safer some how some what warmer, almost at home. She hoped he understood her meaning.

"Listen to the fireplace roar." Still in awe of Noel, Nic stutters out the first thing he can, oblivious to her previous statement. He felt so silly; he was getting drunk on her very presence, he could feel it. She could see him turning red, couldn't she? Or at least would she if not for the glow of the flames. Was he saved by the flames from the burn of embarrassment?

"Where is the little elf room?" Noel asked, hoping to get him to turn any color but that particular shade of red.

"The little elf room??? Oh, Oh, sorry.. right over there to the left, only door on that side. It is can't miss"

"So Id really better scurry," Noel let out as she hurried to her feet and began to move towards the restroom with some obvious expediency.

"Please, No hurry." Nic couldn't believe his luck. Here he was in his own home with a beautiful woman, willingly even, on Christmas Eve of all nights. In real life, nerds like him don't get these kinds of nights, this is that 25 Days of Christmas Hallmark stuff, real rom-com life happenings; even if it doesn't go the way he is hoping, this will still already have been one of the best nights of his long miserable, lonely life. His mixture of enthusiasm and classic self-loathing has its spell broken only by the rhythmic song that is her voice.

"Well, maybe just about half a cup more?" that was all it took for him to want to pour a thousand cups more.

Music to his ears, as the lyrics play from the perfect instrument. The symphony of chords and lyrics from her mouth, her mind the exact words he had hoped to hear, playing his tune...that's it, music.

"Siri..Put some music on while I pour." Nic walked over to the coffee and shakily poured a second cup, again basic black for him, this time hoping the strength would give him the soberness he sorely needed right now to fight her intoxicating stare and left her to build her cup as she saw fit, again this time two sugars more and one shot of the pumpkin spice creamer. Consistent, she knows what she likes, and he likes that.

The neighbors might think.....

"Oh, ba..by, Its...It's bad out thare" Nic stood looking out the large bay window as he struggled to finish his coffee, seeing the snow now at full blizzard condition, stumbling over his words like he was on the slip-in sidewalk again.

"Say, whats in this drink?" Noel joked, looking down at his coffee cup, giving him a quizzical but somehow still-knowing look. "Oh goodness, no one hailing a cab out there," wondering to herself what implication that statement will give him. His eyes turned to meet hers, answering the question she never asked with the loudest answer you can give without saying anything. Those eyes answered so many questions, but they asked more, some she wasn't sure she knew how to answer.

I wish I knew how......

. . .

Nic stepped forward, shaking from the excitement or maybe from the two extra cups of go-go juice, or maybe his heart was beating so fast it might escape his chest and his body was trying to fight the inevitable. Whatever the reason he earthquake wobbled towards Noel.

"Your eyes...they are like starlight now, with the tree and the reflection from the snow..they sparkle."

He brushed the bangs from around her glasses, revealing her glimmering eyes, as green as any Christmas tree, dancing in and out of the shadows of the fireplace. Their gaze locks for but a moment.

To break this spell.....

Nic playfully removed Noel's beanie, "I'll take your hat." Noel sends a death grin right through him, "Your hair looks amazing" It's red glittering bright in the room's toasty cozy colors and the ambiance around them. Here he was, feet away from a young Ann-Margret-looking beauty; wow, he felt like a nerd as he referenced a woman who was last famous 30 years before he was born.

I should say no, no, not this time.....

Nic touches Noel's cheek with his hand, "Do you mind if I move a little closer?" He knows not what he does; forgive him, forgive me, I can't fight that fight. Why would he ask you, to? Does he not understand what he does, or does he not want you to fight it, does he want you to give in?

At least, I'm going to say that I tried.....

"Why does my head feel so fried?" Nic was beginning to have issues concentrating, his anxiety now beginning to overcome him. What was going on? Was his anxiety effecting him that bad? Was he actually drunk on her beauty? Is that a real thing? No, is it?

"I really can't say," Noel said as she sat back next to the fireplace. Clearly ignoring Nic's slightly tipsy speech. Smiling and shrugging her shoulders to physically repeat what her words had already said. Nic stumbled his way over and plopped down next to the tree with her. Erasing the distance between them with: a lean to the left, an over correction to the right and a quick shuffle to realign with his target, answering the ungiven invitation to join her with an aggressive yes.

Ahh, but I'm cold inside...

Nic leaned in for a kiss, Noel didn't exactly pull away. Not at first, at least, she liked Nic, like she said, he deserved better than what was in store for him. He was a caring, kind guy that was just kinda awkward but attractive, kinda guy you hoped for but think you would be settling with if you ended up with him, but the kind of guy you love your best friend to end up with. But quickly, the reality of what this was popped into her head, and fighting against her instincts, she gently placed a hand on his shoulder, creating space between their lips for words to just squeeze through:

"I simply must go."

Nic smiles, trying to convince her without words, asking with a glance, begging with but a look and aiming for charm, landing dangerously close to the reality of desperate instead.

"Baby, it's cold....outside." Nic tries to lean back in, but as he does, he leans a bit too far forward and falls flat on the floor, face first, snorting at his flop. His laughter practically paralyzing him as the muscles were too busy reacting to his amusement to bother trying to fix the situation.

"The answer is no." Noel let the words shudder out between her silent chuckles, battling to hide her amusement behind the facade of concern. While that looked painful, she couldn't help but be both concerned and tickled by the flop.

"Ohhhh babay. Its.. its colddd outslide" Nic tried with all his might to organize his thoughts and get the words out as he struggled to push himself up again, fighting every instinct of his body to simply just go to sleep. Noel sits herself down next to him, lowering herself to his level as Nic tries with his every fiber to rise back up to hers.

"This welcome has been been..." Nic's arms finally give out, having exhausted all the defiance they had left in them, slamming him skull first on the ceramic floor, cracking it in the process, signaling his unconsciousness throughout the house, if not the neighborhood. The reverb shakes the windows. "I'm lucky you dropped in..." Now, not even hiding her mounting laughter at this point, fully dropping the mask now. Rising up from the floor throughout the house, she began to explore. "It is so nice and warm," she mockingly expressed kindly to no one in particular, knowing the only other occupant of the home was unresponsive on the floor, drooling to himself. Examining the tree, inspecting its size, and admiring its decorations as well as its base, she lets her eyes trek through the house until they end up landing on the raging storm outside the window.

"Nic, oh Nic, look out the window at that storm; it's so beautiful out there; you simply must see," she implored, knowing he was completely unable to move. Unable to respond, unable to do anything but be a victim. Her victim.

My sister will be suspicious.....

Gripping her fingers into his shoulders, Noel forced Nic to roll over, not against his will, as there was none there to even try to resist. Gazing into the paralyzed but wide awake face of the young man whose chest she was currently mounting. Slowly, she leaned in till her face brushed against his lips, almost to just remind him that although he could not move, he certainly could still feel. "Man, your lips look so delicious," Noel inhumanly growled the words out as she reached down and squeezed her teeth around Nic's quivering bottom lip. She allowed her upper teeth to meet her bottom teeth through his flesh, meeting no resistance. She decided to remove the piece in question with one swift motion.

My brother will be there at the door.....

As the Christmas crimson covered Nic's face, Noel couldn't help but be struck by his deep blue eyes; those eyes, they were like "Waves upon a tropical shore," darting back and forth. Noel was unsure if it was fear or pleasure her new friend was experiencing; the two experiences can be hard to tell apart visually; she knew she had seen herself in both enough times, but either way, she wanted no need to give him more. She knew all too well that sometimes you have to learn to like the fun times.

My mind is vicious......

"Gosh, your lips look so delicious." Noel gave Nic another "Special" kiss to Nic, making sure his upper lip would not feel cheated out of the exchange. She knew he appreciated a girl who knew what she wanted, and she loved that about him. She admired the new matching set of 'hickeys' she had given her new Christmas beau; swallowing her reward down, she sat back and reached into her coat. Noel lets out a bored sigh, "Well, maybe just a smoke more.." she notices the storm has again increased in intensity, no longer a snow shower but now a full-fledged blizzard of 1964 out there, "Never such a blizzard before.." she felt the need to narrate her thoughts to Nic; he deserved to know what was happening to him and why it was. With a smile at her current plaything, Noel pulled a large hypodermic needle from within her coat pocket. She loved the way the syringe felt in her hand, the weight of the form; it was perfect like God herself sculpted it to fit into her slender hands. She began by running the tip around his face, being sure to poke him enough that he could see the blood run over his face but not enough to cause any real harm, well no real, lasting harm anyway, at least until she started scratching his cornea, again being sure to damage them without truly puncturing them, just a few scratches each, not enough to ruin their perfection, just enough to get a nice reaction for their game. She made him see the needle and the liquid it contained within, teasing injecting it in various places for as long as possible, then telling him never mind and starting to put it back into her pocket before slamming it into his chest, instantly separating him from the realm of the conscious.

Thud. Thud. Thud. After about the third or maybe fourth time Noel smacked the rubber end of the hammer against his head, it finally stirred his soul enough to bring life to his eyes.

"I've got to get home."

Nic struggled to understand what was going on. Why couldn't he move, why couldn't he feel his legs, why did his mouth hurt, why did he taste blood, what was stuffed in his mouth, why cant he think straight, why was his front door open, is that why he's so cold, what was he tied to, why was he naked, and why was he moving towards the door?

"Oh baby, You will freeze out there," Noel told him matter of factually, stating to Nic his intended fate, the feigned concern not even attempting to seem genuine as what would be the point; she continued to wheel him on the Christmas Tree dolly he was hung from towards the open front door. "Oh, say, lend me your coat?" Noel asked as if again playing the role of the innocent good girl. While she put the coat on as mockingly as possible in front of the shivering Nic, she sat the tree down momentarily, allowing Nic to see the floor and, with it, realize why he had no feelings in his legs; Noel had roughly sawed them off from the knees down. Silent mumbled screams were all Nic could force into whatever it was that was stuffed down his throat, never even reaching the vacant space where his lips used to belong. It was the only fight Nic had left, and he used all of it that he had, but to no gain whatsoever. It was a futile struggle. Feeling the tree shake as he tensed and thrashed, Noel knew what he had discovered. "It's a bad storm tonight; it's up to your knees out there." Noel, unable to contain her amusement at her own morbid sense of humor let out that laugh, that same laugh that only hours ago had been the light of innocence on a Christmas Night; that same laugh was now the harbinger of darkness; how could the same laugh sound so different so quickly? The Choir to the Horns.

"You have really been grand." Noel caressed the blood-stained cheek of her recent plaything. Again she stopped at the sight of his eyes, so breathtaking. "Your eyes are like starlight now....but..."she cupped his jaw in her hands, his chin resting in the palms, her thumbs against his bloody red cheeks, wiping a blood-soaked tear away with her right thumb as she used the left to remove what in her mind was the offending optical orb. Gurgles of objection is the only sound that manages to free itself from the prison that Nic's body is now in. "How can you do this...thing to me?" she asked, shoving his left eye in front of his right, making sure he knew what she had fixed. She scanned the face of her Christmas Prince, looking for the gratitude she was owed for having helped him in such a caring way, but she didn't see it; she saw nothing but fear. It feels so good to have someone like him, but...With a push, they were out the door...she does not need such blatant disrespect for a caring gesture. Plopped into the front yard like a yard dart, he would now be a morbid display for the holiday on his own lawn. Hopefully, that will teach him to appreciate gestures such as hers.

"There is bound to be talk tomorrow," Noel teased as she took her phone out from the pilfered coat's pocket and snapped an "elfie" in front of her art project. "Going to make my holiday long," Noel took a spike and a hammer out from her new coat pocket, ", and full of sorrow...," and then began to line it up on his chest, dead center"now hold still, don't want to miss" she drew back the hammer and with one smashing blow drove the spike into his rib cage, shattering both his ribs and any hope his lungs had of surviving this night unscathed "...at least there will be plenty implied,"

Nic wheezed through the newly created hole in his chest, air and blood gurgling in a well-orchestrated symphony of agony. "I will think you caught pneumonia and died." Noel walked back to the house and removed the snow-covered wreath from the door, no longer sliding on the sidewalk, but no longer gliding as she once had, still slippery but more of a slither now, she walked back to Nic to hang it from the recently created hanger. Noel thought his eye socket looked empty, most of the bleeding having stopped; it just seemed, I don't know, hollow somehow. After a moment of thought, Noel had an idea. She hurried back to the house for a moment and returned with a box; she withdrew a few candy canes from the box and proceeded to jam them into the opening. Seeing the lack of balance in design, she hung a few Christmas balls through the eyebrow on the right side, double hooked to ensure safety. Noel took a few more photos after hanging more decorations on her display and finally crowning him with one of his dear mother's angels, which surprisingly only took a few stiff hammer shots to secure in place. She stayed with him, holding his hand tightly until the first rays of sunlight reached their faces. As the sun began to expose the scene to the light, Noel made her way into the darkness, blending in as both disappeared with the day, Noel leaving with a final kiss to Nic's cheek and one final note.

"I really can not stay; get over that old doubt, Baby. It's cold out."

Note from the Author:

Now that you have completed a nice read thorough, I would like to recommend on your next read-through, after you have gathered your comforting drink of choice, be it on ice or in that warm coffee cup, and got your reading nest, be it that couch, your pillow fort or the warm embrace of your blankets that you go ahead and find the song this story takes both its structure and much of its dialogue from. It is available on both Spotify and YouTube with but a search. I won't include a link as those change constantly, and I do not want to accidentally link to something awful, like Viva Laughlin or Emily's Reasons Why Not. But find it and put it on for your next reread; it adds to both the atmosphere and the immersion; yes, I know that's some cross-media asking strangeness, but give it a try; if you don't like it, you cut the music off, no loss. I would also like to take this opportunity to thank the late Frank Loesser, who wrote the song way back in 1944. I'd also like to tip the hat to some of the performers whose take on the song influenced my work: Ella Fitzgerald, Dean Martin, Ray Charles, Idina Menzel and Michael Buble, Doris Day, and Bob Hope. Without these performers and many more, the story you just read would not exist. (Apologies to any or all of those who are shamed to hear this.)

The Christmas Wish
Mike Rusetsky

When Sam ducked into the kitchen to take a phone call from an unknown number, he hadn't suspected it would ruin his Christmas.

In fact, this call, which turned out to be a police officer bearing news of tragic import, ruined far more than Sam's holiday spirit. When he heard the officer identify himself, his body went numb. Some part of him must've already known. Krista was flying back from her work conference in Oregon today, but he hadn't heard from her in hours. The last snippet of an update came just after Sam fed lunch to their son Devin. He was cleaning up when his phone buzzed. Krista's number.

"We finally got the go-ahead for takeoff. Only three hours late! So sorry, hon. Kiss D for me, Momma's coming home!"

She attached three kissy-faced emojis to emphasize the point. Showing the message to Devin only mildly pacified him; he wanted to see Momma *now*.

"It's okay, D. Keep your shorts on."

"I'm not even wearing shorts, Dad. It's too cold!"

Sam smiled. "It's just an expression, bud. Your mom's going to be here before you know it. The pilot thought it prudent to wait out the snowstorm. But she's on her way now."

Devin kept sulking. "But she *promised*, Dad! She said she'd be home for Christmas Eve."

"I know, little man. I miss her too. I'm not sure if you know this, but your momma's a big deal at her work. *And* she's the breadwinner in our family. Very important," he clarified, seeing Devin's confused look. "Nothing happens at her company or in our family without her being right there in the heart of it. So don't you worry, she'll be here soon."

"Will she tuck me in tonight?"

Sam hesitated before answering. He didn't want to be the parent who casually dispensed promises he couldn't keep. Krista already missed her transfer flight in Detroit due to the snow delay, so she might not make it back even by Christmas morning unless she worked her extrovert magic on the Delta reps. But that's no kind of news to share with a worried seven-year-old boy.

"She's going to do her darndest," he said, splitting the difference.

"Okay," Devin sighed, not fully buying his dad's diplomatic wording.

That was just after lunchtime, but now that dinner was over, their annual viewing of *Rudolph the Red-Nosed Reindeer* was interrupted by a strange call. Sam almost let it go to voicemail, but some uneasy stirring within him caused him to pick up.

The news was jolting, confusing, and downright illogical. The cop on the line didn't mince any words, and Sam struggled with the directness of the information. Phrases like "extreme turbulence" and "unplanned landing" gave way to weirder, more nonsensical ones, like "unfortunate fire" and "search for survivors." How could any of this information relate to

Sam's family? He'd consumed a glass of eggnog with a shot of OYO's Honey Vanilla Bean Vodka mixed in, but surely his faculties were still with him. Why was he getting this call?

He asked the cop as much and got a brief silence in return. Then the man on the line cleared his throat and launched into it.

"We have reason to believe your wife was on this flight, sir. The boarding pass records confirm it. More to the point, her purse and wallet were found at the crash site, with some burn damage to them, but identifiable. Unlike... the rest of her, I'm afraid."

Sam shook his head. This was wrong. He was the wrong Sam, or they called the wrong Krista's spouse. It wasn't helping that Devin just turned up the volume in the living room and began singing along to "There's Always Tomorrow," competing with the officer's disturbing information in Sam's other ear.

"What exactly are you saying?" he asked, growing irritated. Why the hell was this cop calling unverified parties with bogus information?

"Your wife, Krista Amos. I'm afraid her plane experienced an emergency landing due to poor weather and worse luck, and the fuel tank sustained a blow that set the whole thing on fire. It's a messy site down here, Mr. Amos. Lots of charred, twisted metal. The plane went up in flames, and... well, the debris radius is damn near a mile. Firefighters are doing their best, but... I'm sure you can imagine the carnage."

He couldn't imagine it and didn't have to. Why was this asshole trying to ruin Christmas for him? Sam was winding down a cozy night with his son, and he had no time for this foolishness.

"I don't know who you *think* you're trying to reach," he said, his voice shaking for some reason. "But it's not this household. My kid and I are trying to have a nice Christmas Eve, and this 'real cop' act of yours is pathetic! Go try your crank call bullshit on someone more susceptible."

But the caller didn't seem surprised to be accused this way. If anything, his voice sounded more calm than before and tinged with tiredness.

"I understand how you must feel, Mr. Amos. Take your time absorbing this news, since it's the worst kind of news a man can get. Hold your kids tight tonight, tell 'em you love 'em. But just know that come tomorrow, this won't go away. In the coming days, you'll get more pesky phone calls, especially as we identify… parts of the passengers. Mrs. Amos's remains will be shipped to the funeral home of your choosing. In cases like this, autopsy wastes taxpayer dollars, so we typically ship the remains directly. But those details will come, so don't you worry. Just be there for your family now, and—"

Sam hung up. Enough was enough.

Settling back on the couch, he slipped under the Christmas-themed Paw Patrol blanket he and Devin shared. *This* is reality, he thought. Right here on this cushioned couch, his son warming his side like a little personal oven.

"You okay, Dad?"

The question made him jump. "Um, yeah. Of course, bud. Just glad to be here with you."

"Was it Momma? On the phone?"

"Oh, that?" Sam's voice was threateningly close to cracking. "It was nobody. Christmas crank call. You know how those kids on the naughty list are."

But Devin kept staring at him, his milk chocolate eyes never leaving Sam's. "You sure you're okay?"

"Uh-huh. Let's watch the rest and get ready for bed, D."

Finally, the movie reclaimed Devin's attention, and Sam relaxed a spine he had no idea was stiff with tension. He stared ahead at the screen without seeing the visuals, although normally, he enjoyed watching Rudolph get his redemptive arc. That phone call was like a rusty tack he'd stepped on, its pointed edge burrowing deeper with every stride, the possibility of tetanus not just a distant chance but a bacterial certainty.

#

"Aaw, are you *sure* we can't wait for Momma?"

"I'm sure, D. You need your sleep, or Santa can't deliver your presents, and then his
schedule gets all out of whack. We don't want that, do we?"

Devin sighed. "No."

"Good boy! Now go brush your teeth, and show me how clean you got 'em."

Devin looked burdened with the weight of the universe. "Do I *have* to?"

Sam smiled, sitting down on his son's bed next to him. "Have I ever told you about a magical thing some kids get to do once a year?"

That got his attention, as Sam thought it might. "No! What magical thing?"

Sam lowered his voice conspiratorially. "You can't tell anyone about this because Santa wants to keep it on the down-low. Only the top five percent of the kids on his good list get a cool bonus gift."

"What kind of gift? Ooh, is it a videogame?"

His father chuckled. "No, D. Way better."

Devin looked skeptical. "What's better than a videogame?"

"A wish, kiddo! A very special Christmas wish."

"Ohhh..."

"That's right. If a child is pure of heart – and clean of teeth – he or she can make a special wish on Christmas Eve. It's bound to come true because it's in Santa's fulfillment clause. It's full of small print and legal jargon, and I'm sure you don't care."

"I do! I do!"

He had him now.

"Okay. Well, if you do a nice thorough job washing up and brushing your teeth, you might be ready for your Christmas wish. I'll get you all tucked in, and you can whisper your secret wish to Santa. He had his elves hide special augmenting sensors everywhere so he would hear you loud and clear."

"I'll brush and wash, I promise! Oh, and Dad, do you wanna know what my wish is?"

Sam shook his head solemnly. "Birthday wish rules apply. It's all part of the Sanity- clause."

He knew the wordplay would sail straight over the kid's head but couldn't help himself. That kind of joke would've landed with Krista, who'd give him a lopsided grin and an exaggerated eye-roll. She love-hated his occasional punny witticisms. Something that felt dangerously close to tears stung in his eyes, and Sam had to blink it away.

"Birthday wish rules," Devin repeated, mesmerized by this new secret knowledge and completely missing his father's emotional turmoil.

"Exactly, bud. So get those teeth brushed, and I'll wait here to inspect them!"

Highly motivated to oblige, Devin disappeared into the bathroom. Sam sat on his son's bed, listening to the running faucet and trying to dissociate from the version of reality that the phone call forced into his structured life. What if...? But no, he couldn't possibly think that way. Crank call. Why hadn't the cop – if that's who it was – called him back after Sam hung up on him? A professional wouldn't have left it there. Unless they had a lot more phone calls to get to tonight... How many passengers were on that flight, anyway?

"All clean!" Devin announced, startling Sam.

"Alright, great job, D! Let me see those chompers."

Devin presented them in a showy grimace, the very face of youthful exuberance. Sam felt something breaking inside himself just looking at Devin's excited face. Was this the last time he would see his son so jovial? If the phone call wasn't bullshit, that meant... but no. Sam had to hold it together. He wrapped his son in a tight hug and felt the boy's little arms squeeze him in return. Somehow, he avoided waterworks before the child, but it was a close battle.

"Good night, sweet prince!" he called, closing the door behind himself.

"Night, Daddy!"

Left to his own devices, Devin immediately went to the wish-making business. He watched the red and green candy canes crawling up his walls and ceiling, the effect of an illusion-casting light globe on his bed stand. The candy canes had a hypnotizing quality, and Devin relaxed his eyes.

"I wish..." he said, then yawned. It's been a good day with his Daddy but a long one as well. He was all tuckered out, as Momma says. "I wish.." he repeated, slower and slightly slurred now. His eyelids were getting heavy, and the silent candy canes sliding across the room made his blinks longer.

"I wish..." He considered what would be the most fun thing to get. That new Roblox game looked awesome, and the playthroughs he watched on streaming sites confirmed it. But he felt Santa already knew about this desire, and St. Nick was likely already en route to deliver it. So what else was there?

"I wish... Momma came home to tuck me in."

There. That felt right. Devin smiled through leaden lids. It wouldn't feel like Christmas without Momma around. Seemed so weird to only be tucked in by Daddy. He loved his daddy for sure, but without Momma, something essential was missing. That would be the best Christmas gift ever if she could join them.

Thinking these innocent thoughts, Devin gave into the soporific effect of the ever-crawling candy canes. Then, all through the house, the night settled in silence.

#

Try though he might, Sam just couldn't fall asleep. The bed felt off-balance, with an empty half where Krista should've been. And oddly, he missed hearing the steady hissing of her CPAP machine. He never thought it would bother him not to hear it, but she'd packed the machine with her luggage. Sam reached for his phone. No new texts or calls.

He frowned and rubbed at his eyes, more out of frustration than sleepiness.

Then he ran a quick Google search, which was something he'd been avoiding doing for the last two hours.

Immediately, several developing news stories emerged on the results page. Images of a fire blazing in a wooded area where a commercial flight had crash landed. Where was it? He clicked and began to read. Then he went back to the results screen and read everything he could, from social media posts to the official statement from the airline. Delta. Krista's preferred airline was not because their service was great or consistent, but because of the loyalty point system she'd had with them forever.

Some early-breaking stories mentioned an area search for survivors. But the current live reports all confirmed the same two-word verdict.

No survivors.

Sam's heart didn't break – it imploded with each successive click and scroll. There was no room for doubt now, and everything echoed the gruff caller's claims. Stripped of excuses or bargaining rights, Sam had to face the truth. He and Devin were alone in the world. Krista, with her sexy lopsided smirk and her "secret-squirrel" hazelnut pancake recipe, with her nerdish love of historic Parisian architecture and her zest for life in all its expressions, was gone.

Sam sobbed into his pillow. Then he began to punch it.

#

It was past midnight, and the living room was lit only by the Christmas tree that the Amos family had decorated together a few weeks before. Sam left the festive lights on overnight, fighting a fatherly urge to save electricity because "Nobody's gonna see it anyway." His dad's voice showed through, something he had to shut down on sight. No way would he be turning into his old man. Hence, the decorations shine on overnight, inside and outside the house.

The stoop by the front door creaked. It could be the wind out there, but more likely, it was the wooden floorboards, as the stoop greeted any weight placement with a similar sound. Inside, lit by the multicolor lights of the Christmas tree, the front door handle began to move. Softly at first, then increasingly faster, in an up-and-down motion that suggested growing impatience from the guest out in the cold.

Once the handle went still, the door began to shake with loud knocking. It came with a force that seemed unnecessary for the late hour. Reverberating through the house, the rapping noises reached Devin Amos's young ears.

"Hmm?" he said, sleep-drunk. "Momma?"

He slipped out of bed and crossed the room, pausing at the door. Yes, someone was downstairs, knocking. Daddy wasn't up, it seemed, so it was up to him to answer the door. The boy raced downstairs, excited to see his mother. He hadn't forgotten his parents' directive to never open the door to strangers. That word of caution was eclipsed by his aching desire to see her.

"I'm coming, Momma!" he shouted, gliding across the hardwood. His hand grappled with the latch, even as the knocking persisted. "Just a sec!" he assured the visitor, finally unlatching the first of two bolts.

The rapping continued, insistent and strangely unaccompanied by any spoken words. They used to have a Nest camera a while ago, but then Momma did some research and said she didn't want it in the house anymore. Something about who else can see what the camera sees. Devin didn't know what that was all about, only that in his present situation, he couldn't check who was at the door, as the old-fashioned peephole was about two feet above his eye level. He grasped the second lock, beginning to twist it.

"Hang on, Momma! Almost there!" he called, at last budging the lock. That's when a grown hand enveloped his own.

"D! What the hell are you thinking?!"

His dad was there, his meaty palm gripping Devin's small fingers.

"It's Momma, she came back! Open up, Daddy!"

"Calm down, son. I just heard you squealing down here. You're saying someone was at the door?"

Devin already looked done with this conversation. "Yes, I'm sure it's Momma! Open the door already!"

Sam took in his son's disheveled appearance. Some part of him was concerned for what tomorrow would bring in terms of breaking the difficult news to the boy. But another part wanted to protect him from all harm, to snatch him up and secure him inside a preservation chamber where the tragedies and awfulness of this world would never reach him. But that was crazy, of course. Devin would eventually grow up and learn to confront all the pain triggers that life had in store for anyone with a pulse. But knowing this didn't make what Sam had to do any easier.

As there was no longer any knocking (if there was any in the first place), Sam put his hands on his son's shoulders.

"Bud, I think we need to talk. You remember that phone call I got tonight during *Rudolph*?"

"Uh-huh. You said it was a cranky call."

"Well, that's what I thought. Turns out it was a police officer. I didn't believe it was real then, but it wasn't a... cranky call, after all."

Devin seemed confused by this information. "But... you didn't call 911 though."

"Right."

"So 911 called *you*?"

"Kind of. Look, the point is that officer had a very sad update to share with me. Krista... your mommy..." Sam's voice caught, and he couldn't continue.

Devin's expression never wavered from confusion. "What about Momma? Did the pilot go to the wrong place?"

That was all the prompting Sam needed to lose his grip on his emotions. The tears came, and he hugged Devin tightly, burying his face in the boy's raven curls.

"It's okay, Daddy. Maybe the copilot knows the way home."

This reassurance only made Sam weep harder. He understood now that this was not the time or place for this conversation. There's no way in hell he could keep his shit together enough to calmly say what needed to be said. Devin was a smart kid but a sensitive one as well. Sam needed time to do a little research on child psychology and the nature of grief. He shouldn't break this devastating news to him here, by the front door, in the middle of the night.

"Why don't you go upstairs and hop back in bed," Sam suggested, tearing himself away. "It's been a weird night, and we'll both need some rest before Christmas morning."

"But Daaad," he whined. "What about the knocking?"

"What knocking? Did you have a bad dream, D?"

Sam knew of his son's struggle with separation anxiety, which especially flared up during his parents' date night outings and his mom's business trips. Little did he know... but no, that would come later. For now, sleep was the answer. Oblivion, if for a few more hours.

"Someone was at the door. I swear!"

"Okay. Let's peep the perp."

He peered into the peephole, lingering longer than he needed to for Devin's benefit. The shadows on the front porch were mostly cast by the giant inflatable Santa riding his sleigh, which the two of them had put up on an uncharacteristically sunny day. The inflatable was lit from the inside, and what looked whimsical by daylight skewed a bit devilish at night, Santa's body sending deep red shadows across the front lawn. But outside Santa, there was nobody there.

"It's all clear out here, D."

"Really?"

The mixture of disappointment and anxiety in Devin's voice made Sam sigh and turn the second latch. "Here, look for yourself."

He opened the door to reveal the snow-strewn lawn and the gently swaying inflatable Santa Claus riding on his sleigh. Devin poked his head out, looking around eagerly, but even he could see no visitors out there.

"Satisfied?"

"I guess," Devin said. His breath became steam as he spoke, and Sam figured that was enough exposure to the cold air.

But as he closed the door, Sam caught a glimpse of something strange on the lawn. Later.

"Alright, back to bed, buddy!" he demanded and made sure Devin was all the way upstairs before he cracked the door open again.

Stepping out on the porch in his house slippers, he examined the odd new feature on his lawn: footprints in the snow. Except... were they? They looked vaguely human-made, except this person must have been drunk off his ass. One foot had been dragged sideways, while the other seemed entirely shoeless. He saw the big toe's imprint in the snow. How much partying would you need to do to lose a damn shoe?

Sam shook his head, darkly amused. Was someone getting wasted on Christmas schnapps and stumbling around the neighborhood? He made a mental note to check all the locks inside the house after he bolted the front door. Who knew what possessed someone to trespass like this? Thank God he caught Devin before he opened the door.

He turned back towards the house when his nose detected a touch of something familiar. Was someone barbecuing at one in the morning? Sam could smell cooked meat. Not just cooked but burned outright. He wrinkled his nose. He hated to see a good steak wasted on a fool who wanted it well done.

Sam stepped back inside and locked the door behind him.

#

Checking the other means of egress was a good idea, but it seemed someone had already beaten him to it. The garage door remained locked and secured, but he felt a chill in the air when he entered the dining room. That wasn't right; they had forced air heating, and at no point should he be feeling a cold draft on his skin. Some quick detective work led him to the sliding door – which was not only unlatched but a few inches open.

Sam didn't like this one bit. He slid the door shut, cutting off the cold air, but felt no calmer for it. Somebody might have gotten inside his house. A person with an erratic gait and unpredictable behavioral pattern, perhaps? It was time to take matters into his own hands. Suddenly, the quietude of the house didn't seem so peaceful. There was an underlying menace to it, not unlike the moment when a predator crouches in the shadows before pouncing on its prey. Sure, it's a quiet moment, but the spring is loaded.

Speaking of loading... Sam quickly assessed the floorplan. One thing he got from his father that he didn't regret (could be the *only* thing) was his penchant for protective measures. Namely, guns. An avid shooter, his dad never missed the first day of deer hunting season and always dragged little Sam along. "Grow you some balls to kill yer own dinner." Sam didn't relish the memory, but those lengthy trips gave him a lifelong respect for firearms, their proper maintenance, and their potential for ending a life.

After his old man passed, Sam inherited his entire weapon arsenal (much to Krista's chagrin and dismay), and for a while, he kept it locked up in a storage unit. But then, a house in the neighborhood suffered a violent break-in, and Krista changed her tune. "If you're super careful and keep the damn things out of Devin's reach..." That was all she needed to say. He'd gone and fetched the entire gun collection the following afternoon. Then he and Krista drew a map: their house's floorplan, marked with red X's where he'd secreted away each gun. Every piece was placed inside a safe or container with a combination lock. Only Sam and Krista knew the combination, which was the same for all the safe boxes. Once every six months, when Devin was away at a sleepover, Sam would enact his gun maintenance protocol. He retrieved the weapons from all the hidey holes on the map cleaned and lubricated the stocks and barrels, and locked them away when Devin came home.

But now, the occasion called for an unscheduled retrieval. Sam took a step towards the kitchen and stopped. He listened to the house, its little creaks and sighs. Was the intruder waiting around the fridge? Sam had a safe box hidden in a cabinet above the fridge. Still, he would have to walk past the pantry closet to get into the kitchen. He had the creeping worry that once he passed the pantry door, the intruder would spring out of it with a knife, slashing at Sam from behind.

No. Better get armed first. Sam took three steps backward towards the living room. In the L-shaped family couch was a compartment he'd cut out with a jigsaw. Inside was a lockbox with a popgun, almost nothing of a thing, but the .22 would get the job done at close range.

He crossed the living room, matching each step to a breath as the multicolor Christmas lights glided over him silently. It felt like he was trudging through a dream, sneaking around his home under the glow of whimsical decorations. But with the ceiling lights out, the place looked more like the set of a festive slasher movie than his own house. The shadows and silhouettes didn't seem right and kept giving him a false sense of motion in his periphery. He finally reached the couch and carefully lifted the corner piece, unhitching it from its longer counterpart.

He checked behind him for movement and saw none. Just breathe... and get the gun.

Sam removed the smallish safe box and entered the four-digit code. 0-4-1-5. His and Krista's wedding anniversary. Borne of an inside joke that getting married on Tax Day would seal their union forever, and it also referenced Krista's job as CFO of her company. They giggled while formatting the wedding invites, settling on an informal design incorporating dollar signs and percentage symbols. Everything seemed so easy and light-hearted back then...

Was that a shuffling noise behind him?

Sam grabbed the gun, cocking it in one quick move. But the room remained still in its eerily lit dead-of-night ambiance. He had time for a quick sigh of relief when he caught a glimpse of a shadow in the far hall. Someone was ambling up the stairs.

"Oh no, you don't!" he shouted, taking off for the staircase. Two steps in, he tripped over the mound of gifts sitting under the tree, lost his balance, and fell forward. The gun went clattering on the hardwood. Breathing a curse, Sam kicked at the gift box that got in his way (the oblong-shaped one, probably the stupid hoverboard he'd insisted they get for Devin) and got to his feet, nervous sweat pouring into his eyes.

"Hey! Fuckin' hold it!" he screamed, rage and panic mixing. He scooped the gun off the floor and raced towards the stranger, who'd disappeared up the stairs by now.

Terrible images danced before his eyes as he cleared the steps three at a time. Intrusive thoughts of a violent drunk stumbling into Devin's room, maybe holding a knife he picked up downstairs or a jagged-toothed bottle of Jack. The man lifts the bottle/knife and stabs the shit out of Devin's bed, making dark-red stains bloom through the blanket. The poor kid inside is trapped, shocked, and suffering... As a parent, Sam would murder anyone who did this to his child and then possibly kill himself. He was already teetering on the edge of sanity and didn't need the extra push.

Upstairs now, he saw it. The shape was more shadow than

person in form. Reaching a dark limb and placing it on Devin's door handle. No more warnings. Sam drew the gun and fired.

Once! Twice! Three reports.

The hand hesitated, and the person – clearly unsteady on their feet – turned back towards Sam. He could see more of the outline now. Long hair, a skirt... one shoe, the other one lost to time and space. Surprisingly, the intruder was disabled, one arm ending in a nub at the elbow. The figure seemed to hesitate, seeing Sam with his gun trained.

"I'm not fucking around, friend. Move away from that door."

Silence. Sam felt like he was being watched. Studied.

"I'm serious! I'll double those wounds if I have to. Step. Back!"

The figure cocked its head like a puppy trying to understand. Then it shuffled forward. He opened fire, aiming for the head.

Seemingly undeterred by the bullets tearing through it, the person slammed into Sam, and for the second time in the last two minutes, he felt himself losing balance.

"Fuck.." he breathed, trying to claw at the wall for purchase, but the attacker's weight brought him down, landing on top of him.

Oh no. The meat smell invaded his nostrils again. Same barbecue stench from earlier. Too well done.

Suddenly, the hall lights came on, and the stranger's face was illuminated. Sam stopped struggling under the weight, his eyes going wide.

"What the... no. No, it can't be..."

He stared into the milk-chocolate eyes he knew so well. Devin's eyes, but predating his son by two decades. The long hair, the skirt—it all made sense now. But how? Didn't the officer on the phone say...

"Daddy? Is that you?"

Devin. Right, he must've been the one who flipped the light switch. I woke him up. *We* woke him up.

The human-shaped form atop him quivered. He saw the eyes roll back out of pain rather than sarcasm, as he'd been used to her doing. She'd lost her eyelids and had no means to make a natural expression in this state. Her skin was missing in so many places that Sam lost count. One cheekbone protruded completely, ivory bone slicing through like a macabre puzzle piece. Some of her hair was still hanging on, but many patches were missing, the fire-scorched scalp underneath browned to a crisp.

Well done, he thought.

Then she met his eyes. And what was left of her lips attempted to shape something.

"Baby?" he asked, sitting up. He took her head in his arms, and it felt both cold and too hot at the same time. "Baby, talk to me. Krista!"

Her lips parted and let out a muted, hissing croak.

"I don't understand!" Sam was openly weeping now. He was in hell. *Was* this hell? "Daddy, what's going on? Is that Momma?"

Devin was standing over them, rubbing sleep and confusion from his eyes.

"Stay back, son! Momma's hurt. She's hurt bad."

But Devin refused to stand back. He sat down and picked up the blackened, dry twig that was now Krista's remaining hand. Holding it tenderly, he began to cry.

"Go to bed, D. Let me call 911 and get Momma some help, okay?"

Devin wouldn't hear of it, though. This moment would not be taken away from him, and who knew if that wasn't for the best? Sam abandoned the mindset of a protective father and embraced his wife's meager form.

"I'm so sorry, baby. I put all those slugs in you. So damn sorry."

She gave a weak nod, her eyes rolling back into her skull. It seemed that whatever energy animated her was now waning, and he didn't know what to do. He avoided looking at the bullet holes his gun shredded in her neck, chest, and left temple. What the hell was the protocol for this? How should one deal with the dying of a woman who was already dead?

"Love you, Momma," Devin managed between sobs. "I'm glad Santa heard my wish."

The fire roasted Krista's throat, most of her esophagus gone. But she managed a soft sigh that may have been the letter D.

They held her in the hallway until there was nobody left to hold. Then they held each other.

#

Christmas morning came, bright and forcefully cheery through the downstairs windows.

Sam awoke on the living room couch, a weight pinning him down. After a panicked second, he remembered Devin had drifted off to sleep beside him. Indeed, he glanced down to see Devin's black curls. The boy was asleep, his head resting on Sam's chest.

Was it a dream? A misshapen nightmare sculpted from anxiety and worst-case scenarios?

Sam moved to sit up and looked around. The Christmas tree was still fully lit, of course. An annual fuck-you to his miserly father's ways. He looked down and saw a single gift lying in the middle of the floor. His heart dropped.

That was the box he'd tripped over on his way to fill the love of his life full of lead. Now he remembered. But Devin was stirring now and Sam had to be strong for his son. "Morning, sunshine!" he tried, attempting joyfulness.

"Hey, Dad."

"Merry Christmas, D."

Devin stretched and gave a yawn. "Merry Christmas to you, too."

"How about we start opening some presents, eh? Looks like Santa gave you a bunch this year. You must've been real good!"

Devin seemed distracted. "I guess," he said. Then: "I feel like I already got the most important gift."

Dreading to acknowledge it and still unwilling to name it aloud, Sam nodded. "I guess so, kiddo."

"Daddy?"

"Hmm?"

"Do you think you could make us some of those pancakes? The squirrel ones?"

Amazingly, Sam laughed. "You mean the secret squirrel recipe your Momma used to make?"

"Yeah. That sounds yummy right now."

"You know what, D? That *does* sound yummy! Let me see if I can find where your mom stashed the hazelnut spread."

"She hides it 'cause you're always trying to sneak it!" Devin laughed. "I do not!" Sam protested, feigning offense.

"Do too!"

Soon, the aroma of frying oil and batter filled the house. The pancakes didn't turn out exactly as they'd remembered, but they were still pretty damn tasty. Chewing a mouthful, Sam reflected on the recipe, the recipe's originator, and the magic of Christmas that somehow brought a child's wish to reality. And as good as the pancake tasted, he had to elude intrusive thoughts about his wife's midnight return.

Life felt uncertain, but one thing Sam knew for sure. Whatever their Christmas dinner meal was tonight, it would not involve steak. Or grilled meat of any kind.

"How about some sushi tonight?"

Devin made a face. "Gross. I'd eat some pizza, though!"

Sam raised his eyebrows. "Christmas pizza?"

"Yeah. It's a new thing."

Sam nodded, looking off. "Yeah. Let's start a new thing."

Outside, it began to snow.

SACK

A.J BROWN

The kid was taken from his home in a brown sack cinched tight with twine. I only know this because he was my brother, and I saw it happen. It was Christmas of 1980 —the eve of, to be exact. Or maybe it was Christmas morning. I can't remember. What I do recall is still sketchy at best, like a grainy black-and-white movie, complete with white voids in the film and black splotches to go along with them.

This is what I remember:

I woke in the middle of the night to a noise coming from down the hall. I thought it was … well, I don't know what I thought it was. I got up to find out, but also because I had to pee. I had an overactive bladder back then (back then? As if that ever changed). I wasn't supposed to be awake. If Santa showed up and I was out of bed, then he would fly on by, no ho ho ho, no presents left behind. Still, I had to go, and anyone with a weak bladder would tell you, when it is time, *it is time*.

I opened the door and peeked down the hall. A nightlight sat near the bathroom, halfway between me and the spare room (really, it was a catch-all, where all the junk Mom and Dad didn't have space for anywhere else in the house went). I didn't know what the noise was when I woke, but standing outside my door, I realized it sounded like something was pulled across the floor, accompanied by bells jingling.

Being a kid, two things were true: I thought it was Santa Clause dragging presents from the chimney, and I was curious, not like the cat, but more like the monkey. I made my way down the hall on the balls of my toes, careful to be as quiet as possible. At the end of the hall was the front room, complete with a couch and two chairs, a coffee table in the center of the room, and a television with a remote control tethered to it by a long cord. Beyond the living room was the kitchen off to the right, closed off by a swinging door, and the den to the left. The den is where the sounds came from. There was a third sound, something I didn't hear earlier: crying.

I walked through the living room, almost tripping over the outstretched cord. I stepped over it and took a few more steps. From where I stood, almost in the center of the room, I could see various colors reflected off the den wall. Red, yellow, green, orange, and pink, each of them lights on the tree that sat in the corner where Dad's desk would normally have been. Though I couldn't see the tree, a couple more steps aligned me with where it should have been, but where something else stood, its back to me, blocking the tree from view. It wore a red outfit that was dirty and grimy and looked as if it hadn't been washed in years. There was no cap on its head. Instead, wild black hair streaked with gray hung past its shoulders. And it wasn't terribly round (I don't believe it was jolly, either).

This is where things get fuzzy. What I thought was Santa Claus turned to the side just enough for me to see the long nose and drooping skin on its face and dark eyes too big to be real.

Wrapped around its neck and shoulders were chains with bells on them. As it moved, the bells jingled.

In its hair-covered hands was a brown sack. Something thrashed around inside the bag; then I realized what that something was. A person managed to get one hand out. That hand is what I remember the clearest. It wasn't large like Dad's, and it wasn't small like mine. It was the hand of another child, one older than me.

"Stop squirming," the thing said and grabbed the hand, pulling the kid partially out of the bag. There was brown hair and red pajamas, the top sporting a faded Spiderman. He had flushed cheeks and wide, blue eyes. The thing pulled the kid's face close and bit off his nose. There was blood and a scream, but it was muffled when the boy was shoved back into the sack, and the twine pulled tightly around the opening. The sack went over the thing's shoulder. A dark spot formed where the kid's head was.

Before disappearing into the fireplace (and presumably up the chimney), it spoke. "You'll make a fine dinner." Then it turned to me and bared its terrible teeth. A fly flew from its mouth. "And you will, too."

I woke up.

My bladder had let go, and my mattress was soaked. But I was in bed. I wasn't in the hall or the living room or standing at the entrance to the den, and there was no creature biting noses off of kids, and he hadn't looked at me and ... and ... it had all been a horrible dream.

The nightmare faded, and as it did, I forgot about it, the creature, that night, and my brother.

Until two nights ago.

I woke from the same dream I had had when I was a kid. It felt real, and the creature's voice was clear in my ears. *You'll make a fine dinner. And you will, too.*

It had said those words before it took my brother. I am certain of this. And I had forgotten.

Dad had passed away by then, but Mom was still around. Though we never had the best relationship, I visited her (as I drove over, I realized something I had never done before: Mom loved me before that Christmas in 1980. After it, not so much. It was a sad epiphany). She wasn't quite ready for bed when I arrived without calling, but she didn't shoo me off either, though I halfway expected her to.

We sat at the kitchen table. There was a bowl of half-eaten oatmeal in front of her and one untouched in front of me. We both had a cup of coffee, hers in both hands as if she were cold, mine sitting next to my bowl of uneaten oatmeal.

When I asked her about my brother, she laughed, shook her head, and said, "You don't have a brother, Cale. You've never had a brother."

She was lying. I could see it in her face, hear it in the nervousness in her voice and the way she turned the coffee cup in her hands. I could sense it in the way she wouldn't meet my eyes.

"What was his name, Mom?"

"You don't have a brother, Cale," she repeated.

"You're lying. What was his name?"

She stood from the table, took her coffee cup and bowl, and dropped them in the sink, which was unlike her. She had always been a neat freak and never left dishes in the drain. She turned to me. I expected her face to hold an expression of hurt or sadness, but I saw anger, pure and dangerous. She then walked away with an, "I'm going to bed now. If you don't mind, show your way out."

I watched her go until she went through the swinging door. Then I listened as she made her way up the stairs and into her bedroom, where her door closed with a whisper and a click.

I showed myself out, more convinced that my dream hadn't been a dream at all. I drove around, my mind stuck in a blackout of memories. I tried to recall anything about my brother. He had brown hair and blue eyes. His cheeks had been flushed in what I thought had been a dream. His nose had been small, and he screamed when the thing bit it off. He had been missing one tooth, a detail I remember from the second time the nightmare played itself out for me two nights ago.

That's all I remember.

It was late when I arrived home. The porch light was on. Charley had gone to bed already, if she even got up that day. The last couple of days, she had been distant, as if something were on her mind that she didn't want to talk about. When I asked if she was okay, she shut me down with a quick, "I'm fine," which is woman speak for, *'Yes, there is something wrong, something very, very wrong.'*

I sat in the recliner across from the entertainment center and pressed the remote—this one not tethered to a cord—and the television came on. The glow from the tube lit up the room, and shadows formed where there had been none a few seconds earlier. I saw a picture hanging on the wall above the couch. It was Charley and me, and we were in our Sunday bests. We were both smiling, but there was something wrong with the picture.

I stood, turned the light on, and went to the picture. At first, I couldn't place my finger on the issue. She wore a pink skirt and a white blouse. I wore a white shirt and a blue tie, my dark slacks rounding out the outfit. We were smiling. We looked like a happy couple except…

"There's a gap," I said and touched the picture. I ran a finger between her and me. Definitely a gap. I went to the entertainment center. Another picture sat on top of it, just above the television. We wore the same clothes, but we stood hip to hip, and my arm was around her waist—there was no gap. I grabbed the picture and went back to the one on the wall. Side by side, it was obvious something was missing in the bigger image.

I set the smaller picture back on the entertainment center and went through the house and into the bedroom. The light went on, and I opened the closet door, pulling the chain inside so the light would also come on.

"Cale, what are you doing?" Charley asked, her voice soft and sleepy.

"I'm looking for something."

"It's almost one in the morning, Cale."

"I know. I can't sleep."

"Well, I was."

"Sorry, Babe, but I need to find the photo album from my childhood." I turned to her in time to see her drop off the elbow she had been propped up on.

"You're kidding, right?"

"No."

"It's on the top shelf somewhere."

I rummaged along the shelf. There were many books and small boxes, a few of which fell to the floor.

"Cale, you're making a mess."

"I'll clean it up," I said when I spotted the brown spine with the faded gold emboss on the edges. I pulled it from the shelf, knocked off another box as I did so, and went to the bed. The mattress gave slightly beneath me. My heart was suddenly racing. In the back of my mind, I think I already knew what I was looking for and what I would find.

"Cale, I'm trying to sleep here."

"I'll only be a minute." I flipped through the pages. Most of the pictures were of me in various stages of my childhood. Me playing basketball as a teenager and a few of them when I was maybe two, chubby with a head full of curly brown hair. In one of them, I was sitting on the floor in an Easter outfit, a picture that was staged. That was the first image that looked odd. It appeared as if something (or maybe someone) had been behind me when the picture had been taken, but whatever it had been, it was not in the picture somehow. In another photo, taken the same day, there was chocolate all over my hands, face, and clothes (nothing unusual). There was one of me on crutches during winter. I wore a blue coat I thought was cool.

"Can't you go in the living room, kitchen, or spare room and reminisce about your childhood?"

"Yeah, I could, but ..."

The family portrait stopped me. Mom and Dad stood in the picture (another one staged, but this time in a studio for the Holy Album of Our People of Whatever Church we were going to at the time). I stood in front of Mom. One of her hands was on my shoulder.

"Babe, look at this picture and tell me what's wrong with it."

"Cale, I'm tired."

"Just look at it."

With a huff, she sat up in bed and gave me a dirty look. Whatever had been wrong with her the last couple of days may not have been my fault initially, but right then, I believed it was. She took the photo album and stared down at the picture for only a second or two.

"It's a picture of your family. Big deal."

"Charley, please," I said, my voice soft. "Look at it—*really* look at it."

She stared briefly, then plopped the photo album on the bed. "I don't know what I'm supposed to see here, but ..."

"Why am I standing in front of Mom in that picture?"

"What?"

"Why am I standing in front of Mom? Why am I not in the center between my parents?"

"I don't know. Why does it matter?"

"I'm standing in front of my mom because my brother stood in front of Dad."

"Cale, you don't have a brother."

"I did."

"You're an only child."

I had not been an only child. I was positive of it. I was also certain of something else, something that had been niggling at my brain all night long, really for the previous two days. Since Christmas Eve. I wasn't entirely sure, but I thought I also knew what was wrong with her.

"Charley, get up," I said and stood, the album in one hand. I pulled the covers from the bed with the other. She still wore her nightclothes from the night before and the night before.

"What are you doing?"

"What's our son's name?"

I saw the lie on her face before she spoke. "We don't have a son."

"We do. And you know it."

She shook her head 'No,' but the tears that formed in her eyes said just the opposite.

"Cale …"

"Get up," I said, this time gently. I took her hand. Though she protested weakly, she rose, stood, and followed me out of the room and down the hall to where our picture hung on the wall. I set the photo album on the entertainment center and grabbed the lone picture from on top of it. I held it up next to the one on the wall.

"Look at the two pictures, Charley. They are different."

"I … I …" Tears spilled down her face.

"Look at them."

When she did, her face flushed, and she shook her head as if in denial of something terrible. In truth, that's exactly what it was.

I took her hand and went back down the hall, but I stopped in front of the spare room instead of our bedroom. I opened the door, flipped on the light, and went inside. The walls had been painted canary yellow. There was a dresser on the opposite wall and some boxes on the floor. Other than that, there was nothing else in the room. Everything looked normal except for a spot near the door that was maybe three feet wide by about four feet long where the carpet appeared fuller. And were those indentions where the feet of a piece of furniture once stood?

"What was his name?"

"Cale ..."

"What was his name?" It was bad enough having a brother I didn't remember, but a son as well, one I knew she had given birth to, even if I didn't know when or where or even how old he had been, was far worse.

"James," she finally said.

"James?"

She nodded. The name sounded right, but there was more to it. It sounded like my brother's name. Memories, long dead and buried, surfaced, flooding my mind with images, conversations, and events involving a kid two years older than me.

We fished at the pond while sitting on a crate pallet we had dragged there. He beat me at Monopoly every time we played until I finally won, thanks to the purchases of three railroads, Boardwalk and Park Place (with houses to boot), and a little brotherly confidence builder. He carried his books home using his belt looped like a noose, the buckle holding everything in place. I always wanted to carry my books that way. He used to shoot hoops with me in the backyard, teaching me how to play the game he loved probably more than I did. We ate oatmeal and cinnamon toast and drank milk while watching Saturday morning cartoons in front of the television. Then he had been pulled from his room and shoved into a sack by a creature and had his nose bitten off and ...

"It ate him."

Charley slumped to the floor, her face in her hands, her shoulders bobbing up and down as she cried.

"It ate my brother?" Now tears fell down my face. I had seen the thing take my brother, and I did nothing to stop it, except wet my bed and believe it was all a bad dream. Then something else dawned on me, making my stomach flip and my head swoon.

"Where is our son, Charley?"

She began to wail, her head down and her eyes on the floor. "It's not my fault," she said between sobs.

"What's not your fault?"

"It was your momma."

"What about her?"

"She took him."

I could have waited for her to fill in all the details, and I could take the time to go into those details as well, but I didn't, and I won't. Just understand a few things:

1) Mom was bad—she didn't like me. I knew this, but I doubt Dad did. If he did, I think he would have died a lot sooner than age sixty-one.
2) There was a curse on the women of the Blackburn clan, to which I belong (First name: Cale. Last name: Blackburn). The first-born male to each woman was to be eaten by the Krampus—something like the anti-Santa Clause, who punishes bad kids. Supposedly, all first-born boys were evil.
3) Mom was the Krampus. That's the short version.

4) Finally—the child couldn't be eaten until The Feast of the Holy Family, which, according to Charley, falls on the Sunday after Christmas or December 30th. I didn't understand this, but I didn't argue with her. In this case, Christmas had been on a Wednesday.
5) There's one more: It was now early Sunday morning, and my son would be eaten soon.

The drive to Mom's house was only twenty minutes on a normal, all-is-well, ride, but things were anything but normal, and I made it there in nine, my heart pounding and hands sweating. My mouth had gone dry, and to be honest, my mind was a complete blank. I had had a brother. I had a son, though I couldn't tell you anything about him. Their memories had been wiped away, and the only people who remembered them were their mothers—'it's a maternal thing,' Charley said.

The front lights were off, and only one room in the house was lit up—Mom's bedroom. I didn't bother with the front door, knocking, or even calling to let her know I was there. She wasn't going to answer the door or the phone. Call it filial instincts if you want.

A key in the flowerpot was at the base of the steps to the back deck. It sat under a little ceramic turtle I had painted in second grade. One of the feet had been chipped at some point, and the paint had faded, but the turtle was still there. So was the key.

The back door opened into the kitchen. I closed it softly behind me. The kitchen sink still held Mom's coffee cup and the half-eaten bowl of oatmeal. My cup and bowl sat on the table, still untouched. If Mom had come down after I left and saw it, she would have been even madder at me than before I left. I took a couple of steps toward the door that led to the living room—it was a swinging door on pivot hinges that was normally loud if you hurried through it. On the opposite side of the entrance was the doorway to the den. To the left was the hall that led to the bedrooms and bathroom.

My hand was on the door between the kitchen and living room when I heard a distinct jingling sound. Even though I wore a coat, my skin became cold. The jingling grew closer, but it no longer held my attention. The sound of a crying child did. I heard it over the bells that seemed to jingle with each step someone—or *something*—took.

I was a kid again in need of peeing, the weight heavy on my bladder. The hall was dark, and the nightlight cast just enough light in a circle to let me know the bathroom was to the right and the spare room (the one that had been my brother's room) was to the left. If I followed the sound, I would surely see Santa Claus putting out presents.

That isn't Santa Clause, Cale.

I turned from the door and went to the counter. The drawer to the left of the sink held the utensils. I opened it and saw the cutting block and knives sitting next to the drainer. I took the largest one. Why settle for small when you might need something more substantial?

Back at the door, I gave it a soft push with one hand. It opened enough for me to peer out and see the glow of Christmas lights coming from the den. The shadow that moved along the floor and jingled and jangled with each step it took told me the creature was almost to the den. The crying of the child was muffled. When I stepped completely through the door, careful not to let it swing shut and make a lot of noise, I saw the sack slung over the creature's shoulder and knew my son was there.

Is that the same sack James had been in?

I hoped not, but it was possible.

"Oh, you are going to taste so good."

I took a couple of steps, hoping to catch it off guard. It set the bag on the floor before the Christmas tree, the child still screaming from inside it. Though I couldn't see its arms and legs, I could see the sack bulge where the child swung its limbs.

"And so will you."

It turned to me. I could see the same expression in its dark eyes that I saw in Mom's earlier that night. I knew then Charley had told the truth.

"You should have stayed away," Mom hissed. Her teeth were yellow and rotting, and the skin on her face hung loose, as if it were sliding off. Her hair had gotten longer and grayer, and her nose was thick and pointy at the tip.

"Get away from my son."

She cackled like a woman who had lost her mind. One hairy-knuckled finger pointed at me, and my bladder became weak.

"He is mine."

"Get away from him."

She smiled, and a fly flew from her mouth and into the air in zigs and zags.

"I will come for you when I am done with him."

She bared her teeth, growling as she did so. Then she bent down to pick up the sack with my son in it. Life slowed down as I ran toward her. She untied the twine that held it shut and reached in. Drool slid from her bottom lip and dripped from her chin. The edges of the sack's opening fell away, and I saw the child—he couldn't have been over a year old. His eyes were tear-weary, and his face was red. His brown hair was a cowlick mess. He looked at me, then reached out.

She went to pick him up just as I reached her, the knife coming down across her face and down into her chest. We crashed into the tree, our bodies tangled in limbs, lights, and each other. I tried to stand and found I couldn't. Something was wrong with my sides, and air escaped me. I raised the knife and ...

I woke up in my bed.

Charley lay beside me. My side of the bed was slightly damp. The sun was out and shone through the curtains. I stood from the bed and fell to my knees. The pain in my ribs was sudden and sharp, and for several seconds, I was on my hands and knees, trying to catch my breath. When I did, I sat back on my legs and lifted my nightshirt. Both of my sides held bruises and scabbing lacerations. They were still fresh. But if the wounds were real and I were still alive ...

I reached my feet and stumbled down the hall, passing the spare bedroom. In the living room, I turned the light on and stared at the picture on the wall. Charley was on the left. I was on the right. On Charley's hip was a child, not quite a year old. I knew his name immediately: James Terrance Blackburn. My heart lifted. I remembered the night before, putting him to bed in the crib in his room. He wore a red jumper that would keep him warm if he kicked his blankets off, which he did almost every night.

I remembered. I remembered.

Then I ran back down the hall, not trying to be quiet, when I swung the door open to his room—what had been the spare bedroom the night before—and turned the light on. There he was, standing in the crib, having pulled himself up. He turned to me and smiled. A fly flew from his mouth, and his eyes were dark. He giggled.

Afterword

As we reach the end of *Christmas Chaos*, I want to thank each of you who braved the pages of this twisted holiday collection. There's something especially chilling about the darkness that hides behind the festive lights and cheer. The holidays, after all, aren't always filled with warmth and wonder. Sometimes, they bring shadows, old fears, and the unsettling realization that not everything can be wrapped in holiday magic.

In *Christmas Chaos*, we sought to explore the sinister side of the season—where mystery, folklore, and hidden fears converge amid the winter chill. Each story in this anthology unearths a piece of the darkness that lurks just out of sight, reminding us that even in the season of joy, there's room for terror and surprise.

As you put this book down, I hope you carry a bit of its haunted holiday spirit with you. Let it be a reminder that the warmth of the season isn't complete without the shadows that dance at its edges, waiting to be discovered.

Thank you for joining us in this descent into the darker side of the holidays. May your season be merry, bright... and just a little bit haunted.

With eerie holiday wishes,

Outsider Publishing Company

Acknowledgments

Nate Walton-Let me start by thanking our kickstarter backers, you guys have your own section, but I needed to let you know that this truly wouldn't be in readers hands without you, thank you for contributing to making dreams come true, you guys did the thing and someday this book might be the reason a great writer exists and you will have helped that become reality, thank you. I also want to acknowledge the work both creative and on the publishing side of my creative partner Tiffany Vega, she put the sweat and tears in to get this in your hands, I cannot thank you enough Tiff, thank you. I also want to thank all the writers and editors that helped contribute to this project. We appreciate your creative efforts and hope you are as proud of this work as much as we are.

I want to thank my wife Jonna Walton and my daughter Haibay, without them I could not do this, from either a mental or physical standpoint. A big thank you to the rest of my friends and family as well for the support and strength they have given me over the years. A further thank you goes to Grandma Charlotte as I can never thank her enough for all she did for me.

I also want to thank all the creators of Holiday Horror, rather in film, literature, music or art. Bob Clark, John Carpenter, Victor Miller, Sean Cunningham, Charles Dickens, and everyone else I'll feel dumb as hell for forgetting. You have given joy and happiness to so many and I hope you at least feel a percentage of the joy I get from your work, not to mention the millions others you have reached.

Tiffany Vega- First I want to acknowledge all the writers that help make this anthology a creepy and haunting read. It would never had been made if you the writers didn't have a story that needed to be told. Some of you I feel like we will be working side by side for a long time. This is what we planned when we started Outsider Publishing was giving voices to those that need to be heard. And these 13 writers needed to be heard. They have done some of the best work and stories that brought a chill to my spine.

Next I would like to acknowledge those that back the Kick starter, you took a chance on a small press working on their first anthology. With out you this would never have been funded. You are truly our Outsider Stars. I don't think that there is words in the world to express how much I appreciate you and the support that you have shown us. Please understand that my words fail me but know my heart is filled with joy and love for you all.

Of course, as always my kids, thank you for listening, working with me and be the shoulder I need when I was ready to give up and say forget this. There has been many times I wanted to give up and one more time then that you were there telling me to not give up. I love you all to the moon and back.

A special thanks to Zachary my youngest, who give me strength in every step of the process. He gave me his advice and was there when I broke down and didn't let me give up. He been my CFO and my ride or die through this whole thing.

Next I want to acknowledge Nate, my partner in this, my brother, my best friend. The one person that understood me growing up. The one that help me dream big and not know any other way to dream. If it was not for spending our childhood dreaming of writing I would have never started my writing journey. I am so glad that it is now us doing it and not me alone. **After all we are the rebels of the written word.**

Outsider Stars

We owe you a tremendous thank you for your incredible support in bringing *Christmas Chaos* to life! You braved the dark and twisted corners of our imaginations and joined us on this journey, making it possible for our haunting holiday visions to become reality. Without your courage and backing, *Christmas Chaos* might still be lurking in the shadows, waiting for a voice. You guys are really stars!

Liviu Ioan Codreanu
Jessica Enfante
Frejs
Judy McClain
Rebecca M. Senese
Sean
Mars
Zack Fissel
Giusy Rippa
Ed Abbott

Donald E Brown
Madilynn Dale
Kristina Meschi
Aaron Henton
Dino Hicks
Denise Geerling
Jacob
Thomas Aaron Nottingham
Bloodevil Studios

About the Authors

Justin Brimhall- I've been a storyteller my whole life and my passion was always film/tv. My parents called me rerun because I would always quote lines from movies and tv shows. As I grew, I found a passion for writing.

After graduating from the university of Utah with a degree in English Literature, I got to work. I've published two books so far and tirelessly continue work on many more to come. When I'm not writing, I'm lifting weights, reading, playing video games, or hanging with my family. You can find me @ Instagram is justin_d_brimhall, TikTok is @justin_d_brimhall.

Max Wright - Max is a writer living in Dallas, Texas. His more than 20 stories have appeared in a number of magazines, e-zines and anthologies, most notably Mother's Revenge, which was shortlisted for the Stoker Awards for best anthology in 2017. When he's not trying to scare people, he enjoys tennis, vintage Volkswagens and bad horror films. You can follow him on Facebook at https://www.facebook.com/max.wright.737.

V. Franklin lives in a double-wide in the Pacific Northwest with two cats, two goats, four sheep, two horses, a couple thousand bees, two humans, and maybe some ghosts. The carpet is filthy and we're almost out of coffee.

J. Bradford Engelsman mainly writes non-fiction about lactation support, infant care, and gender diversity under the name Jacob Engelsman but he has recently begun dabbling in the realms of science fiction, fantasy, and horror. This is his first story someone else has agreed to publish but he should have his first novella available on either substack or amazon by the time you read this.

He likes to keep many irons in the fire and is currently outlining books on his favorite defunct bar, ultramarathoning, historical alchemists, infant care, and a memoir on everything he has ever failed to do.

When he isn't writing and taking care of babies he enjoys climbing, running, cycling, baking, fermenting, playing board games, and running roleplaying games in sunny Atlanta, GA with his spouse and cats. He's always happy to talk about babies, writing, or Star Trek; feel free to give him a shout on Instagram @jacobibclc.

Ray Prew was originally from Rhode Island, but now lives in Florida. He is a graduate of the New England Institute of Technology. Ray has been a blue-collar worker all his life, and started writing as a hobby. He spent 9 enjoyable years as a phone psychic. Ray's work has been published in several online magazines as well as a few anthologies. Ray has 2 books of his own on Amazon, Delightful Nightmares and The Collectors. Ray has a video on

YouTube based on one of his stories. Ray Prew Let Me Out. Can you find Ray's other work here.

John DeLaughter, M.Div, MS, works as a Data Security Analyst. In 2024, John's fiction appeared in the *Mind's Eye Publication's*, "Journ-E: The Journal of Imaginative Literature Vernal Equinox Edition (March 2024)," *Savage Realms Monthly* (May 2024), *Wicked Shadow Press's*, "Flash of the Undead" (May 2024), *"Schlock Webzine"* (June 2024), *Obsidian Butterfly's* "Necronomi-Romcom: Dark Volume" (July 2024), *Red Cape Publishing's*, "Whisperer in Valhalla: The North Sea Trilogy Book 2" (September 2024), *Eerie River Publishing's* "Wand Anthology" (September 2024), *Wick Shadow Press's* "Flash of the Dead" (October 2024), *Judith Sonnet's*, "Screams" anthology (December, 2024), and Outsider Publishing's, "Christmas Chaos" Anthology (December 2024).

Tiffany Vega is a native Arizonan. She dreamt of being a writer her whole life. She loves gardening and crocheting. Dancing in the rain and worshipping the moon. She is a mother of three incredible men and a mother of two fur-babies. Cake and Sage. She is also working on two novel that will be coming out next year. You can find her work at www.booksbytiffanyvega.com

Solomon Forse is the founder of HOWL Society. When he's not hanging on the Discord server or handling publisher and audiobook duties, Solomon spends his time role-playing horror with tabletop RPGs like Call of Cthulhu or shredding horror on the guitar in his Lovecraftian metal band Crafteon. Learn more about his works at solomonforse.com.

Alexander Jose Martinez is a high school social studies teacher who currently resides in Pittsburgh. During his time at Duquesne University he frequently worked on creative fiction, predominantly in the horror and suspense genres. After over a decade hiatus to establish himself as an educator Alexander has recently returned to his passion of writing. He has recently had multiple short stories as well as a novelette published by *NightScribe*. Between lecturing about the nuances of the influence of the progressive movement and coaching football, wrestling and track, Alexander loves to spend time outdoors with his wife and daughter. As a former college athlete he often incorporates themes of sports as well as family, school, and the great outdoors to craft relatable characters in vivid settings. Currently, Alexander is working on a longer work that blends suspense and cosmic horror. He plans to publish an anthology of short stories and novellas in 2025.

Mark Daponte has sold five short stories that have appeared in short story anthologies, and punches up screenplays—because they don't punch back. He also is a Staff Writer for Culture Sonar website; a pop culture and music website (https://www.culturesonar.com/author/mark-daponte/) Mark has had five one act plays performed by in Los Angeles, (Sacred Fools), Sacramento, CA (Sacramento

Actors Theater Company), Dover, NJ (Dover Little Theater) Ellicott City, MD (Thunderous Productions, and Galway, Ireland (Teacher's Club). When he isn't in Cobble Hill Park waiting for the perfect cumulus cloud to float by to hear his latest nonsensical rant, he can be found seeking signs of intelligent life in his hometown of Brooklyn, NY.

Sam C. Tumminello Jr-A lifelong fan of science fiction and horror, he has spent much of his life pondering the airless badlands of worlds on the edge of galaxies and all too familiar dark ominous places. Incidentally this interest dovetailed into a love of history, which in turn lead to a master's degree in political science and history. Steeped into such a multitude of stories, he is excited to be able to share some of his own creations. This is his first published work.

Jude Deluca's a nonbinary aegosexual Capricorn. Specifically, a Christmas Capricorn. They grew up devouring Christmas horror stories. As a kid they'd record Christmas episodes of TV shows onto blank tapes. Now they're finally writing their own Christmas stories and ruining the holiday season for everyone! Their primary interests are in slasher fiction, magical girls, YA horror, superhero dads, and big beautiful men. As a professional detective of horror media they've rediscovered several short stories such as Goosebumps: Dead Dogs Still Fetch by R.L. Stine and Braden Gardner.

They can be found on Twitter as @judedeluca, and on Instagram, Bluesky, and Tumblr as @judedeluca.

They would like to dedicate their story to Jennifer Jeanne

McArdle and Michael W. Phillips Jr. of From Beyond Press, as thanks for publishing the first Generation Dead story in *Escalators To Hell*.

Nate Walton, despite the rumors is not a thousand monkeys at a thousand typewriters but instead one 44 year old pop culture nerd. Growing up with the works of King, Claremont, Marz, Barker, John Ostrander and the films of Craven and Lynch he is probably writing something right now, that or debating the latest DC reboot online. Currently resides with his wife Jonna and daughter Hayley in Amish Country.

Mike Rusetsky grew up in Ukraine, reading Russian translations of works by Agatha Christie, Stephen King and Roger Zelazny. At 13, he moved to Ohio to attend Junior High and write cringeworthy poetry in his third language, English. Post-college, several of his original play scripts received local stage productions, and his one-act plays *Angel of Death* and *The Plight of Smitty* were met with critical acclaim. Mike has written three stage adaptations for a children's theater in Columbus, Ohio and has attempted stand-up comedy four times, usually to impress a girl. He has written two yet-unpublished novels, 13 play scripts, and 50+ short stories. He continues writing today, always seeking a trifold balance between the fantastical, the horrific, and the humorous -- and trying to mind the tricky grey spaces in between.

Facebook - https://www.facebook.com/mykhaylo.rusetsky

Instagram - https://www.instagram.com/beatnikjuice/profilecard/?igsh=MXR4cHI4cW96Z3RzdA==

Twitter/X - https://x.com/RussetSky?s=09

A.J. Brown is a southern-born writer who tells emotionally charged, character driven stories that often delve into the darker parts of the human psyche. Most of his stories have the southern country feel of his childhood.

Though he writes mostly darker stories, he does so without unnecessary gore, coarse language, or sex.

More than 200 of his stories have been published in various online and print publications. His story *Mother Weeps* was nominated for a Pushcart Award in 2010. Another story, *Picket Fences*, was the editor's choice story for Necrotic Tissue in October of 2010. The story, *Numbers*, won the quarterly contest at WilyWriters.com in June of 2013.

If you would like to learn more about A.J. you can check out his blog, Type AJ Negative (https://typeajnegative.wordpress.com). You can also find him on Facebook (https://www.facebook.com/typeajnegative).

Review

If these twisted holiday tales filled you with festive fear, consider leaving us an honest review on Amazon and Goodreads. Your feedback helps keep the dark magic alive—and ensures more chilling tales find their way to you next Christmas!